To Moira,

Art And The Abductor

The Second 'L-Shaped Village' Novel

Thank you so much!

By

Lee J H Fomes

© 2012 Lee J. H. Fomes. All rights reserved.

No part of this book may be reproduced, stored in a retrieval system, or transmitted by any means without the written permission of the author.

Published by EllShapyan Imprint, June 2012
ISBN 978-1-4717-3989-7

Cover background art: © Claudia Knights 2012
Character art: © Rob Fuzzard 2012
Quotation from Charles Dickens "A Christmas Carol"

All characters depicted in this work are fictional. Any similarity, real or implied, to anyone real people is purely coincidental.

I am fundraising in support of Help for Heroes; with the aim to raise at least £1,000. Help For Heroes do fantastic work supporting our service personnel and their families and I am sure that they would be extremely grateful for any help or donation that you can give. Please go to my fundraising page to see what I have donated already: www.bmycharity.com/lshapedvillage.

Acknowledgements

As is always the case with any publication, there are a number of people I must thank for their help and support.
Thanks to Claudia and Rob, whose artistic genius has once again brought to life Art's fabulous world; to my editors Helen and Luath, for their unrivalled skill in all things literary; to my wife Hannah, my live-in proof reader; to my joint number one fans Holly, Tiana and Rebecca; to the Cookseys for spreading the word to the Midlands; and last but certainly not least, to the one and only Jools Holland, for his wonderful endorsement.

For Hannah, Molly and William

" *"There are some upon this earth of ours," returned the Spirit, "who lay claim to know us, and who do their deeds of passion, pride, ill-will, hatred, envy, bigotry, and selfishness in our name, who are as strange to us and all our kith and kin, as if they had never lived. Remember that, and charge their doings on themselves, not us."* "

Charles Dickens,
"A Christmas Carol".

PROLOGUE

'Hurry up, dear – you'll be late for school.'

'Ok mum – stop worrying,' he shouted down from his room. The little boy pulled himself out of his bed and his eyes met a pile of school clothes neatly stacked on the red plastic chair next to his bed. He sighed. Yet another day of school lay ahead; the same classroom, the same people, the same teachers. The memory of it seemed oddly distant, but still somehow just as vivid as always when he woke up on a Monday morning. It was always the same – the week days would drag on and on, and the weekends would slip by as if nothing had happened. Every Monday morning the weekend seemed like a memory that had been implanted to make it seem like he had had some time off, as if there had been no weekend at all. But then a flash of yellow caught his eye, and the invitation tacked to his wall jarred his memory of the party he was going to after school – a strange day for a party, but that just made it more appealing - and he threw his clothes on as fast as he could.

He dashed down the stairs and into the kitchen, where breakfast had been laid on the little round oak table. His older sister and brother were sat opposite one another, and so were his mother and father, leaving one empty chair with less room than everyone else.

'Move your chair round Michael – make some room for your brother.' Michael made a half-hearted attempt to shift his chair over, moving maybe an inch or two, grunting disapprovingly as he did.

The little boy sidled into his seat, ignoring the sneer his brother gave him, and reached out for a white china bowl.

'What time are you picking me up tonight, dad?' he said.

'Jacob's mother said about seven-ish. You'll have to do double homework tomorrow to make up for it, ok?'

'Yeah yeah.' The little boy poured himself some cereal and reached for the milk.

'That Jacob's such a wimp,' said Michael. 'What's his party gonna be – poodle grooming?' He burst out laughing, loudly and a little too deliberately. The little boy paused just as he was about to pour his milk. Taunts from his brother and sister were just part of his daily routine, and usually, he reserved himself to the fact that if he ignored them, they would soon get bored. But today was different. A strange anger was welling up inside him, starting from the pit of his stomach.

His mother raised her eyebrows at Michael. 'You leave him alone – Jacob's a nice boy, thank you very much.'

Michael just laughed even louder. 'Yeah I heard that too – I heard he's a very nice boy!' His sister joined in, and they both hooted with laughter.

The little boy's mother put her hand on his shoulder. 'Just ignore them dear, like you always do. You always were more grown-up than the pair of them put together.' She stared at them both as she said the last bit. But the little boy was having a hard time ignoring them this time. For some reason the bubble of anger in his stomach was growing and growing the louder they laughed.

Michael hadn't finished. 'Actually, he's probably the perfect friend for you! Are you gonna stay behind when the party's over and do your nails together?' Michael and his sister both hooted with laughter again.

The little boy, who had the jug of milk in his hand, suddenly saw red like never before. The bubble of anger had boiled over, and his eyes hardened and his thoughts darkened. His hand gripped the handle of the jug so hard his fingers turned white. His father noticed something unfamiliar in his son's expression, but before he could do anything, the little boy threw the whole jug of milk over his brother's head without a second's further hesitation, and an impossibly loud voice boomed from his little chest.

'WHOM I DECIDE TO BEFRIEND IS NO CONCERN OF YOURS, IMBECILE – NOW HOLD YOUR TONGUE OR YOU'LL BE WEARING YOUR OWN BREAKFAST AS WELL!'

The whole table froze, including the little boy, who looked perhaps the most shocked of all. His voice had been so loud it didn't seem possible that his throat could have produced it. His brother looked white with fright, but it was hard to tell if it was just milk dripping off his face. His mother looked totally bewildered and confused; never had she heard such language from her son. Not that it was rude as such, just totally out of character and ... well, frightening.

His father was the first to speak.

'What the HELL do you think you're doing? Clear up this mess NOW! No – on second thoughts, get upstairs and stay there. And it's straight home from school for you – no party!'

The little boy looked at the empty jug of milk in his hands, then slowly and gingerly placed it down on the table. His chair scraped loudly on the floor as he slowly stood to his full height, which was not much more than his brother sitting down. His whole family stared at him as he backed out of the room and climbed the stairs.

From his room he could hear the bustle of clearing up from the kitchen, but he could hear very little talking. He sat down on his bed feeling rather numb and confused. The sounds of the clear-up operation carried on below, and soon he heard someone ascending the stairs as well. The footsteps reached the landing, and paused outside the door to the little boy's bedroom. There was a loud knock, then another, then another. It was his brother's usual knock – slow and condescending. He always wondered why his older brother would knock on his door – it never stopped him coming in if there was no answer. Sure enough, the door flung open and in he came. He headed straight for the little boy and wasted no time in giving him a dead arm. Yet another knuckle punch to the nerve cluster just below the joint that stung just as much as the last, even though it did seem a while since he had had one.

'You ever do anything like that again you little stinker and I'll stick your head down the toilet!' Michael left the room and slammed the door behind him.

This time the little boy felt no anger, no bubble of raw hatred coming from inside him, in fact, the incident in the kitchen was the first time he had lost his temper at all. His brother and sister had never acted like older children, they had always been immature and petty as long as he could remember. His mother and had always smiled at the way he dealt with them; whatever they did, he just ignored them and got on with whatever he was doing. Sometimes it was a problem, as they were both bigger and stronger than him, and he occasionally suffered with dead legs and arms, but they usually lost interest after a while and busied themselves in TV programs or computer games. And some of the time, he actually got on well with them if they were in a particularly good mood.

But his father was different. They would lie to him about things he had supposedly done, and he would believe them, every time. He never saw their immature side like their mother did – they would hide it whenever he was around, and he bought it hook, line and sinker. He would be in trouble time after time, although usually innocent, and they would sneer at him as he was dragged off and shouted at until his ears rang. His mother would protest his innocence for him, but it never did any good. Eventually his father would convince her too.

Downstairs, his mother and father finished cleaning up the mess. 'I just don't understand it,' said his mother, 'he's usually so level-headed. He's never done anything like that before.'

His father sighed. 'I've heard of him behaving like that before, but I've never actually seen it. I don't mean what he was saying either, but ... how it sounded.'

His mother sighed too and began polishing the table with a cloth. 'I don't think I've ever heard Danny speak like that before.'

Chapter One
THE RETURN

The room slowly came into focus as Art awoke from the heaviest slumber he had ever known, but the bliss of those first few moments when you know nothing of the happenings of the night before was absent. He knew *exactly* where he had been, and *exactly* what he was waking up from.

Only days ago, fresh back to school from the Christmas holidays, strange things had started happening to him that he couldn't explain. Well, *he* couldn't, but oddly enough his Grandmother could. And he would make sure she explained it to him a whole lot better when he saw her – which was the first thing on his mind.

The memory of where he had been was strikingly real in his head – it could *not* be mistaken for a dream. A small amulet called the Fragment had transported him to a pretty little snow-covered settlement called The L-Shaped Village, in a strange world full of magic and wonder. There, he had found overwhelming evidence that yearly visits from the mythical figure often referred to as Santa Claus, was *not*, in fact, mythical at all. He had met several families from the village, which Art discovered was an *Artisan* village, where every member of the community was a crafts person or artist of some kind. But he had perhaps been the most taken with a group of them who called themselves an army, led by a charismatic character called Scem. He and his second in command Sergeant, had tried to teach him the ways of a village warrior, using small magical weapons that inflicted no harm on an opponent. In doing so, he had met the feared leader of an opposing army, who turned out to be little more than a small boy, trapped for decades in a world he could not escape from, growing no older in body, but ageing considerably in mind.

The last thing Art could remember was coming back through to his own world again, *with* that little boy, in a bid to reunite him with his family. But someone else had come through with them as well. A child from one of the Artisan families. A very special child. A magical child. And this memory *did* hit Art like a tonne of bricks, and for good reason – the child was a younger version of someone he *already knew* in this world – his magical friend Maga. And all the while, his Grandma had known about it all. He would give her a piece of his mind when he saw her.

As his mind adjusted to consciousness again, he slowly became aware of his position; he was lying down on his bed, head just below the pillow, his left leg hanging off the side. His head was throbbing, and his ears were ringing as though he'd been at a live concert. He noticed his hands were clasping the sheets, so he released them and held them in the air to inspect. The Fragment was still secured around his wrist by the leather twine, but there was no life in it; no hint of the warm glow that he remembered had protected him from the cold of the L-Shaped Village's unique weather system. It was just an odd looking charm crafted in metal, tied to his wrist with worn leather rope. His arms weren't shrouded in the dull, but comfortable, clothes he had been dressed in at the Village either – he was back in his school uniform. Despite this, there was no doubt whatsoever in his mind that he'd been there; it was quite simply a *fact*. The first question that came to his mind was – *when* was he? He remembered that the first time he had been through a Portal, which was how he had been transported to the village, the Fragment had taken him. But going *back* had been down to two people, two strange people from that world called Pud and Jimma, sitting somewhere in a room with some 'tech' – whatever that meant. And they had promised him that they would deliver him back to exactly the same time and place as he had been when he had left.

He became aware of a presence in the room, and it shocked him to the core; he didn't know who it was but he felt immediately threatened. He sat bolt upright and came face to face with Tina, his closest friend, who wore an expression of pure shock. He screamed in her face at the sight, and she screamed back. Art clawed at the sheets to get away from her, and without realising it, he clawed at his side for the little weapon they had given him at the village - his Sta'an – but the sheath it had been nestled in was not there anymore. But gradually his memory of Tina returned, and slowly he calmed himself down. His ears were still ringing, and he realised she was talking to him, but he couldn't hear her. He shook his head and bashed his ears, and slowly the ringing started to subside.

'Art – are you ok?'

It sounded like she was talking from the other side of a very thick door, and Art could only just make out what she had said. 'Erm, yes I ... I'm fine. What happened? What time is it?'

'You fainted Art. I got your text and rushed round here, and ... and your eyes just lolled up into your head and you flopped down on the bed ... I couldn't wake you up. I ran downstairs to get some help but there wasn't anyone here, so I came back up but ... you'd ... *gone*. You disappeared Art – where did you go?'

Art thought quickly; obviously Pud and Jimma had been close, but not exact. 'How long was I ... *gone* ... for?' he said.

Tina put her hand to his forehead. 'I thought you'd woken up and gone to the bathroom or something, so I went looking – but when I walked past your room again to go downstairs you were back on your bed. You were even lying in the same way you fell. What *happened*?'

It sounded like Pud and Jimma had only been off by a few seconds – maybe he could get away with it. 'I was feeling a bit queasy - I did go to the loo – but I ... er ... used mum and dad's en suite. I must have missed you on the landing. I'm fine now though.'

Tina scoffed. 'I don't think so, Art – you *fainted*. You're going to a hospital. Is your Grandma still in? She can drive you.'

Art was about to protest, but stopped himself at the last second; Grandma was *exactly* the person he needed to see. And ask a *lot* of questions. Tina helped him up, and Art wasn't sure whether he'd have to fake being unsteady on his feet or not – he realised he actually *didn't* feel completely right. It must be something to do with travelling through a Portal, though he couldn't remember feeling like this the first time he had gone through. He filed it away as one of the many questions he would ask Grandma when he saw her.

After a while, Art *did* have to fake it – when they eventually got out into the street the fresh air was like a tonic, and Art started to feel strong again. The trouble was he wasn't very good at faking, and it seemed to Tina like he was getting worse as he 'stumbled' and 'tripped' every now and then. When they eventually got to Art's Grandma's house, Tina was genuinely worried, and she started calling out for help. Grandma's face appeared in the front window and seconds later the front door flew open.

'Quick – Art fainted at home and I think he's getting worse!' Tina called. 'We need to get him to a hospital!'

Grandma rushed to his other side and helped Tina manhandle him through the front door, into the front room and onto the sofa. 'How long was he out for dear?' she asked.

Tina rubbed the side of her head, still looking very worried. 'I don't know – it can't have been more than a minute – not even that – but you should have seen his *face* - it was awful! Is he gonna be ok?'

'He'll be fine dear. Arthur's brother, Walt, is still here – he's in the other room playing on the Puu console. Do me a favour would you dear – rush back to the house and wait for his ma and pa – and tell them that he's safe.'

'What should I tell them?'

'Just what I said – that he's safe.'

Tina was unsure at what she'd been asked. 'Are you ... not going to take him to a hospital?'

Grandma frowned. 'I don't think there's any need for that, dear. Run along now.'

Tina stood her ground. 'But he *fainted* – he needs medical help! You can't just leave him like that – it might happen again!'

Grandma just smiled in his direction. 'Aye, so it will,' she said under her breath. Then she turned to Tina again, and stared at her almost unkindly. '*Run along now, dear.*' There was a definite edge to her voice that Tina wasn't sure about. She stared back, and intended to stare for as long as it took, but something in Grandma Elfee's eye made her lose her nerve, and she sighed angrily and headed for the front door again.

'First Evi, then Art. I'm losing friends rapidly,' Tina said to herself as she turned.

'What do you mean by that, dear?' said Grandma.

Tina turned back reluctantly. 'Evi fell in hockey today and broke her wrist. She's in hospital right now.'

Art nearly lost his composure as he heard this news. He had had feelings for Evi as soon as she arrived at the school in their third year, and she was Tina's best friend.

Grandma glared hard at Tina, with a knowing look on her face. 'Run along now dear,' she said again.

As soon as the front door clicked shut, Art sprang up from the sofa and confronted his Grandmother. She didn't seem in the least bit surprised that he had been faking. '*You* – have some *serious* explaining to do.' He held up his wrist, where the strange amulet, the Fragment, nestled snugly. 'And you can start with this.'

Her eyes lit up at the sight of it, and she rushed closer to inspect it.

'You found it, so you did!'

'Actually, it sort of found me.'

She looked at him oddly, then smiled. 'Not the Fragment, you eejut – the *Village*! You found the L-Shaped Village!'

Art felt a flash of anger. 'I am *not* here so you can reminisce! You KNEW before I went there! You asked me about *this*...' He waved the Fragment under her nose again. 'You knew about this and didn't tell me! And you even knew about Maga!' He pulled a chair out from the dining table and sat down matter-of-factly. 'Explain. NOW.'

Grandma slowly pulled out the chair next to him and sat down. 'You first...'

'NO – *YOU* FIRST!' he spat. She recoiled slightly, then narrowed her eyes as if trying to work something out.

'You've changed, so you have. What have you seen?' She smiled slyly again. 'More to the point – *who* – have you seen?'

Art leaned forward. 'Like I said – you first.'

She sighed. 'Well now – the problem I have is I wouldn't know where to start. And I mean that. I take it you learned a thing or two while you were there.'

Art glared at her. 'I'll take that as a yes, so I will.' she said. 'And I'm guessing a lot of it would have been about ... *Time* ... am I right?'

More glaring.

'Thought so. So here's the thing. I don't know what I can or can't talk about unless I know a bit about your visit. If I start talking about the *wrong* visit, well – you can see the danger in that.'

Art broke his silence. 'What do you mean *the wrong visit*?'

Grandma sucked her teeth. 'There you go, you see? Even that could be damaging – now you know you go there again.'

Art thought for a moment. 'But surely you just recall the first one and ...' Art's eyes widened. 'You ... you mean you ... *remember* ... them? Like they're ... in your *past*?' His eyes glazed over as his head was lost in thought, but with thoughts he *couldn't* fathom. It was as if his brain was a computer processor overloaded with tasks, rendered unable to do anything.

Grandma rose from the table and headed for the kitchen to put a pan of water on the stove. When it had boiled she took two tubs of powder from the back of the top cupboard and made two steaming hot drinks. She calmly walked back to the table and placed one in front of Art. The smell seemed to rescue him from his painful thoughts, and as he reached for it a memory returned.

'You made this for me the last time I was here! The day I went! This is ... Stroth-Brew! I had loads of this stuff at the Village.'

Grandma Elfee smiled. 'That's right, dear.'

'And ... the picture that was hanging just there – the one you gave me of the L-Shaped Village - you said it was your *home* – and that it would soon be ... *my* home too.'

Grandma smiled again. 'So I did.'

Art folded his arms on the table and rested his head on them. He looked exhausted. Grandma rested a hand on his elbow. 'You see dear, I have to know about your trip first before I can tell you what *I* know. If I make a connection *for* you, it could be disastrous. So come on now dear – drink your Stroth-Brew and spill the beans. You'll feel better so you will.'

Art heaved his head slowly up, and cradled the mug. He looked at the liquid still spinning around slightly from a vigorous stir. He looked up at his Grandma. Or whoever she was. 'Any honey or milk? I hate this stuff without it.' Grandma glanced to the centre of the table – Art looked in that direction and there were two small china jugs, containing honey and milk, resting on the table. 'I hear they were down to you. Bravo, dear,' she said. Art stirred a little of each into his drink, and reluctantly started talking.

He told her everything he could remember; when he had found the Fragment and secured it to his wrist, waking up in the woods and finding the Hut, walking through the snow to the Village and meeting everyone, going on the mission and making that fateful mistake, exploring the Village with a younger version of Maga, fighting beside Shay-la in the Battle for the Village, and discovering Danny. Grandma watched, rather than listened, as Art talked animatedly about everything, and whenever he talked about the Village his face seemed to glow, and his expression, although not beaming with a smile, seemed as though it wouldn't fit a frown anymore. She sighed as he talked, marvelling at the detail he could remember, as though she were reliving, through him, a memory of years past. She rested her head on her hand, and after a while was so lost in thought she didn't hear his question.

'Grandma! What does it mean?'

She started. 'Oh. Er – what does *what* mean, dear?'

'Have you been listening at all?'

'I'm sorry – it's just the way you talk about it. Reminds me of ... ' Her eyes glazed over again.

'Grandma! Snap out of it! This is the part where you give me answers!'

She started again. 'Oh I'm sorry dear. Just back-track a wee bit, would you?'

Art sighed, swilled his Stroth-Brew around and took a sip before carrying on. 'Just as I was leaving – Hité said something. I still can't quite believe it – I mean it can't mean what I *think* it means ... can it?'

Grandma smiled knowingly. 'What did she say dear?'

'Well ... I asked her how I could get in touch with her. You know, communicate between this world and that. And she told me to write a letter, on paper, and ... throw it on the fire.'

Grandma's face broke into the biggest smile Art had ever seen. 'And ... you don't know what it means?' she said.

Art paused. 'It's more that I can't quite believe it.'

'Well now,' Grandma said, 'forget about belief for just a second, and just tell me what you think it means, and I'll tell you if you're close to the mark. But here's a tip. Don't be thinking too much about what you *know* as the truth – think about where you've been and what you've seen, and don't be afraid to add two and two – even if you're certain you'll get five.'

Art looked at her as though she had just picked words at random from the dictionary and strung them together, but to his amazement he could see some sense in them. He took a deep breath, placed his hands flat on the table and steadied himself. 'I can't quite believe I'm even going to *say* it ...'

'Go on, dear ...' Grandma encouraged.

'From what they all told me ...'

'Yes ...'

'and from what Hité said just at that moment ... I thought it meant ...'

'Come on, dear – just say it ... try the words out for size ...'

'I mean that's how children communicate with ...'

'*Say* it ...'

'Sss ... San ... ta ..... Claus?'

'There we are now!' Grandma threw her hands in the air.

Even though Art felt the words leaving his mouth, it felt as though someone else had said them. He stared at Grandma incredulously. 'You mean ... he's real? He exists?'

She chuckled. 'It's not *quite* as simple as that. For a start we're not really talking about a *person* as such. And certainly don't be thinking about a cuddly fella in a red suit either. Now that *would* be silly. Although sometimes they do wear red, so they do ...'

Just as Art thought he was getting some answers, and he'd really strained his knowledge of reality to do it, more questions were posing themselves. It was just like talking to Hité again.

'So what *are* we talking about?' he demanded.

'Well, now. That's a hard question to answer. I suppose you could say it's more like a set of ideologies.'

'That doesn't make any sense either. We've gone from talking about a person to ... I don't know, a set of ideas or something. Which is it?'

'Well you can't have one without the other you know,' she answered.

Art caught himself. 'Hang on – just a second ago you said *they* – like there's ... *more than one*!'

Grandma nodded. 'That's right, dear. You have to understand - this whole thing is far bigger than just *one* person.'

Art took a deep breath. 'This is doing my head in. Okay – start from the beginning. Tell me everything.'

Grandma added some milk and honey to her own Stroth-Brew and took a sip. 'Ok then. Here goes. The world is a tough place to be in. Life is hard – in some countries harder than others. But even in countries where people have everything they need, there is still terrible injustice everywhere you look, and most of those injustices are down to *people*. Now – where nature runs smoothly, where species live in an eco-system that works, it's because there's a *balance*. And in the case of humans – injustices have to be balanced out by something else. Something opposite. And if it's down to the people that there's injustice, it's down to the people to balance it out. The only problem is – human nature doesn't create enough of the good ones to do all of the balancing themselves – they need a bit of help, so they do. So they borrow some goodness from a realm where there's too *much*.'

Art thought for a moment. 'So ... you use *this* realm to ... what, hand out presents at Christmas?'

Grandma chuckled again. 'Oh, Art. That's just one teeny, tiny part of the whole thing. It's infinitely bigger than that. But let's concentrate on that part for the moment if you want to.'

Art scratched his head. 'Ok,' he said. 'Let's start with that then. How does that work?'

Grandma took another sip from her mug. 'Well, that's the part people know about. And they only know about it because somebody was seen. An operative by the name of *Jauger Clause*, from Austria. He was enjoying his semi-retirement from the agency with a nice little delivery job - three days a week. He was in Scotland at the time, wearing his usual fur-lined red coat. He was a traditionalist – liked the old methods of transport. Wouldn't travel by anything motorised if he could help it. Certainly not by shuttle like most of them do.' Grandma grinned at Art. 'I'll bet you can guess how he travelled.'

Art said it like it was a silly thing to say. 'A sleigh?'

'That's right.'

'Oh, come on!' Art said. 'You're kidding me, right?'

'Will you *listen*?'

Art fell silent.

'Thank you. He was placed down the line a fair few centuries. He believed the best disguise was to hide in plain sight, and for the most part he was right. But one evening he was spotted and followed. No one knows who by, but they followed him the entire night, watched everything he did. They didn't quite understand everything they saw, but whoever that person was, they started a rumour that spread like wildfire. No one quite believed it, but every year they expected him, so much so that people would buy presents for their children and say they were from him. And so started a tradition that still exists today.'

Art thought for a moment. 'There's got to be more to it than *that*.'

'Well, of course there is – traditions don't just start one day and carry on forever. *Something* gave this particular one weight, we still don't know what, but even so it took a fair few generations to catch on.'

'Oh.' said Art. 'Okay ... so supposing that's all true. Didn't he do himself out of a job by being spotted?'

Grandma laughed. 'Oh no. Funny how things work out – he actually made his job easier.'

'How do you figure that?'

'It was easier to leave presents without drawing attention to himself. In fact he made it easier for every operative the further the tradition spread – if any presents were found and not recognised, it was just blamed on Clause.'

Art still looked very confused. 'I'm still not getting this at all. *How* did they find out his name? And, why would someone leave presents in people's houses every evening, for a *job*, in the first place?'

'Like I said. There's a balance to be kept. That is just one small way it can be done. And as for his name, that's still a mystery as to how they found it out. But as time went on, the name warped somehow into the words you uttered a few minutes ago.'

Art thought for a bit longer. 'But – where does the L-Shaped Village come into that? I mean, they're just a village of artisans – what can they poss ...' And then he remembered the long building making up the bottom length of the L-shape of the village. He remembered Maga wouldn't tell him what went on in there, and that they were all on holiday from something.

'I don't believe it!' he said, incredulously. 'How can I *not* have worked that out?'

Grandma smiled. 'There we go. More connections – I guess they didn't tell you it was a toy factory. That sounds like Hité. But again, they're only one small part of it too. Their biggest contribution to it all is their Portal technology. It's essential to everything we do.'

Art sipped his drink in yet more thought. 'Hang on – when you say *everything*, what do you mean? What *else* do you do? And how come it's involving *you* all of a sudden?'

Grandma smiled again. 'You'll find out how it involves me in time. And as for what else we do, I can't give you details, but I can tell you what it's about.'

'Well,' Art said, 'go on, then.'

'Okay. Did you learn anything about *prophecies* at all?'

'Yes – Danny told me about them, and it didn't sound like they're a good thing.'

'He's right, so he is. They can be very damaging. A prophecy tells of something that happens in the future – very dangerous. But what few people know is that the opposite of a prophecy ... is a *tradition*. They tell a story of something that happened in the past, and they can be very beneficial, very healing for the balance. So – in a nutshell, that's what we do, Art. We create traditions.'

Art's face washed over with understanding. 'Aah – so the present thing was started to develop into a tradition,' he said.

Grandma shifted. 'Well not *entirely*. We never intended that to develop into a tradition. That was just something nice that was started to try and even the balance, one of the first things we tried when the call for help came. We were all starting out back then, and we tried every idea that came to the table. We didn't expect it to be as huge as it is today. How that one developed taught us all how we *could* do it; taught us the value of traditions. You could say it started everything off.'

Art rubbed his head. 'So it's still going on today then? There's actually someone who delivers presents at Christmas? *Really?*'

'I already told you Art, it isn't *one* person. There are thousands of operatives – the technology doesn't exist that would allow one person to do all that in one night. It is still going on today – but only just.'

'Oh.' Art said, deflated. 'Why only just?'

'A century or so ago, it became harder and harder to leave presents that everyone would assume someone *else* had bought. The more control people had over their lives, the harder it was to let the big man take the credit. So as we go further up the centuries, presents had to be more or less replaced with ... well ... random acts of kindness, from anonymous benefactors. And while we're on that subject of the big *man*, half the operatives were *women* – male chauvinism turned it into a big *man* in a sleigh, so it did.' She folded her arms defiantly.

'So ... there's not much left to do then? That part's nearly all finished?' said Art.

Grandma dropped her arms down on the table. 'Art – didn't you learn *anything* about Time when you were there? It'll *never* be finished.'

'Okay, okay, take it easy. But you said it wasn't going on much today ...' Grandma sighed heavily. 'Listen. The village's Portal technology, and everything we learned about it, means that we have access to all Times simultaneously. Delivering to *every* house in the world, even for just *one* night of every year, takes *millions* of trips – we'll pretty much never be finished delivering into the past. It's not happening nearly as extensively today as we sit here in *this* point in Time, but the sheer size of the task means we have to keep going back in Time, night after night, year after year, to where we left off, and carry on. It'll take centuries, and we're not sure how many. But it all works out because Time knows that we eventually catch up. And someday we will, but it's a long way away. A *very* long way away. And that's only one department of the whole agency, so it is.'

Art was beginning to understand, but the concept was making his mind boggle. 'Just *one* department? There's more? What else do you have to do?'

Grandma laughed. 'Oh Art ... where to start? It's endless so it is. And like I said, it's better you find out gradually. But ... I'll let you in on one of them if you like.'

Art perked up. 'Go on,' he said.

'We choose Agents and Operatives from all over Time – so, obviously there's a department that deals with recruitment and training.'

Art looked at her oddly. 'What do you mean by that?' he said.

'You'll find out, so you will. Probably very soon. Remember I said it though.'

'Erm, okay,' he said. He sat in thought for a minute, then spoke out loud without realising. 'So there's no actual Santa Claus.'

Grandma started. 'What? I wouldn't say *that* now!'

'But you just said ...'

'I know what I said, but you have to read between the lines. Remember what I said about the whole thing – it's *huge*. So many different departments spanning so many millennia, so to speak. There has to be someone leading all that, someone co-ordinating every department, making sure everything runs smoothly. If history has taught us anything, it's that leadership *works*; something that big can't operate without it. So I suppose, by today's understanding of the legend, *that* person could be thought of as Santa Claus, yes.' She sat back and folded her arms, regarding Art silently.

Art rested his head in his hands. 'Whoa,' he managed. And then he heard movement from the hallway – footsteps approaching the door. Grandma heard it too, and sat up straight again.

'Now remember what I said about the recruitment department.'

And then, the young version of Maga that Art had travelled back from The L-Shaped Village with strolled in, as casually as anything. Art dropped his hot drink into his lap.

Chapter Two
REBORN

The door to Danny's bedroom flew open; he was still in bed, and wide-eyed at the intrusion. Michael grabbed Danny's arm and yanked him out of bed. 'Mum said *GET UP*! Can't you hear from up here, you idiot? You're right above the kitchen!' Michael laughed at the sight of his little brother clattering to the floor – the first bruises of the day. Michael waltzed out of the door and yelled down the stairs as he went.

'Mum – I asked him to get up but he just swore at me. Dad said the next time he did that he'd lose his pocket money.'

Danny pulled himself upright. Another morning. Another day of dealing with Michael and Amiele. They usually woke him up somehow in the morning, but today was particularly rough. The feeling of the slight bubble of anger sparked inside him again. He took a deep breath, fought it back, and seemed to be winning. He heard his brother carrying on, but managed to shut it out. He walked out of his room and tried the bathroom door. It was locked. He knocked gingerly. 'Are you gonna be long? I need the loo ...'

'Get lost Dan. I'm in here and I'll be out when I'm ready,' came the snarl of his sister. He walked back to his room to get dressed. This was nothing out of the ordinary for Danny, the way they spoke to him. He had never known any better, which was a shame for a young boy still in infant school, but for some reason he wasn't dealing with it as well as he always had. He had fought back the bubble of anger in the pit of his stomach, but it wasn't *gone*, just shrunk to a manageable level.

When he got back to his room, however, his father was waiting for him inside.

'What did you say to him?' he demanded.

'I didn't say anything, honestly!'

'Michael said you swore at him. I told you yesterday you'd lose your pocket money if you did it again!'

'I did not!' Danny protested.

'DON'T ARGUE WITH ME! YOUR BROTHER IS OLDER THAN YOU – HE DOESN'T LIE!'

'HE DOES! ALL THE TIME!' His father looked at him with wide eyes of anger.

'NO POCKET MONEY! AND IF YOU CARRY ON, THERE'LL BE NONE NEXT WEEK EITHER! NOW HURRY UP AND GET DRESSED!' His father stormed out of the room, slamming the door behind him.

Danny sat on the side of his bed, deflated. He hadn't had any pocket money for so long, he couldn't remember the last time he could actually *buy* something from the shop on the way to school. The bubble of anger was growing again, and it was getting harder to control. He slowly finished getting dressed, and was just heading for the door when Michael burst in again. He headed straight for Danny's money box resting on the top of his chest of drawers.

'Michael – what are you doing?'

'Shut up! I haven't got any money for sweets today, so I'm taking some of your savings. Is this all you've got?'

'But that's for my model aeroplane! Leave it alone!'

Michael ignored him, and carried on emptying his money box. Danny ran over to try and stop him, but Michael shoved him to the floor by his face, and laughed at the sight of his little brother falling down.

Danny looked up at his brother laughing at him, and he felt himself losing control. The bubble of anger he had been controlling suddenly exploded in his stomach, and it made him feel sick. He was so angry he couldn't see straight, and the pain of it made him cry out; he lay on the floor, blinded and paralysed by confusion. The sound of Michael laughing at him wasn't helping, nor was the sound of his money box becoming more and more empty. Then all of a sudden, pain filled his head as if it was splitting apart, and he clutched at it, crying out again. Through the pain he felt his mind filling with images and feelings, his brain swelling to bursting point as forty years of memories exploded through from the back of his brain, forcing their way to the forefront, and embedding themselves, never to be removed. They were just a jumble of scenes and exchanges, mixed up, out of order, and seemingly not his own. He couldn't understand what he was seeing, and why there was such searing pain whenever he tried to make sense of them. He may have been screaming the whole time, but he wasn't aware of what his body was doing any more. Four decades of memories in one jumbled knot of confusion threw themselves at his consciousness all at once, far too much for any brain to process, let alone that of a seven year-old. His brain seemed to settle for the main memory for now, anger, and it filled his whole body like an electric shock, and he writhed like a snake, trying to rid himself of the feeling.

Slowly, but still painfully, the memories started to stretch out into separate pools, and as each tendril stretched and snapped, spasms of pain shot through his brain and down the length of his body. Each pool of images and feelings seemed to order itself relative to the next, and before long the whole four decades stretched back behind him like a long straight road that he daren't look back at. And then just as slowly, the pain started to gradually subside as the images and sounds felt familiar again, and started to mingle with his existing memories of his seven Earth years. And all of a sudden he realised they *were* his memories, lost for an instant, but now back, to stay, defining him and shaping him. And the very next thing he felt, was that he was not the sort of person to suffer a 'young' fool like Michael.

He was breathing heavily, angry, upset, tears streaming down his face from the lessening pain, as he slowly rose to his feet. His face was contorted into an expression of pure hatred, and his eyes were suddenly surrounded by deep age lines, the whites of his eyes lined with red blood vessels.

Michael was still laughing, thinking he had just witnessed a tantrum, oblivious to whom he was now facing. The memories of Danny's discovery were still there, but he hadn't looked for them yet, the need masked by the rage streaming through his system, and to all intents and purposes, he stood before his brother as the formidable General of the Blue Triangle army.

The thought that his youth had blinded him from seeing how caustic Michael was, and that he actually had some brotherly feelings for him sickened him, and he clenched his fists, turning his knuckles white.

Three memories forced their way to the front of his mind as he thought of how to tackle his opponent - the rules of engagement that he had leant about during his time in that strange land; his respect for those rules that lessened the more time he spent with his supposed second-in-command; and the fact that he was not in that world now – the rules did *not* apply. But at the same time, his infinitely more mature mind reminded him that he was *not* his brother, *not* so cruel.

Quick as a flash, Danny ran forward and batted the money box out of his brother's hand, and delivered a stinging open-handed slap to the side of his face, and not the closed fist blow that he knew Michael would not hesitate to use. Michael reeled, shock and anger showing on his face.

'Why you little ...' Another slap landed on the other side of his face, the force of it sending him over sideways. He nearly fell, but managed to steady himself.

'What are you doi...' another landed home, his cheek beginning to redden, and this time he lost his balance and folded onto the floor, the shock and anger on his face replaced by confusion. His tiny, unassuming little brother had reacted impossibly fast, and his movements seemed calculated and precise. As was the voice that erupted from his tiny chest.

'You have annoyed me for the last time, *brother*,' Danny fumed.

Michael shot up onto his feet again, and aimed a blow to the usual spot on Danny's arm. It seemed slow and clumsy to Danny now, and quicker than the eye could see he pushed the muscular part of his forearm upwards and blocked the blow in the middle of his brother's exposed forearm bones.

Michael howled in pain at the blow he had tried to inflict, and another stinging slap landed on his face. Danny had landed four in the same place now, and the area was beginning to glow red.

'How much more can you take, brother? I can last all day. Can you say the same?'

Michael hesitated, then raised his hand to try another blow, but his face exploded with more pain as another slap landed home from nowhere, and he crumpled to the floor again. Danny lowered a pressing knee to his brother's chest, and grabbed him by the scruff of his neck. Michael's eyes grew wide, and wild.

'Run along now, sibling. Run to 'daddy' – tell him everything. You can be safe in the knowledge that you are not lying this time.' Michael's face was beginning to fill with fear on the back of confusion, and he made no attempt to fight. Danny moved his face to within an inch of Michael's.

'But a word of warning. Every time you ... *report* ... an incident such as this, however far-fetched, I will ENSURE it comes true. After all, I must *earn* the reputation you have given me, mustn't I?'

Michael's face was filled with definite fear now at the sight of Danny's hatred-filled eyes. The strength in Danny's hands grasping at his collar was frightening, and the speed with which he had countered Michael's every attempt to fight back had shocked him. Danny released his brother's collar and slowly rose. He walked over to where his money box was lying on the floor, picked up the loose change that surrounded it, and flung it all at Michael.

'Enjoy your ... *sweets*,' Danny spat. 'Now *get out*.'

Michael scrambled to his feet and fled the room. Danny walked over to the mirror and regarded his reflection. He looked deep into his own face, and sighed heavily, noting the change in his eyes.

'You are so old ... and so young,' he mused. He narrowed his eyes, and smiled darkly. 'What shall you do with it, I wonder?'

From the hallway he heard the bathroom door swing open, and the sound of padding feet as his sister emerged.

'Dan – bathroom's free. You'll need to get a towel though – I used yours,' she shouted through his door.

A grim smile broke out on Danny's face. 'Ah yes. Sister.'

He strode towards his bedroom door, opened it, and swept through. Ameile was still making her way back to her room when Danny emerged on the landing.

'From now on,' he piped up, 'you will be out of the bathroom at seven o'clock precisely. Or woe betide you.' He stepped into the bathroom and shut the door behind him. Ameile laughed in shock at his audacity.

'I don't think so,' she said to herself as she strode into her room.

Danny rummaged through the bathroom cabinet, and found what he was looking for in amongst his sister's bathroom products: two bottles, remarkably similar in design, vastly different contents. He swapped the labels over, then swapped the positions of the bottles over, closed the cabinet with a grin, and went about having a shower.

Seven year-old children very rarely have a shower in the morning, usually opting for a bath in the evening instead, until their pride gets the better of them and they shape into young adults, wanting privacy to preen. But Danny wasn't even a *young* adult anymore, and he opted for a long hot shower, revelling in the luxury. He eventually turned the mixer taps off, dried himself down, and wrapped a towel around himself to walk back to his room.

But then he caught sight of himself in the mirror, a blurry image of the seven year-old through the misted glass, and he stopped. He rubbed his hand along it, clearing a path of pure reflection, and he started to remember the blurry edges of everything around him as he was transported from one place to the next. The memory grew more vivid, and he remembered something, just a whisper of a memory, something *he* had said, just before he ... but the memory wasn't strong enough yet. What had he said? It seemed important, like something he should do. He concentrated hard. It was a 'P' word, he was sure of that. But what was it – *pro*-something. *Pro – mice?* Promise! A Promise!

His memory of Hité suddenly emerged, standing before him as the outlines of her image grew clearer, and of something he had promised her. What *would* he have promised her? He leant on the side of the sink and thought hard. What had she asked him – *go and be the person you* want *to be*. And he remembered agreeing, and thanking her, before ... before ... two people standing either side of him ... still unclear ... but fondness for both of them, he was sure of that. He searched his mind for their names. A ... Art – and a Mage, definitely a mage. Maga! Art and Maga! His two friends from ... the battle. The Battle?

His eyes widened as he remembered the battle between his own forces and those of the little village. Only this time, he was remembering it from his *own* mind, his *own* emotions, not false ones placed there by someone elusive and dark. Someone who always came to him with a smile but blackened his thoughts whenever he did. His memories of the things he had done whilst under the influence of this evil character sickened him, and he almost threw up in the sink. And out of desperation he searched his mind for redemption of any kind, some hope that he wasn't that person anymore. And then he found it. The memory of sitting among the people of the village he had attacked, with the Mind-Charm who had saved him, and who had seen him for the innocent that he was, for the most part. Art and Maga were by his side, reassuring him, welcoming him, despite everything. And he remembered Hité telling him how he had been manipulated, how the legitimate hatred had been turned into anger and rage by the man with the staff. He remembered his anger, and how he had forgiven the people of the village for what had caused it, and how they had forgiven him. And he remembered how it had ended; a promise – a favour really – to be *himself*, just himself, as he would choose to be, only this time armed with knowledge and experience far beyond his human years.

But he caught himself. Hatred had been a part of his life for so long; he was unsure he would be *able* to choose the right path. But a promise was a promise, and he resigned himself to trying, at all costs.

There was a part of his mind that found the goodness hard to accept, however. *I could have some fun with this,* it thought. But then he thought of Art and Maga, out there somewhere, just children, and how he was uniquely qualified to help them. How he *wanted* to help them, a strange feeling after so many years of hatred for anyone resembling them.

He walked back to his room, ideas filling his head of how he could find them, and then how he could help when he did. He enjoyed the feeling of the friendship that had grown between them in the short time he had known them. But the part of his mind that had promised him a little fun was not that easily dimmed.

Chapter Three
THE STUDENT

For some reason, Art had almost totally forgotten about Maga. He had been so preoccupied with finding out his Grandma's role in all of this, both Maga and Danny had completely slipped his mind. Was that also due to the effects of travelling through a Portal? He had remembered travelling through very clearly, and the things Hité had said moments before it happened, so how had he forgotten about his travelling companions?

Maga smiled reticently. 'Hello Art. Erm, how's things?'

Art stood up slowly. He walked over to Maga, and prodded him with his index finger. 'You're ... really *here*.'

'Yes, I'm here. I *think* I arrived at exactly the same time as you did. Just not *where* you did.'

Art looked at Grandma, incredulously. She looked totally nonplussed. 'You ... *knew* he was coming here?'

'Come on now Art. Remember what I was talking about,' she said.

Art could hardly believe it. 'You're one of Maga's *Instructors*?'

'Oh no, nothing so grand.' She replied. 'But someone has to keep an eye on him while he's here, so they do. He can't just go wandering the streets now, can he?'

Art sat down again, and Grandma refilled his mug. Maga took a seat as well, but he declined a mug from Grandma when she offered.

'Maga will be staying here with me,' she started. 'I had a communication from his Instructors at the Faculty a while ago – they didn't give me much time to prepare, but

I think I've got everything arranged. Maga will pose as my foster child. I'll look after him like my own, and see that his training goes smoothly. Not that his training will be down to *me*.'

Art looked up. Even Maga started a little. 'Who will be training me?' Maga said.

'Not even I know that, dear. The chances are you won't even meet him or her.'

Maga looked a little nervous. 'So what will happen then?' he asked.

'What will happen will happen,' she said simply.

'That's not good enough,' Art cut in. 'You must know more than that. Come on – out with it.' Art was becoming quite good at being direct, and even Grandma looked impressed. Maga just looked grateful for the support.

Eventually, Grandma relented, with a heavy sigh. 'Okay, okay. I'll tell you what I know, but I'm afraid that's not a lot. One of Maga's instructors is here, somewhere. He or she will arrange a series of very basic academic lessons for you to learn, and the odd written test based on those lessons, and monitor how you get on. I probably won't meet him or her, but you will.'

Maga looked deflated. 'That's it? That's all I'm here to do? Just some lessons?'

'I told you I don't know much.'

'But I'm training to be a Mage. Shouldn't I be learning how to ... do *magic* and stuff?'

'Maga – you have so much to learn. He or she may teach you *some* magic, but certainly nothing that requires a Staff. Experience of life is one of the most important things you can gain - teaching someone advanced magic before they know where and when to use it is extremely dangerous.'

Art could see the disappointment in Maga's eyes. He wanted to tell him again how great he would turn out to be, all the things he had seen the older Maga do every year, and how dearly he was friends with him.

Grandma stood up and wandered over to the dresser. She opened a drawer and lifted out a pile of folded clothes – Art recognised them as the school uniform of the primary school that fed to the school he was at now.

'Maga – how old are you?' Art said.

Maga sighed. 'Fourteen. Just turned.' Art could see him recalling something. He could tell Maga was missing home already.

'Well I'm afraid you don't look anywhere near fourteen years in this world- you're just too tiny. You may just pass as a year two if you're lucky.'

Grandma was grateful for the input. 'That's right dear. You're expected at Bush Mill Primary first thing tomorrow.

Maga looked up. '*School*? You're kidding me! I've nearly *finished* lessons at home – don't tell me I have to start again?'

Art was beginning to feel for Maga now. 'He has a point, Grandma. Does he have to start straight away? He's just got here after all – he has to have *some* time to settle in.'

'I'm sorry Maga,' she said. 'Part of the training is life experience as a human – it has to start straight away. The people at the Faculty were very specific.'

Just then the door swung open, and Walt breezed in. Art felt a pang of emotion – after all, he hadn't seen his brother in over three days, though it had been only minutes for Walt.

'Hey Art,' he said. 'Gran – have you got any more cake? Oh ... hello.' Walt spotted the new face at the table.

'Sorry – where are my manners, now?' Grandma said. 'Walt, this is ... Nicholas. Nicholas – this is Art's younger brother Walt.'

Maga was frozen to the spot, as if he had seen a ghost. Grandma nudged him out of his stupor with her elbow. 'Er ... hello Wa ... Walt.'

'Nicholas is staying with me for a while,' Grandma said. 'I'm fostering him until he can be with his parents again.'

Maga's reaction hadn't gone unnoticed by Art. What was it – recognition? It was a shock of *some* sort.

'Hello Nicholas,' Walt said with a smile. 'Do you want to play on the computer?' His caring side kicked in for the young nervous looking boy, who was actually bordering on the same age as him.

'I'm okay thanks,' he said, but Grandma elbowed him again. 'Er, I mean ... okay. Thanks.'

'Just before you two go off,' Grandma started, 'Walt – do you think you could make sure Nicholas gets to school okay tomorrow? He's a little nervous – first day and all.'

Walt's chest swelled a bit. 'Oh yeah - 'course I can. You'll like Bush Mill Nicholas – I used to go there – so did Art. There's this teacher there who looks like he's wearing a false nose, glasses and moustache – but he isn't! Don't laugh at him though. He's alright.' They both walked out of the room together, Walt with his arm around Maga's little shoulders.

Walt called back through the doorway. 'I haven't forgotten about the cake, Grandma.'

Grandma watched them go, with fondness in her eyes. 'You see Art – Maga will be fine here. And I know he'll do well. You mark my words.'

'Yeah I know,' said Art, 'but making him start school again? That's just cruel.'

'Oh it won't be forever. He'll only be here a year – two if he doesn't work hard, but I'm sure he'll manage.'

Grandma went back to the drawer in the dresser again; she pulled it open and fished out a brown envelope. The writing on the front looked familiar; it was an unknown language, but Art had seen it before - the letter Scem had received from the Blue Triangle army had been written in the same strange dialect. Grandma returned to the table and handed it to him.

Art accepted it, looking more than sceptical.

'Well go on then – open it,' she said. Art looked at the writing on the front. It was in thick black ink, strange symbols in a seemingly random pattern, separated into two words, if that's what they were. One was a three letter word, the other a four letter word. He looked at his Grandma.

'What does this say?' he said.

She smiled, encouragingly. 'Well, I've handed the envelope to *you*, so ... what do you think it says?'

He looked again. 'But how can this be my name – Elfee has *five* letters.' He held it up for her to see.

'Well now that's a puzzle, isn't it? Go on – open it up.' She handed Art a letter knife and he opened up the letter. Inside was a piece of cream-coloured paper, folded into four. It looked like the sort of paper the Amarly map had been printed on from the mission in the village. He unfolded it. It was a brief message, maybe eight or nine words long, written in the same strange hand as his name was supposedly written in on the envelope. He recognised the same two words at the top – his name in this strange language.

'I ... I can't read this,' he said. 'What am I supposed to do with it?'

'That's your first assignment,' she said. She went to the drawer a third time, and pulled out a little package wrapped in brown paper.

'What do you mean *my first assignment*? I'm not training for anything – *Maga* is.'

'Okay, you don't have to think of it as an assignment. Think of it as something that will greatly help Maga out if *you* can also read and understand this language. He has some trying times ahead – he'll need you.' She unwrapped the package, and handed Art the most incredible leather-bound notebook he had ever seen. It was light brown, beautifully sewn together with gold thread, about half the size of a piece of office paper, and at least two inches thick. The pages were made of thick cream paper, and the edges were gilded in gold ink.

'Use this journal - decipher the language in the letter and write it in here. It's the only way you'll learn.'

Art was leafing through the journal. All the pages had a little symbol at the bottom, each one different, but then some appeared again beside another, the further he flicked through. Page numbers.

'But how am I going to do that? This is total nonsense to me. How can I even begin to do this?'

Grandma stirred her drink absentmindedly. 'This is an ancient and very powerful language, Arthur, deeply rooted in magic, the likes of which neither of us will ever understand. But the beauty of it is we don't *have* to understand. Just like a caveman from centuries ago wouldn't have a clue how an electric razor works, if you showed him how, he could *use* it. The same applies here. If you heard this language spoken it would be as alien to you as this world is to Maga. But if you apply the symbols to the letters of our language's alphabet, it will translate *itself*.'

Art picked the letter back up again, staring at the language with renewed interest. 'But – this is *magic. I'm* not here to learn that. And you said it was dangerous to teach it when ...'

'This is *not* learning to create magic. That's what Maga will eventually learn to do. And once he, or any other Mage, creates it, *anyone* can use it. And Art – not everyone is aware of that, and it should probably stay that way.

Art looked confused. 'How do you mean *anyone can use it*?'

'Okay. Let's use an analogy. Now what can I use ... aha!' She picked up the table clock and took the battery out of the back; she held the power cell up to Art. 'Do you have any idea how to *make* one of these?'

'Erm, well no.'

'Exactly. But once you've got one, you can use its power, right?'

'Oh. Oh, I see.'

'There you are then. The language of EllShapyan uses magic created centuries ago, that permeates it and defines it. Certain people, even some *humans*, can learn to use its power, Mage or not. But remember what I said just now – not everyone is aware of that. And er, I wouldn't mention this to Maga, okay? It'll probably *look* like I'm teaching you magic, and I saw the disappointment in his eyes earlier too, so I did.'

'Oh,' said Art, looking crestfallen. He didn't like keeping secrets from Maga, not when he was feeling so homesick. 'Well why can't he learn this too?'

'He knows the *language*, dear. Everyone from Amarly does. But he's not aware of the *power* it can create – that's what I want to teach you.'

Art thought for a bit. 'But ... it's not really power, is it? I mean, its just translating from one language to another. Where's the power in that?'

Grandma leaned forward. 'I'll show you.' She rummaged around in the brown paper that the journal was wrapped in, and found a pencil. Then she smoothed out the brown paper and wrote something on it, in EllShapyan. 'Now ... try and pick that up,' she said.

Art looked at her oddly, and reached out for the paper. To his utter surprise, it was so heavy he could hardly get his fingers under any of the edges, and when he did he couldn't lift it off the tabletop more than an inch or two; it simply wouldn't budge.

'Whoa! How did ...'

Grandma turned the pencil over, and rubbed the word out with the eraser; the paper gave a small judder, and looked its normal weight again. Then she wrote something else on it, and before Art's eyes, the brown paper turned transparent. It was like a sheet of acetate. She picked it up, and handed it to Art.

'There's your *second* assignment, then. Work out how I did this. Or even better, turn it back. *Without* erasing the word.'

'Wow,' Art said. 'That's impressive.'

'It's the first stages of magic. Paper magic, or Lithogrics. Maga's instructors will get him onto it in no time, trust me. But this little project – this is just for you, understand?'

'Yeah. Yeah I do,' he said eagerly. 'But how do I start?'

'I told you. Learn to translate the letter.'

'But how do I learn to do that?'

She grinned. 'I'll give you a head start. You see your name on the envelope?'

'Er, yes – here it is.' He handed it to her.

'Well, this word is your first name. Art.'

Art could make out the three distinct symbols in the word. 'Okay,' he said.

She pointed to the second word. 'And this is your surname. Elfee.'

'But I told you, it can't be. There are only four symbols there.'

'Ah,' she said. 'but look closely at the fourth symbol. What do you notice about it?' Art studied it. It looked a little like a squashed small-case letter 'e'. Sort of. But there was something else; above it there were two dots, one on top of the other. Art assumed they were just part of the symbol.

'I don't see anything,' he said.

Grandma circled them with her pencil. 'Those little dots - they're *punctuation*. They mean there are *two* of that letter.'

Understanding washed over him. 'Oh I *see*. So there *are* five letters.'

'That's right,' Grandma beamed. 'So now you know what seven of the symbols are, and how they can be written. If I were you I'd write those down in your journal right now. That's a good head start, don't you think? You'll have the rest in no time.'

To his surprise, Art found his heart was pounding in his chest. His excitement was making his hands shake slightly as he smoothed out the envelope, and opened the journal to what he supposed was page one. He wrote his name in large letters, then wrote each of the symbols of his name in EllShapyan under them. But instead of writing the strange symbol that was the 'e' of his last name twice, he copied the punctuation, and wrote it once, with two small dots to the bottom right of it.

'Bravo, dear,' Grandma said. 'That's a good start so it is. Now see what you can do with the rest when you get the chance. Don't leave it too long now, okay? Come on, pack that all up and we'll all go and see what Maga's making of a games console, shall we?'

Art folded the clear paper up into four and put it in the pages of his journal, along with the letter. He went to follow her into the sitting room, when he suddenly remembered about Evi – she was in hospital. With a sharp intake of breath, he darted for the front door.

'Grandma – gotta go! Evi!' he managed, and disappeared behind the thick front door as it slammed shut.

DIALOGUE FOUR

'Morning Jimma.'
'Oh. Hello Pud. How long have you been here?'
'I stayed late. I fell asleep on the rug at about three.'
'You've been here all night? Have you had a shower?'
'Yes, down at the gym. I've done three thousand cents this morning.'
'Three thousand? That's further than you've done for a while. Are you okay. Pud?'
'I'm fine. Really.'
'Oh hang on – I know what this is all about. It's the Paradox alarm again, isn't it?'
'........ I just can't work it out ......'
'You don't need to. And pulling an all-nighter isn't going to make any difference.'
'Yes, but why did it go off? With all this extra surveillance we're doing, we should have some idea. Even in the unlikely instance that it's a future event, there should be some indication somewhere.'
'Pud – just forget about it. The thing about Paradoxes is ...'
'Yeah I know – you always spot them in the end. It's just ... there's only ever been one alarm before, and that turned out to be a near Time Extinction Event. I'm just edgy, that's all.'
'Listen – there's literally nothing we can do until we spot something. It's a waiting game – how long have we been in this business – you should know that by now.'
'Yeah I know, but ...'
'But nothing. We have the same discussion, every morning. And I'm getting a bit sick of it. And you're letting it affect your work now – I mean look at you – you're

exhausted.'

'Jimma, I'm fine. Since when has overworking affected me?'

'Pud ...'

'Yes ...'

'You're stirring your Stroth-Brew with the laser-wand. It's boring through the bottom of your tankard.'

'Oh tchu-fitzs! *It's gone everywhere!'*

'LANGUAGE PUD! Now clear that up, and go home. I'll see you back here after lunch.'

'No I'm fine, rea.....'

'GO HOME! Do I have to pull rank?'

'Yeah – you'd better, while you can. One rotation and counting 'till I get my fourth Star.'

'So still only three then. GET OUT!'

'Okay, okay. Leaving. Just before I go though, the communication's come back from the Faculty. It has an e-seal – dare I say it – Four Star clearance only. Want a look?'

'Oh. Well I'd better, yes. Flash it over to my screen. Thanks for that, by the way – having my own screen makes all the difference.'

'Not a problem. Flashing it over. Should be there .... nn ... now.'

'Got it. Now off you go.'

'What does it say?'

'I'll let you know, okay? Now get off with ......'

'Jimma? What is it? Jimma?...'

'Whoa .....'

'Jimma!'

'Erm, it's err ... it's nothing. I'll deal with it. Go on – get off.'

'I know that look. In fact I remember that look – it's not nothing, is it?'

'Pud, it's fine – I'll deal with it.'

'No WAY!'

'Pud, I ...'

'It's the Paradox, isn't it? You've found something!'

'No I ... look, just go, alright?'

'You HAVE! I knew it! What is it? I'm not going anywhere now, so you may as well tell me.'

'Look, it might be, alright? But I can handle it. We've got loads of time on this.'

'Show me. Flash it back over.'

'I can't do that, Pud. I ... hey! What are you doing?'

'I've got it. Let me have a look ...'

'PUD! Did you just steal that back? How did you ... STOP THAT!'

'We can look at the Seal, right? Just not at the main body of the text. Where is it, where is it ... Aha! There it ... oh. Oh ... that's not good.'

'I'll deal with this blatant insubordination later. But you've seen it now – you may as well give me your thoughts.'

'Well, they've selected the new Mage's instructor. But it's .... I mean that's a blatant Paradox – what are they doing?'

'I know – is it even possible, Pud?'

'Well, no. It's really not.'

'That's what I thought. And there's more - we have to arrange his transfer through the Portal and contact him with the details.'

'But that would mean we're involved. Why didn't it register? I mean the alarm went off, sure, but there's been nothing on the scans at all. And it won't be easy either – I mean, he's not even an instructor – how are we going to find him?'

'Well, according to the personnel list he's been a Shadow Instructor for the past four years – that'll be why it isn't listed.'

'Really?'

'Really. Access to the personnel files takes a slightly higher clearance than you have, Pud. It's a need-to-know basis thing.'

'And I suppose I don't need to know.'

'I don't make the rules up, Pud. Sometimes I wish I did ...'

'Yeah, because then you'd give me access, wouldn't you?'

'Probably not, no.'

'I was being sarcastic. It's a need-to-know thing.'

'Steady, Pud.'

'Okay, so what do we do?'

'Well, I'm not getting involved in this unless we have clearance, and an explanation.'

'From who? The Boss? Uniform Red again?'

'I suppose we don't have a choice. But I think this requires a bit more discretion – I don't want the Faculty knowing we were questioning them.'

'How do we go about it then?'

'We need to send an encrypted alert, priority one, directly to his console.'

'Oh, that'll be easy – this console can communicate with any other console through a little back-door programme your uncle wrote for just such a situation.'

'Really?'

'He didn't want anyone to find it, so he hid it well. But hey – I'm sneaky - it didn't take me long to spot the anomaly.'

'Why didn't I know about that?'

'Need-to-know. You didn't ...'

'I'M YOUR SUPERIOR!'

'I know, but ...'

'NO "BUT"S! How am I supposed to compile my Chronology Of Console History book if you keep things like that from me? What else haven't you told me?'

'Nothing. Honestly.'

'Why don't I believe you?'

'Erm ... no idea. Do you want to send this message or not?'

'This is not over, you understand?'

'Okay, okay. So the message reads ...'

'Right. Hang on, just let me think about it for a moment. ..... Okay – erm, "Dear Sir, Faculty planning a blatant Paradox involving the instruction of the newest Mage. Please advise."'

'That's it?'

'That's it. Send it over. CAREFULLY.'

'Okay. Sending – tracing – ooo that was close – just a bit longer – it's there.'

'What happened?'

'Someone's tracking communications.'

'Who?'

'I'm guessing the Faculty. They're intercepting everything using a sneaky programme that's almost as clever as your uncle's.'

'You're kidding me! We'll have to report that!'

'No point -it's untraceable. Can't prove it. And anyway, the lines of communication we just used aren't exactly legitimate.'

'Fair point. Okay – I'll wait on the response; you get off. See you after lunch.'

'What? I can't go home now! You know how much this has been bothering me – I want to find out what's going on!'

'Okay, okay. Go and lie down in the bunk and I'll call you if we get a response.'

'Well, that's better than nothing. Stroth-Brew?'

'Please.'

'Dough-Drops?'

'Oh yes.'

Chapter Four
evi wise

Art tore around the corner and into the forecourt of St. David's Hospital, nearly losing his footing as he went. He rushed up the steps and nearly smashed into the automatic doors as they swung open way too slowly for him.

Waiting at the side of the main doors was a figure, dark and blurry; but as Art went to look, he decided it wasn't worth looking at, and dismissed it. He searched his mental map of the hospital, etched into his brain after so many years, and raced towards the children's ward. He wasn't sure Evi would be there, as she was sixteen – slightly older than Art. But he would give it a try first. He navigated his way through the various floors and doors, eventually arriving at the main entrance to the ward. He pushed through the doors, and rushed up to the desk, and came face to face with Jenny Hopkins, the staff nurse that he, Dawn Levvy and Maga schemed, every year, to outwit as part of the plan to leave presents in the Children's Ward. He was sure *she* wouldn't know *him* however, as he had only ever seen her face in photographs himself – Maga's planning was always well presented.

'May I help you?' she said, calmly. She eyed the teenager, out of breath and scruffy from running. Art stared for a moment, before he checked himself.

'Erm, yes – erm – I'm looking for Evi. Evi Wise. She broke her wrist earlier today – is she here?'

'Evi Wise?' Jenny said, 'No, I don't think so. Are you talking about Nathan Wise's sister?'

'Yes. Yes I think so.'

'First him and now her, poor things. Well I can find out where she is for you – just let me log on.' She tapped away at the computer for what seemed like an age. Art was impatient, but was careful not to show it for fear of giving himself away to her, even though that was impossible. She eventually finished typing, and stared at the screen.

'Aha - there she is. Blue corridor, downstairs – ward 5. 'I can draw you a...'

'Thank you!' Art sang as he turned on his heels and sprinted for the doors again. He knew exactly where it was.

He landed at the bottom of the stairs with a bump and flew through the doors. Blue corridor was just up ahead, but as he hurried towards it, another figure was standing at the side, again blurry and somehow unclear. Again, as he went to look he dismissed it as nothing important.

He entered the fracture area and found ward 5. He rushed up to the desk to ask where Evi was, but he spotted her out of the corner of his eye, lying on one of the beds on the left. He ran over, but as he did he realised he didn't know what to say.

He arrived at the bed, and there she was, lying in a hospital gown, but still looking as radiant as ever. And as usual, Art's tongue tied itself in knots.

Evi's eyes lit up. 'Oh! Hello! What are you doing here?' she said, expectantly.

Art wondered how long he could stand there like a lemon, not saying anything, when he suddenly found his voice from nowhere. 'Erm, coming to see you. Are ... are you okay?'

She smiled. 'I will be. How did you know I was here?'

'Erm, Tina told me. Said you'd err ...' he pointed to her wrist.

'Yeah. It was hockey. I didn't even have the ball, I just tripped up near the goal and fell awkwardly on it, and it just snapped.'

Art winced. He knew what broken bones felt like. He noticed that her wrist was resting in an open brace, covered over loosely with lint; it hadn't been set in plaster yet.

'Well ... how long are you going to be in here?' he said.

'I don't know. They have to operate to straighten it out. Come and sit down.' She patted the chair to the side of her bed with her good hand; Art felt his face flush. He walked over sheepishly, like he was being told off, and sat down in the chair. The cushion was huge, and the air hissed out of it as he sank down, creating an embarrassing, long silence.

'What's that?' she said, looking at the journal he was still cradling under one arm.

'Oh.' Even he had forgotten about it. 'Erm, Grandma gave it to me. It's a sort of diary. I don't really know why she gave it to me.'

'Oh,' she said, and the silence carried on.

'So erm, where's your family?' Art said.

'Oh, they've been. They've just popped home for some tea and they're coming straight back. Your timing was perfect.'

Art panicked. 'Oh, I didn't ... like ... *plan* it or anything ...'

'I know, I know. But I'm glad you came.' She was looking at him, and it wasn't helping. He looked at her, and his stomach flipped. He looked away again quickly. Then she spoke, ever-so quietly.

'You're still taking me.'

Art knew exactly what she was talking about. She had asked *him* to the New Year's Ball, quite unexpectedly, the day he had been transported away to the L-Shaped Village. Then he realised, with a start, that it was *still* that day; his days away at the L-Shaped Village had messed with his concept of time.

'But ... your wrist ... it'll still be painful,' he said. 'The ball's only in a couple of days. You should rest it.'

She kept her gaze on him, unwavering. 'I don't care. I said pick me up on Thursday, and I meant it.'

'Oh. Well we'll ... we'll see. *You should rest it,*' he said once more. She smiled warmly at him, and his stomach flipped again.

Across the ward, Art noticed the dark figure yet again, this time directly in his eye-line. But this time, unlike before, he didn't immediately lose interest when he looked at it. But when he tried to focus on it, the bit he was looking at seemed to vanish, and then reappear in his peripheral vision when he moved his eyes. He found he couldn't concentrate on it for long, and eventually, he did lose interest.

'Art? What are you looking at? Art?'

He started. 'Oh. Sorry. I thought I saw something. Well, I didn't actually. I don't know what I was looking at ...'

Evi took his hand, and squeezed it. Her skin was soft and warm, unlike anything he had felt before, and he felt his chest pounding.

'Art – are *you* okay? Tina said you'd had a funny turn.'

'Oh. Erm, yes I'm fine. Really.' His stomach was doing back-flips as she squeezed his hand – he definitely was *not* fine. 'How did you know about that, anyway?' he said.

'Tina sent me a text. She was really worried.'

'Oh. I'm okay. It's *you* I'm worried about.'

Evi looked at his hand in hers as she spoke. 'You know, they nearly put me in the Children's Ward. Wheeled me up there and everything.'

Art's ears pricked up.

'Some of the toys were still there. In the play area. I don't know how you did it.'

Art's heart was still pumping in his chest, but he was unsure whether her hand in his was causing it, or her words. 'It ... it wasn't ...'

'I *know* it was you, Art - stop denying it,' she said. 'I think it's really nice.' She squeezed his hand again. He thought she was joking, but when he looked in her eyes there was no hint of sarcasm, only admiration. He felt his face flush again, and wondered what colour it could possibly be, as it was flushed already. He looked down at his hand, paralysed in hers.

'Do ... do you think so?' he said quietly.

Her eyes widened. 'IT WAS YOU! I *knew* it!' she beamed.

Art looked surprised. 'You tricked me ... hey that's not fair!'

'I *knew* it!' she said again. 'I'm sorry – I just had to know. I'm sorry.' She tried to take his hand with both of hers, and shrieked when she tried to move the broken wrist. Art shot to his feet and tried to calm her. There was pain in her eyes and Art felt helpless to do anything.

'Shall I get the doctor?' he said, and felt stupid; it's not as if the doctor could just fix it there and then. Her face relaxed slowly, and she breathed heavily, her eyes closed.

'You should rest that wrist for a while after the operation,' Art said again.

She fixed him with a stare, but it turned into a smile as the pain subsided. 'You wouldn't stand me up, would you?' she said, looking sorry for herself, her lip pouting falsely.

Art smiled at her. 'You can't make me do *anything* with that smile, you know.'

'Yes, I can,' she chuckled. Art knew it was true. She found his hand again, and squeezed it, and he returned the gesture, feeling hopelessly lost in his feelings for her.

'Evi!' came a shriek from some distance away. Art turned, and saw Evi's little brother Nathan cascading down the ward. He had a bright blue cast on his wrist, which was covered with writing and drawings. He was followed by his parents, Jack and Jackie. Art automatically went to take his hand away, but Evi stopped him with an iron grasp. He looked at her, and couldn't help smiling, even though he was more nervous than he had ever felt in his life before.

Her parents, Jack and Jackie, reached the bed. 'Hello, dear. Everything alright? Has the doctor been round yet?' Jackie said. Art saw her eyes dart to their hands, still clasped, and the hint of a smile showed in the corners of her mouth. 'Oh. Erm, you must be Arthur. How are you, dear?'

Art looked at Evi; she had a guilty look on her face. 'Yeah, I'm ... I'm okay thanks,' he managed. Jack stepped up, though his chest was sort of puffed out a bit. He held his hand out for Art to shake, and had a serious look on his face.

'Jack Wise. Pleased to meet you.'

Evi finally released his hand, and Art shook Jack's. 'Art. Art Elfee.'

Jack looked as though he was sizing Art up. 'Mmm. Good strong handshake, that's what I like to see.'

'Oh dad, stop it will you?' Evi chuckled.

Art thought it was best to make his get-away sooner rather than later. 'Well, I'd best be off.' He stood with his hands by his sides, not really knowing what to do. He turned to Evi. 'Erm, I'll see you ... on ... erm ...'

'*Thursday*, yes. See you then,' she smiled. He moved awkwardly backwards, and headed towards the reception desk. Jackie was still wearing an amused smile, and her gaze followed him as he went. He folded himself through the big double doors and began his journey home, a strange feeling in his stomach.

*

Art knocked on Tina's front door, and she answered it almost straight away.

'Art – how are you feeling? Are you okay?' she said, as she ushered him through the door and into the front room.

'I'm okay. I've just come from the hospital.'

She looked concerned. 'What did they say?'

'Oh no, I wasn't there for me, I'm okay – I went to see Evi. She's having an operation tonight.'

'Oh?' she said. Her whole manner changed, and she wore the kind of smile Jackie had been wearing.

'Stop it, will you?' he said.

'Okay, okay, tetchy boy. How is she?'

'She's okay, but it's a pretty bad break. Her family's there now.'

'Oh – they err ... they saw you two together, huh?'

'I said stop it!' Art insisted.

Tina's mum poked her head around the kitchen doorway. 'Hello Art. Cuppatea?'

'Yes please, Mrs. Rosenbaum.' Art was grateful, but really, he yearned for a Stroth-Brew.

Tina spotted the journal under his arm. 'What's that?'

Art was about to say it was nothing, when he had an idea.

'Actually, I was hoping you could help me with something.' He picked out the letter Grandma had given him from amongst the pages of the journal, and unfolded it. He handed it to her.

She took it, and studied the strange writing for a while. 'What's this?' she said.

'It's an encrypted message, from someone. I don't know who sent it, but I'd like to know what it says. Do you think you could help?'

'Well, I don't know. Is it substituting letters from our alphabet?'

Art remembered what Grandma had said about the language translating itself when applied to the alphabet, but he hadn't thought of it in *that* way. He was glad he had asked her now. 'I think so. Actually yes – the envelope has my name on it. So I already know some of the letters.' He flipped open the diary to the first page and showed her. She took the diary, and studied the page.

Tina's mum came in with a cup of tea for them both. 'Would you like to stay for your tea dear?' she said.

'No, it's okay Mrs. Rosenbaum – dad's cooking tonight.'

She grinned. 'So would you like to stay for your tea dear?'

Art laughed. 'His cooking's not *that* bad. I'll man it out.'

She laughed too. 'Well the offer's there if you want it,' she said as she waltzed out into the back garden to carry on with her potting.

Tina was still studying the page of the diary. 'Could you leave this with me?' she said.

Art was unsure. 'My Gran gave it to me and made me promise not to show anyone.'

'Not a problem,' she said, and took out her mobile phone. She lined up the camera over the letter and took a shot, then took one of the first page of the diary.

'Done,' she said simply.

'Wow. D'you think you can do it?'

'I'm not one to dodge a challenge. I'm sure I can work it out. But not tonight.'

Art looked puzzled. 'Why's that?'

She looked at him with that wry smile again. 'Because tonight, we're going to the shopping centre to get you some decent clothes.'

Art scoffed. 'How would *you* know what decent clothes are?'

'I don't. But the shop assistants do. No arguments – you're not going to the ball on Thursday looking like *that*.'

Art rolled his eyes. 'Well of course I'm not going dressed like *this*. I've got a ... er ... tux.'

Now it was Tina's turn to scoff. '*You've* got a tuxedo? Your *own* tuxedo?'

'Well, no,' he said sheepishly.

'Whose then?'

Art rubbed the back of his head. 'It's ... erm, dad's old one.'

'Like I said, we're going shopping. Come straight back after tea, okay?'

Art smiled. 'Thanks, Tina. I'll see you later.'

*

Art arrived home to a warm welcome from his two faithful beagles, Speedy and Steph; they rushed up to him whimpering like they hadn't seen him for weeks. Their paws were covered in mud from the park.

'Hey guys. Did you run mum ragged again?' he said, and wiped their paws clean with the rag by the front door.

He scratched them both behind the ears, then went up to his room. They trailed in behind as usual, and headed straight for their beds. He sat down on his bed and thought hard about the incredible week he had had, even though it was still the same day. His whole life had changed in four eye-opening days in that time, and his whole understanding of the world had been turned upside down.

The Fragment was still secured around his wrist, but hidden under his sleeve. It had all started with that. Then the incredible journey to the L-Shaped Village, where he had learned that strange magic-like powers existed, although they were not as he imagined them to be. He had learned how differently a race of people can live their lives, and he had learned the hard way – by committing a crime that had shocked them all, and even though it was out of the ordinary for Art to have done, it wasn't out of the ordinary for his world. And then something even stranger happened – he had met a young version of one of his best friends, who had never met *him* before. And then he remembered the strange feats he had seen the older Maga perform, and he realised, with a slight jolt of shock, that he actually *wasn't* a stranger to magic at all.

But then, just when he thought things couldn't get any stranger, his time at the village ended and he learned that one of the best known legends of his time actually *wasn't* a legend after all. It was vastly bigger than he ever thought, virtually unrecognisable in fact, but the legend everyone knew as Santa Claus, of a sort, was real.

His head should have been spinning, but he found he could actually deal with it all surprisingly well, as if his mind had grown capable of holding information that ordinary minds couldn't. He had heard several times that only ten percent of the human brain is actually used; maybe dormant parts of his brain, undiscovered parts, capable of dealing with the unbelievable, had been awakened. It would certainly explain why his bedroom, adorned with its many wonders crafted from his own hand, looked decidedly ordinary now. It was as if his home was ... not really his home any more. He knew it was, he felt comfortable in his own familiar surroundings, and he knew he was glad to be back. But there was an unmistakable feeling in his chest that this was one of only two places where he felt perfectly at ease. It felt more like a ... *home from home*. And so was the L-Shaped Village. He was part of them both now, unequivocally, unconditionally. The question was, would he ever have any real reason to go back there? And if not, could he make one up?

His mind was churning with unanswered questions and thoughts that he couldn't quite make sense of, and after a while they left him drained. He headed to the bathroom and brushed his teeth, which he hadn't done for nearly four days now, washed his hands ready for dinner, and padded back to his room. All the while his mind was processing as efficiently as it could, trying to make sense of the last few days. The ordinary was puzzling him now as much as the extraordinary; on the one hand, he had actually spent days away in another world, which took no time at all in this; and on the other, why on Earth would a beautiful being like Evi take even the slightest bit of interest in someone like him? He found them both equally puzzling, which surprised him, as one purely concerned matters of the human heart, and another the realization of a different plane of existence. He lay on his bed and buried his head in his pillow, his body unable to move with all the processing his mind was doing. But before long he heard his father shouting up the stairs that dinner was ready. He sighed, swung his legs around and onto the floor, and padded out of his room.

Chapter Five
THE ABDUCTOR

Danny came down the stairs in his school uniform, with an extremely grumpy expression on his face. He supposed if he was really going to make a go of his second chance of life, he would have to do everything properly, including going to ... eeuugh ... *school*. The thought of it made him sick; drawing, and painting, and learning maths and English, chanting times tables and singing hymns in assembly, and worst of all, *doing what he was told*. He shuddered as he thought of it. Not long ago he was a feared and respected General, with a huge army at his command, and now here he was faced with the prospect of endless 'Yes Miss's' and 'No Miss's'. But then again what else could he do? He had thought with relish about all the things he *could* do with a mind such as his, but a seven year-old boy was pretty limited in the things he would be *allowed* to do without drawing too much attention to himself.

The kitchen was a hive of activity as everyone went about making their breakfast, and as he rounded the hallway and could see through the kitchen doorway, he caught sight of his mother. He stopped. For some reason he hadn't expected to see her, which he immediately knew was silly. There was serious conflict in his mind; his human memories told him he'd seen her just yesterday, but his other memories told him he hadn't seen her for forty *years*. His father came into view, and he became even more confused. Had he seen him half an hour or so ago, or four decades ago? His head swam for a while, trying to process the impossible.

After a while, he took a deep breath, pulled himself together, and strolled into the kitchen.

'Morning, Danny,' his mother said. That was all it took. Without any control he ran up to her and hugged her legs as hard as he could.

'Oh, what's all this? Danny, this is very nice, but you'll be late for school.' She leant down and picked him up, with more than a little effort, and he clung to her neck with a vice-like grip.

He didn't let go. He was fighting back the tears, and doing a good job. He told himself this was silly, but his arms wouldn't slacken. His father was watching, still wearing the grimace from his scolding earlier on.

'Oh come on now, Danny. What's up?' she said, secretly enjoying the attention.

'I stopped his pocket money, that's what,' his father answered. Michael was sitting at the table, but he didn't snigger. His face stayed as still as a statue. Not a flicker.

'Oh, what did you do that for, Ian?' she said.

'He swore again at his brother. Isn't that right, Michael?' Michael said nothing.

Danny was oblivious to the conversation, lost in his thoughts, but the sound of his father's voice jarred him from his mother's grip. He slipped out of her grasp and ran into his father's, who looked shocked and decidedly awkward.

'Whoa. Erm, what's all this then?' he said.

'Nothing, Father,' Danny whispered. 'I've just missed you both, is all.'

'Erm, right, well, erm – lesson learned then. No more swearing, okay?' Ian patted Danny's back awkwardly. 'Come on then young man. Breakfast.'

Danny let go, feeling foolish and emotional at the same time, and sat down at the table. The sight of Michael stirred lesser but similar feelings, but he was more able to throw them aside. Especially as he had already been reacquainted with Michael and Amiele; for some reason it was the sight of his parents that had reawakened those feelings. He poured himself some cereal, and reached for the jug of milk. As he took it, Michael gave him a look, but Danny countered it with a flash of pure anger, and Michael looked down at his breakfast again.

'Milk, Michael?' Danny ribbed.

'That's not funny Dan,' Ian said.

Danny gave a wry smile. 'I know. Sorry Father.'

Ian gave him a quizzical look, as he folded his paper and put it down on the table.

'Father? Do you mind?' Danny gestured towards the paper.

'Erm, of course. You ... you want to ... *read* that?'

'Yes. Do you mind?'

'No. Err, go ahead.'

Danny picked it up and started scanning the front page as he spooned his breakfast into his mouth. Danny's mother and father looked at each other, wondering what was happening. They couldn't believe it. Literally, they *didn't* believe it.

'Erm, Danny,' his mother said, 'wouldn't you like something a little ... easier to read?'

'No, thank you, Mother. What does *abstain* mean?' he narrowed his eyes as he read the unfamiliar word.

Ian looked at him with wide eyes. 'Where does it say that?' he said.

Danny held up the paper so he could see. 'Just there, under *systemic*.'

Ian nearly fell off his chair in shock. 'Wh ... what how ... Liz – have you seen this?'

Danny's mother narrowed her eyes as she too looked at the paper, and then her eyes widened. 'Danny, that's ... that's amazing,' she managed.

'I know,' he answered, 'the government are actually thinking of *not* sending criminals to jail. It *is* amazing.'

Liz sat down next to him, more out of shock than anything else. 'Danny – why are you speaking like that?'

'Speaking like what, Mother?'

'Like ... *that*. You've never called me 'Mother' before. And you're so ... I don't know ... well spoken, and ... you're *reading*, and everything. How ... how can you be reading?'

Danny searched his human memories, and found a tiny snippet of information about the ridiculously easy books he had been given to read at school, and would still struggle with. But his other-worldly memories barged their way to the front and he remembered how he had been forced to learn to read quickly as part of the little jobs he had to do around the village; things got a lot easier for him when he could read the lists he had regularly been given, and managed to decipher what they wanted him to do. He couldn't recall much about *learning* to read after that, only that he just could. He also had a fairly good knowledge of a second language, involving strange symbols that his Mage would sometimes use when he wanted something out-of-the-ordinary to happen.

'I thought you'd be pleased, Mother.'

'Well, I am, I suppose, it's just ...'

'He's not reading that,' Amiele piped up. 'He's having us all on. Silly idiot.'

Michael looked at her in shock, as if he expected Danny to dart over and start slapping her.

But Danny didn't even look up. 'I would mind your tongue if I were you, Sister, or I'll tell Father where you're *really* going this evening.' That piece of information offered itself up to Danny's mind like the sweetest gift. Amiele immediately turned red, and Ian started questioning her. Danny smiled as he carried on eating his breakfast, listening to Amiele trying to lie her way out of trouble.

He flicked through the paper, scanning the pages. He had never actually *read* a paper before, but he had a vague idea of what one was, and he was intrigued. His mind had no trouble in reading relevant snippets of information from the paper whilst enjoying listening to the family argument going on in the background at the same time. Even he was surprised at how agile his mind was. He was enjoying both forms of entertainment, when his eye zeroed in on a picture in the middle pages, and he froze. It was a school portrait from the local secondary school, and even though there were over four hundred faces staring at him, he recognised one face instantly, middle row, far left. He searched his memories for who it could be; the part of his mind containing his seven years as a human youngster offered no suggestions, however hard he tried, even though he was *sure* he had seen this face not long ago. But he didn't think it would fit with his memories of the *other* world either, it was too ... *normal*, too friendly. It couldn't be there, could it? He was sure it couldn't, but where else was there to look? He gingerly stepped into his other memories, even though he told himself it was impossible. It couldn't be. But there it was, right in front of him. The same face just as he remembered it, friendly and welcoming, but strangely out of place. *Art Elfee.*

He quickly looked at the very front page again – it was the *local* paper. He flicked back to the middle pages, searching for whatever information he could glean from the article that went with the photo. He scanned down the column, and found what he was looking for – the name of the school: St. David's Comprehensive.

He jumped down from his chair and headed for the study. He tapped Michael on the shoulder as he went.

'Michael – with me,' he commanded, and though Michael looked at him wide eyed, he found himself blindly following.

Danny went up to the computer in the study, and glared at it. 'How does this thing work?' he said.

Michael looked at him quizzically. 'It's a computer. You just turn it on and type. Simple.'

'Show me then,' Danny snapped.

Michael yanked himself forward and turned the computer on. They both watched as the screen slowly came to life, and the software began to load itself. Danny had vague memories of this contraption, mainly consisting of being told not to touch it by pain of death. But he had an even vaguer recollection of it being good for looking things up.

'What do I do now?' Danny demanded.

'Well ... what do you want to do? Play a game?'

'Of course not, you cretin. I need information. How do I get that?'

'Oh – the internet. You just click on that icon there.'

Danny reached forward and tapped the screen with his finger. Nothing happened.

'Erm, no – with the mouse. I'll do it ...'

'I WILL DO IT. Show me how.'

Michael gave him a crash course on opening a program with the mouse, and entering information in the search engine. It wasn't long before he was matching Michael's speed, and even less time before he left Michael behind.

'Thank you, Michael. Now kindly get out.'

Michael stared at him as if he was about to say something, but Danny fixed him with his caustic stare again, and Michael quickly exited.

Danny looked at the keyboard, and clumsily typed out 'St. David's Comprehensive' in the search box. He tapped the enter key, and immediately the school website was listed along with other matches. He clicked it, and the screen was filled with a picture of a building, with the school name on a large sign to the left of the front entrance. He scanned the page, and clicked the 'pictures' tab. Immediately he was looking at class photographs similar to those he saw in the paper, but Art was not there. There were similar pictures below it, so he pulled the page down, and stopped at the third picture. There he was – Art Elfee, smiling at the top left of the picture. Danny stared at the screen closely – it was definitely him. The picture was clearer and much larger here – there was no mistake.

He clicked on the picture, and a list of the students' names came up – Art's name was near the top, but the writing was in black – clicking on it did nothing. So Danny navigated back to the search engine page, and entered 'Art Elfee' in the search box. He pressed the enter key, and the computer hummed and whirred like it was suddenly very busy. Eventually a list of pages came up, underneath a heading – *34,568 entries found.*

Danny stared at the first listing. *The Sunday Read - The Elfee/Ainsworth case.* The second listing was similar – they all were. The name Elfee had brought up over thirty four thousand listings, mostly related to a court case – Elfee versus Ainsworth. Danny scrolled down the page, and spotted an interesting looking one – *Dorothy Elfee – Abductor or Adopter?* Danny clicked it. It took him to an old newspaper article from 1940.

Dorothy Elfee, the woman at the centre of the Ainsworth Abduction case, is here examined and exposed, revealing a truth most shocking. Why she was allowed to officially adopt the little Ainsworth boy, when the circumstances surrounding the sudden loss of his only remaining parent remained suspicious, is beyond anyone. Here, we examine exactly what Elfee may have been accused of, and some shocking theories as to how she may have influenced the authorities' decision.

Jonathan Ainsworth, the little boy at the centre of it all, was raised by his mother, Ellie Ainsworth, previously Allcott, after the untimely death of her husband Albert, Jonathan's father, in the increasingly violent war against Germany. Ellie became very good friends with Dorothy Elfee, who suddenly moved into the house next door shortly after Albert's death. Dorothy seemed like a very neighbourly woman, and helped Ellie with her three year-old son on a daily basis, but it wasn't long before the records became confusing about exactly where Dorothy was living. As the months went by, Dorothy was seen out with little Jonathan more and more, and the increasingly frail Ellie Ainsworth was seen out less and less. On the 20th of November

1936, the police were called to Ellie's house by her neighbours, and discovered her body in the kitchen. Eye witnesses say the police were inside for a very long time, and after much shouting and screaming, Dorothy Elfee was led out of the house in handcuffs and Jonathan Ainsworth was taken into the temporary care of the police, having no other family to speak of.

However, the following day, Dorothy Elfee was seen going back into the house, with Jonathan Ainsworth, where they lived amid great controversy. She appeared in court no less than ten times, with little Jonathan in tow, and in November 1937, almost a year to the day after Ellie's death, Dorothy officially adopted the little boy. Jonathan Elfee, as he was known from that day on, continues to be raised by Dorothy, even though serious questions about the death of Ellie Ainsworth remain unanswered.

Police records show that Jonathan Ainsworth was petrified of Dorothy for a while after his mother's death, and during his initial interview by police, he identified his mother's killer as none other than Dorothy Elfee herself. However, this is the only mention of the case being anything other than a death by natural causes, which is how the case was concluded just one year after Ellie's death. Dorothy's court appearances during that time were shrouded in secrecy, and the judge and jury remain bound by law. Despite Elfee's best efforts, the story of her involvement in Ainsworth's death soon spread around the area, and while the boy was regarded with great sympathy, Dorothy was regularly attacked by violent verbal outbursts, and she moved from the area to the parish of St. Davids, although no one knows exactly where in the area she resides.

Danny couldn't believe what he was reading. He went back to the listings page and scrolled up to the very top story, which was a more recent article about the infamous court case, and clicked on it.

Twenty years after the final ruling in the Elfee/Ainsworth case, the court transcripts have been leaked to the media, causing much embarrassment to the Prosecution Service. They landed on the desk of one Sunday evening newspaper, and were published the following day. They reveal exactly what Dorothy Elfee, dubbed the Ainsworth Abductor, was charged with. The nickname she was given hardly seems fitting; she was charged with the brutal murder of Ellie Ainsworth, which followed a two-week abduction of Ellie's son Jonathan. The case was made even more confusing by the sudden appearance of Avarice Ainsworth, who claimed to be Albert Ainsworth's brother, Jonathan's uncle, who filed for custody of the boy. In a year-long court hearing, Dorothy Elfee gave evidence no less than ten times, and just before the verdict was due to be announced, Avarice Ainsworth disappeared. His whereabouts are still unknown to this day. Avarice's disappearance threw the case into disarray, and the evidence was ordered to be re-examined. His disappearance paved the way for Dorothy to adopt the Ainsworth boy, although no court in their right mind would allow the adoption of a young man by the alleged murderer of his mother. Even though she was questioned regarding Avarice's whereabouts, and the outcome was inconclusive, the court did allow Elfee to adopt the Ainsworth boy, to the outrage of the country. The evidence was never re-examined, and a verdict was never reached. Elfee was relocated with her newly adopted son, but she refused to change her name. Her whereabouts remain as elusive as Avarice's. The following ten-page dossier outlines the day-to-day proceedings of the court case, and raises some interesting questions itself about the integrity of the criminal justice system.

Danny sat back in his chair. Dorothy Elfee had been relocated to somewhere in the parish of St. David's. He did a rough count of the years in his head – he concluded she must be Art's great-grandmother, if she was related to Art at all. He navigated back to the main search engine page, and typed in *Elfee Family Tree*. He hit enter, and again thousands of entries sprang up. He clicked the first one, and immediately he was looking at a diagram of the Elfee Family Tree, which started, surprisingly, with just one person: Dorothy T. Elfee. There was a line down to her only child, Jonathan Elfee, who was married to Alianor Templar. They had a son and a daughter, Mitchell and Maisie. Mitchell was married to a woman named Claire Sommers, and they had two sons – Arthur and Walter Elfee. The tree ended there.

Danny noticed a thick telephone directory lying next to the computer, and he flicked through it until he found the entry he was looking for: Elfee, Mitchell. Danny looked at the address.

'I know that street,' he said to himself.

Chapter Six
The New Year Ball

Art walked up to the front door of the Wise house. It was a thick wooden door, unpainted and with the grain of the wood clearly showing, even in the dim light; Art liked it. He pulled at the collar of the new shirt Tina had made him buy from the shopping centre – it was nearly strangling him, and the arms were itchy. But according to the shop assistant it was very stylish, though even Tina had to admit she didn't see why. She had also made him buy a new pair of trousers, and though they were tight and itchy, and the legs seemed too short, they were apparently in fashion too. He had a bunch of roses that Tina had picked out, the only thing she didn't let the shopkeepers choose, and suddenly Art felt incredibly stupid. But then the door opened, and Evi was standing there dressed in a blue ballgown, with her hair tied up with blue ribbons, and her cheeks glowing. The blue cast on her wrist seemed to fit perfectly with the whole outfit, and Art almost didn't notice it. A whole host of things to say ran through his head, but he couldn't make sense of any of them; he was lost in her eyes, which were framed with large eyelashes with the faintest hint of blue eye shadow. He surprised even himself with what he eventually said.

'Is your arm okay? I mean, does it hurt?'

A smile broke out across her face, and Art felt dizzy.

'It's fine. I may need to take it steady, but I'll be okay.'

'Erm, okay then. You erm, you look amazing by the way,' he said sheepishly, and he handed her the roses clumsily. Evi took them, then leaned forward and kissed Art on the cheek.

'Thank you,' she said, and she placed them in a vase that stood empty on the telephone table. They heard some sniggering coming from around the corner of the hallway, and Art saw a little foot poking out.

'Nathan,' Evi called, 'come and say hello to Art. He won't bite.' She leaned forward to whisper. 'He said he was going to spy on me when you got here. He's not a very good spy.'

Nathan poked his head around the corner – he had a playful grin on his face.

'Hello, Art,' he said.

'Hi, Nat. How's *your* arm?' Art replied.

Nathan's cast covered more of his arm than Evi's, but he moved his arm like it wasn't even there. 'I've nearly got twenty signatures on here now. And the clown at Ned's party drew a dog on it. Look!' He displayed his cast for Art to see.

'Hey that's cool,' Art said. 'Want another signature?'

'Yeah!' Nathan ran forward and fished a felt tip out of his pocket. 'Here you go!' he said. Art signed it with a flourish in the only remaining blank spot he could see, and Nathan looked at it proudly.

'Cool, thanks! Bye Evi!' And he ran off into the lounge to show off the newest addition to his cast.

Evi smiled, and called after him. 'Mum – I'll be back by ten.'

'You take your time dear,' came the reply. Evi's father was not so liberal.

'You make *sure* you're back by ten, okay?' he called.

'Oh Jack – leave the girl alone. Just be thankful she's going with someone *without* an ASBO.'

'I heard that,' Evi chuckled.

'You were meant to, dear! Now go and have a good time!'

'Bye, then,' Evi called, and she stepped out beside Art and pulled the front door shut. She looked at Art, feigning surprise.

'What?' he said.

'Have you been shopping?' she said. Art pulled at his uncomfortable collar again.

'Is it that obvious?' he said.

Evi chuckled. 'Tina did a good job. Surprisingly. You look great.'

'Well, I didn't want to show you up or anything,' he said.

'Why would you think that?' she said.

'Well I'm, err, and you're …'

'Oh don't be silly. I'd be proud of you if you were in your dad's ghastly old tux.'

Art's face flushed. 'Yeah, imagine that,' he said.

'But you're not,' she said, 'you *do* look great, and we're going to have a wonderful time, okay?'

Art still couldn't quite believe his date for the ball would be the envy of every guy there. He swung his elbow out into a loop, Evi took hold of it with her good hand, and they began the walk along the road to the school hall.

Art walked slowly, which he knew was silly; she had broken her wrist, not her ankle, but she didn't protest. She clung to his arm as they walked, and Art's head was spinning. How on *earth* had he ended up here, on a date with the most beautiful girl anyone had ever seen in St. David's Comprehensive? It was the last thing he had ever expected to happen, and just as he thought nothing could spoil what was the most perfect moment of his life so far, he heard a cruel drawling voice from across the street.

'Evi – what *are* you doing?'

It was one of Evi's friends, walking along in a large group. Art's heart skipped a beat; maybe Evi *would* stop and look at what she was doing, and wonder why she was walking along with the school's resident laughing stock. Maybe she would burst out laughing at any second, and rush across the road to join her friends, laughing at how she had managed to make a fool of him so easily.

But Evi just answered, cool as anything, her smile fixed firmly in place. 'I'm going to the Ball. What are *you* doing?'

'You can't be serious! With *that*?' her friend answered.

'Yes – I have a *date* for the ball. Do you?'

Her friend's face faltered. Everyone in the group was dateless, as far as Art could see.

'We're err … meeting ours there. Are you really going with that?'

Evi faced them, her face still smiling, but somehow full of malice.

'*This* … is Art Elfee, and he is walking me to the ball, like a gentleman should. And would you stop being so *rude*!' she hissed.

Her friend just laughed. 'Well you can't sit at *our* table with him. You'll have to go somewhere else.'

'That's fine. Just as long as you enjoy the party,' Evi replied.

The group rushed off into the distance, talking loudly about how Evi had changed, and how they would be better off without her on their table.

Art felt terrible. Evi was losing her friends because of him, and he didn't like the feeling in his chest that he felt appearing.

'Evi,' he began.

She squeezed his arm even tighter, and her warm smile returned.

'Don't even think about it,' she said.

'I know, but … they're your friends.'

'We're about to leave school, and go to college. They're a good laugh to be with at school, but they haven't *grown up* very much. I was hoping they would have by now.'

'It's funny,' Art said, ' but it seems to be the other way round for me – the boys are talking to me more and more. They're careful not to let on in front of anyone, but it's a whole lot better than it was. It's usually the other way round, isn't it?'

Evi chuckled. 'That's what everyone says. That and "*school days are the best days of your life*". Why do they say that?'

Art looked at the floor, sheepishly. 'I'm actually beginning to get that one,' he said. Evi blushed slightly. He impressed even himself with that comment.

Art could see a figure up ahead. It was too dark to make out fully, but whoever it was, they looked too small to be out at this time of night. The figure walked underneath a streetlamp, but to Art's surprise, the figure remained dark and unclear, even when doused with orange light. His mind flashed back to the elusive character at the hospital, but the figure he had seen then was not even visible, and his mind wouldn't *allow* him to think about it at the time. This figure was different; he could make out the shape quite clearly, and could see the movement of the limbs as it skipped down the street. But he couldn't see any detail – it was like a silhouette.

'Hey – who's that? He said.

'Who's who?'

'That person up ahead. It looks like a child.'

The figure paused, mid-step.

'I don't see anyone,' Evi said, squinting slightly.

Art pointed. 'Just there – right in front of us.'

The figure turned its head and looked directly at Art, but it was still just a silhouette – Art couldn't make out any features. It cocked its head to one side, as if it was looking hard at him.

Evi shrugged. 'Where?'

'Just there. It's standing right under the street light.'

Evi shrugged. 'I still don't see.'

Art jabbed his finger in it's direction. 'It's just *there* – right th...' Then he realised with a start that Evi *couldn't* see the figure.

'Art – are you okay?' Evi said.

'Err, yeah, I'm fine. I err ... thought I saw someone, that's all.'

The figure turned and sprinted away, leaving Art with an uneasy feeling in his stomach. He had a feeling he would be seeing this figure again. And there was something familiar about the way it walked.

They arrived at the school gates, which were adorned with fairy lights, and a huge sign pointing the way to the New Year's Ball. There were people arriving all around them, and Art secretly relished the way they all did a double-take when they saw who his date was. The boy's faces looked the most shocked, but then unlike the girls, their faces would change to one of respect, and some even threw him the 'okay' sign. He looked at Evi, and was shocked to see she was beaming as well, as if she was proud of *her* date. Art shook his head and shrugged it off.

They entered the school sports hall, which had been transformed into an elaborate ballroom, complete with a marquee-style ceiling, round tables and a huge dance floor. There was a small chamber orchestra made up of students from the sixth-form college up the road, who all looked as if they were re-living something. It was led by Art's science teacher, Mrs. Jones, on bassoon; she wore a similar look of nostalgia. On the other side of the hall, however, a DJ behind a set of CD decks was rifling through boxes of music ready for when the dinner had finished. The sight was breath-taking, and somehow the light made Evi's face seem magical, unreal. Art could tell this was a moment he would remember for the rest of his life.

They walked over to the seating plan secured to a large cork board. Evi's face smiled even more when she found their names. They were on the central table, facing the orchestra. They walked over to the drinks table and picked up an orange juice each, then walked over to the crowd of people who had arrived already to mingle. Evi was looking eagerly around, as if searching for someone, and Art found himself trying to see who she was looking for.

'What's up?' he said.

'Never mind. You'll see,' she said with a sly grin.

He met most of his form tutor group, who mostly didn't recognise Art on the first glance because of the clothes he was wearing. Most of them stood awkwardly with a date that they obviously had just chosen so they weren't alone for the ball. But most of them were on the cusp of not caring who they were seen with, and they all looked happy, which was what mattered most.

Suddenly the chamber orchestra struck up with a waltz, and everyone looked round at them, impressed by the sound. But when they turned, almost every jaw dropped at what they saw on the dance-floor. Peter's enormous frame was waltzing effortlessly around the floor, accompanied by a tall brunette, who was mirroring his every move. Peter was dressed in a tuxedo, rather like Art's father's tux, but somehow Peter was pulling it off well. His shoes were shinier than anyone had ever seen, and he had bright gold cufflinks that shone when they caught the light. His mysterious date was dressed in a sequinned red ball-gown that swirled as elaborately as she did. She was wearing bright red shoes, and her dark hair was tied up ornately, adorned with red ribbons tied the same way as Evi's blue ones. Art knew that everyone *would* have laughed at the sight of the two of them, had they not been dancing so expertly. And for once, no one was looking at Evi; everyone was bewitched by the figures on the dance-floor.

Suddenly the orchestra reached the end of the waltz with a flourish from the first violin, and Peter and his mysterious partner finished exactly in time with the music, striking a professional-looking finishing pose. Everyone erupted into ear-splitting applause, and the pair stood for a while longer than they intended, holding their position. Eventually, they relaxed, and started walking over hand-in-hand to where everyone was gathered, still applauding. Even the orchestra gave them both a standing ovation.

As they got closer, Art made out Peter's beaming face, which still looked like an angry gorilla's, but next to his was a face he slowly recognised as it emerged into the light, although he could hardly believe it. It was Tina, looking as he had never seen her before.

'What did I tell you?' Evi whispered, elbowing Art gently.

Tina was almost unrecognisable. Her cheeks were rosy, her lips were bright red, and her eyes were framed with enormous eyelashes. Art had never seen her with even the tiniest hint of makeup before, and along with the broad permanent grin on her face, Art had to narrow his eyes to make sure it was her.

'Tina?' he ventured.

'Hey,' she managed, still out of breath.

'Wow. I mean – WOW – you look amazing!' said Art.

'You don't look so bad yourself. Nice threads. Where d'you get 'em?'

'I went shopping with one of my best friends. I can't see her though,' Art said, still looking incredulous.

Tina blushed. 'I went shopping too,' she said, throwing a glance at Evi.

'I just can't believe it. Well, I *can*,' he added quickly. 'And Peter - wow. *Where* did you learn to lead like that?' Art said turning to his other best friend, and they high-fived. 'In fact, where did you *both* learn to dance like that?'

'Hey,' Peter said, 'I've been called the all-round dancer, I'll have you know. Almost spherical, in fact!' They all burst out laughing.

'Peter taught *me*, actually,' Tina said. 'He's quite the teacher.'

'I can see that!' Art said.

Peter turned to Tina. 'Shall I get you a drink?' he said.

'Thank you,' she replied, blushing slightly again.

'Art? Evi?' he said.

'Oh yeah – same again please. Thanks, Pete.'

Peter trotted off to the drinks table; the crowd parted – some in shock, some in fear, as the giant waded through.

Tina started fishing around in the impossibly small handbag that was part of her outfit.

'Art – I think I've cracked *most* of it,' she said.

Art knew immediately what she meant – the EllShapyan translation.

'Oh, that ... err ... homework I was doing?' he said, throwing her a wink or two.

She paused, looking surprised. 'Erm, yeah. That's it. I've ... err finished it. You can look at it later.' She handed Art a folded piece of paper, and he put it straight into his pocket.

'Right, thanks, Tina. I'll just go and help Pete with the drinks.' He sidled off leaving the two girls talking animatedly about how they each looked.

When he got to the drinks table, he took out the piece of paper and unfolded it. Written on the paper in neat blue ink was a very short message:

Do not let _a_a know who his student is.

The partially translated word was circled in red, with a question mark next to it. Art read the message several times, but it wasn't long before it came to him; Tina was working with *her* knowledge of the English language, and even though she could have guessed that the unfinished word was a name, Art knew it was a name no one of *this* world would probably have heard before: *Maga*.

Art thought hard about what the message meant, and the more he thought about it, the more he thought Tina must have got the translation wrong. Little *Maga* was here to train as a Mage - he was the *student*, not the instructor – that word must be different. It should read *Do not let Maga know who his Instruc...*

Art's eyes widened. With a shock that seemed to vibrate through his whole body, he realised what the message meant. And he realised its implications. The message was *correct* – had he not seen and learnt what he had in the last few days about how Time worked, he wouldn't have got it, but his knowledge of the seemingly-impossible was more extensive than most; young Maga's Instructor was none other than – *his older self*, the version of Maga who appeared every year to help Art plan the Drop at the hospital. The message was telling Art to keep the knowledge of his student *from* him.

But Maga couldn't be teaching an earlier version of *himself*, could he? Art had heard of things like this before – he'd seen films and read books that on more than one occasion had mentioned something called the *Grandfather Paradox* – if you went back in Time and somehow prevented your grandfather from having his children, you wouldn't have been born to go back and stop him, so he would still have had them, which meant you *could* go back in Time to stop him and so forth, causing disastrous effects in Time, usually with dramatic 'universe-ending consequences', whatever they were. Maga being his own Instructor didn't sound quite so serious, but it just didn't sound *possible*. After all – if he instructed *himself* to be a Mage, where would the knowledge have really come from? Himself? How could that be?

Art had no idea why anyone would send a message to him about this, but whoever it was, it sounded as if they were trying to limit those consequences somehow. But then Grandma had given Art the message herself – she must have read it - why hadn't she told him? Why had she just left something as serious as this to chance? What if he hadn't managed to decode the message before the two Magas had met? Art made his mind up about one thing though – if it was somehow wrong for the older Maga to know who he was teaching, Art would make sure the younger Maga didn't know who he was being *taught* by. Art felt it was important, though he didn't know why.

Art was jolted back to reality by Peter, who nudged him. 'Hey – some help would be nice.' Peter's arms were loaded with glasses of drinks. Art pocketed the note and took his and Evi's drinks from him. He decided to put his thoughts to the back of his mind for now.

'They were some seriously impressive moves back there, Pete. And you kept quiet about your date too. I didn't even know you *knew* Tina.'

'Yeah, well. Our families know each other,' he shrugged.

'Really? How's that?'

'Oh I don't know – old school friends or something. She's nice to me, anyway.'

That figured. Tina was almost as kind-hearted as Pete. Almost. She had a naturally nosy side to her that sometimes came across as being rude and interfering, but he couldn't imagine Tina avoiding anyone because of how they looked, like most other people did to Peter.

Art mini-punched Peter's huge arm, with a smirk. 'That she is. I think she's quite taken,' he said.

Peter looked at the floor, turning a shade of red.

Then out of the corner of his eye, Art spotted movement through the window to the changing room that overlooked the sports hall. There was light pouring from it, and when Art looked directly up at it, he saw the strange figure again, silhouetted against the glass.

'Pete – take these will you – I gotta check something.'

He awkwardly handed the drinks back to a protesting Peter.

'Hey I can't carry all these... where you going Art?'

Art pushed his way through the crowd of people towards the high window, keeping his eye on the figure. The silhouette moved slightly, as if startled, like it had been spotted. Art walked towards the doors to the sports hall that would take him to the stairs, and up to the lit changing room. The silhouette looked left and right, panicking, and then darted out of sight. Art picked up his pace as he saw the figure disappear. 'Oh no you don't,' he grunted, as he pushed through the huge doors.

He rushed up the staircase two steps at a time, and sprinted through the doors at the top just in time to see the door on the other end of the changing room swing shut where the shady figure had exited. He sprinted across the room and out of the same door that led to the fire exit staircase – the figure was at the bottom landing and nearly out of the emergency door. To Art's surprise, the figure ran straight through the door without opening it – it just sort of slipped through like it wasn't there. Art reached the door and pushed it open. The figure was sprinting across the tennis courts as fast as it could, but Art kept up with it easily. Art was starting to gain some ground when the figure darted off to the right and into the side entrance to the science labs.

Art cautiously pulled open the door. The familiar smell of gas from the Bunsen Burners hit him as it always did as he entered the labs. He walked slowly between the desks, listening hard as he went. He was almost at the other side when he heard a door swing shut to his left, and he opened up into a run towards it. He rushed through into the adjoining lab, and stopped to listen again. There was absolute silence. Above him he felt the smallest of breezes, and he looked up. A solitary bubble about the size of a tennis ball was floating down towards him, and it popped as it touched his forehead.

His mind started to fog over slowly, as if he was trying to remember something long forgotten, but however hard he tried he couldn't recall it. He looked around; he was in a science lab. *What am I doing here?* he thought. He pushed with his mind, trying to recall what he was doing in a darkened laboratory, and surprisingly, it started coming back to him. He was in school – it was the New Year Ball, and he was chasing something. A figure, a shadow, that had run into the labs, and he had followed it. His mind came back into sharp focus again, and standing directly in front of him was the figure, only now he could make out some of it's facial expressions. It was smiling, smugly, but as it saw that Art was focusing on it again, its face changed to a look of confusion, then horror, and it sprinted away again.

Only this time, Art was too quick. He knew his way around the lab better than the figure; he sprinted in front of it and blocked its way out. It skidded to a halt and ran the other way, but Art headed it off again, navigating his way through the desks with ease. The figure skidded to a halt again, and stood there in a pose of pure fright.

'Nowhere to run. Now who – or *what* – are you?' Art said triumphantly.

Chapter Seven
QUPHORIA

Danny finished his third proper family meal, which he greatly enjoyed. He hadn't tasted proper human cooking for as long as he could remember, and even though there were certain things he was used to and would miss, there was nothing like a proper, hot, home-cooked meal.

'Mother – may I get down please?' Danny said politely.

Liz gave him a sad look. 'Of course, dear. Off you go.'

She had found it hard to cope with the new mannerisms of her youngest son, and Danny felt bad about it, but he honestly couldn't remember how to behave like a seven-year old anymore. He couldn't have even faked the behaviour for her sake.

'Thank you Mother. That was truly superb.' He gave her a melancholy look, and jumped down from the seat and headed towards the door. He touched his brother's shoulder as he passed. 'Michael – a word please.'

Michael looked at his mother as if to protest, but she mistook the look.

'Yes, of course you can get down, Michael. Off you go.'

He begrudgingly got up and followed Danny up the stairs. When they reached the landing, Danny gestured towards Michael's bedroom.

'After you,' he said, and Michael filed in. Danny closed the door behind them, and jumped up on Michael's desk chair.

'Listen, Michael,' he began, 'I'm sure you've noticed by now that Mother isn't happy. She's quite upset about ... well, you know what about.'

Michael looked sceptical.

'So,' Danny carried on, 'I think we should make a concerted effort to get along. To be honest, this whole sibling rivalry thing is getting rather tiresome; I think I've punished you enough. After all, we did have *some* good times, didn't we?'

Michael looked confused.

'True, mostly you've been a monster. But those days are over, now, aren't they? How old are you now – fifteen? There's no reason why we can't get along.'

He paused, gauging Michael's reaction, which wasn't looking good.

'And to be honest, it's not *really* a request,' he carried on, looking at his nails. 'For a start, I am ten times smarter than you, and purely because I *believe* it, I'm also two or three times stronger, as I believe I showed you a few days ago. You've gotta love the human mind.'

Michael put a hand to his face, where the red mark was still just visible.

'And if I were to pay you back in one go for every punch and kick I've ever received from you up until now, I should think you'd be *hospitalised*, with a question mark over whether you'd ever regain conciousness. And I don't think any of us want *that*, do we?'

Michael shook his head slowly.

'There's a good chap. So here's what I propose. We start again – wipe the slate clean - a new beginning. No history at all, everything gone, genuinely. We shake hands, and become friends. I mean *proper* friends – no pretending. After all, we are brothers, and even if that means nothing to you, it certainly does to me, after ... well, anyway.'

Danny had been trying to put aside the brotherly feelings he had for Michael ever since he regained his memories, but he couldn't escape the fact that he was much older now, even if only mentally. Family meant a lot more to him now than it ever had, especially as he had been without it for so long. At first, he relished the revenge and the hold he had over Michael, but now it was paining him. He hadn't *enjoyed* seeing his brother suffer, like he thought he would, despite the things Michael had done to him in the past. He had thought Michael would start to put up a fight – at least then he could respect him a little. But Michael was obviously still too immature, and Danny had been secretly disappointed that the old adage about bullies was true.

And then there was his mother. He really *was* upset that she was finding it so hard to come to terms with how her seven year-old was behaving now. There must be *something* he could do, and this was the best he could think of for now.

He stood up, walked over to Michael, and extended his hand.

'So. What do you say?'

Michael looked at Danny's hand, with a look of disbelief in his eyes. He inhaled, then exhaled sharply, and slowly reached out and took Danny's tiny hand.

'What ... *happened* to you?' Michael said.

'I wish I could tell you, brother. More than that – I wish I could *show* you. But it's not possible, so let's just say I've ... changed.'

Michael chuckled nervously. 'You can say that again.'

'I wasn't joking about the friends part Michael. I really *would* like us to get along – I've ... well, *missed* you. Don't laugh.'

Michael nearly did laugh, but it didn't annoy Danny; he was just glad Michael was able to wear a smile again.

'You're right,' Michael said. 'I suppose I was a bit of a bully. I don't really blame you for ... you know.' He covered his cheek with his hand again. 'Sorry.'

This surprised Danny. Maybe he had been wrong about Michael's maturity.

'That's quite alright,' he said. 'And anyway – just think what a team we'll make now! Unstoppable!'

Michael gave him a confused look. 'Unstoppable in what?'

'Oh. You know. Stuff. Anyway – I want to ask you a favour.'

'Go on.'

Danny jumped back up onto Michael's desk chair again, and lowered his voice.

'I have a mission ... I mean ... something to do tonight, and I need you to cover for me,' he whispered.

'What's that?' Michael said.

'Nothing special, I just need to get out and about by myself tonight. I need some more ... information is all. Can you help?'

'Well of course, but ... will you be alright on your own? I mean, you're still only little, even if ...' he gestured to Danny's head, as even he was unsure of what he meant.

Danny chuckled.

'I'll be fine. Woe betide any *human* who crosses me, Michael.'

'What do you mean by that?' Michael said.

'Just that. Look me in the eyes, and think about the things I've said and done in the last few days. Are you sure they're the actions of a mere *human*, Michael?'

Michael shuddered. 'Stop it – you're freaking me out now.'

Danny chuckled again. 'Exactly. Like I said – I'll be fine. As soon as mother has tucked me in, and read me a ... uurrg ... *story*, I need you to keep them busy while I slip out. I'll be no more than an hour. Can you do that?'

'Not a problem, Dan.'

'Good man. Right – I'll jump in the shower, then I'll get ready.'

Michael hesitated.

'What?' Danny said.

'Erm, I think mum's expecting you to have a *bath*. That's what seven year-olds do.'

Danny sighed. 'Really? I could read two chapters of Tolstoy in the time it takes to have a bath. Oh well. I'll go play 'the son' then. See you later. Be ready just after my bedtime, okay?'

'You goddit,' Michael said, and Danny jumped down from the chair to leave.

'Dan ...' Michael said.

'Yes?'

'Erm, you wanna play on the computer?'

'What do you mean?'

'Well there's still an hour before bedtime for you. I've got two guns. Want a go?'

Danny thought about it. A bonding session with Michael; it was almost laughable. But at the same time, Michael was obviously making an effort now that they were talking on somewhere near the same level, and it made Danny smile. Besides, he had no idea what 'playing on the computer' entailed, and he was intrigued.

'What do I do?' Danny said.

'Now you're talking!'

*

Danny listened as his mother read from the colour story book. He made out that he hated being read to like a child, but actually he loved the one-to-one time he had with her. Many years ago he had resigned himself to the fact that he would never see her again, and the pain had been almost unbearable. But here he was, for the third night running, being pampered by the woman he had most wanted when nearly freezing to death on the streets of the L-Shaped Village. A part of him was still angry for the time that had been stolen from him as a child, but a bigger part of him was grateful for the gift of wisdom. Art had made him see that. And whenever he felt he was straying from the path, all he had to do was think of how Art had helped him, and it made him focus again.

'... and that's the story of the whalebeast's breakfast.' Liz finished.

'Mother that was amazing. A truly inspiring story, really.'

She sighed. 'Oh Danny. What's happened to you?' she said, with a heavy heart.

A sharp pain shot through Danny's chest. In many ways, she had lost the son she knew, even though he had never been away as far as she was concerned. It was ironic really, as it was really *he* who had lost *her* for so many years. He placed a hand on hers.

'Mother please. I'm fine, honestly. And ... I've missed you. I really have.'

'But what *has* happened to you? You're so *different*.'

There was no way he could explain it to her. To these people, the unbelievable was still just that – unbelievable.

'Mother – it's still me. I don't know what's happened either, but *I'm* still here. Remember the day we got the guinea pig – and had to take it back because ...'

'... your father was allergic. Yes, I remember,' she said.

'And the day we got stuck in the car in the snow, and you read me every book in the Mr. Men series until father came and dug us out?'

She chuckled. '*Every* book? Really?'

'Every one. I'll never forget it. And the day in summer when we both got stung by stinging nettles and spent ages rubbing our legs with dock leaves. You remember that?'

'Yes I do. I can't believe *you* still remember that, though.'

'There you are then,' he implored. 'Those are *our* memories. I can't deny I've changed; I can't explain it any more than you can, but it *is* me. Okay?'

She sighed, and kissed his cheek. 'Okay, Daniel. Just promise me one thing.'

'Anything, Mother.'

'Stop calling me Mother.'

Danny chuckled this time. 'Okay. I don't think I can stretch to 'mummy' though. Will 'mum' do?'

'Perfect. And ... stop growing up. There's so many books I still want to read to you, and *I* want to know how they go.'

'So do I, err ... mum,' he said.

Liz sighed again, but this time with a small smile. 'Okay then. Night night.'

'Goodnight mum.'

She stood up, and walked out of the room, turning off the main light as she went.

Danny heard her tramp down the stairs, and listened for whatever Michael had planned. He heard Michael's bedroom door open, and another set of feet tramped down the stairs, and a muffled conversation started right below his room. It sounded as if it was turning into an argument, and before long the kitchen was erupting with angry people. Michael had come through.

Danny threw off his duvet and jumped down from his bed, dressed in whatever black clothes he had found earlier that evening in his wardrobe. He slipped some black trainers on, grabbed his thick dark coat and headed for his bedroom window. He opened it, and lightly jumped down onto the garage roof. Before long he was running down the street, steam rising from his mouth with every breath of cold night air.

He knew exactly where he was going – he was looking for number Twenty-seven, Pear Tree Avenue – the listed address for Mitchel Elfee. Pear Tree Avenue was roughly three streets along, and ran parallel with his own street. The exercise was exhilarating, and he was almost saddened when he found the correct street sign. He checked the first house number on his left – two hundred and thirty-eight. A long street. He ran down it, and before long he passed St. David's Comprehensive, where he could hear an orchestra playing from the sports hall. The houses started again shortly afterwards – number one hundred and ninety-five to his left. He ran faster, aware of the time he had been gone already. But after only a few minutes, he spotted something he couldn't quite believe. It was a bright pink house, with red window shutters and a green roof. But that *wasn't* the unbelievable part. The garden was in full bloom, literally bursting at the seams with flowers and plants of every kind, blossoming despite the time of year.

He stopped. Something was wrong. Even for someone with limited experience of the human world, it looked out of place. He walked up to the fence that was doing its best to keep the garden enclosed, and stared in disbelief. His seven years of human memories hadn't furnished him with much knowledge of flora and fauna, and he couldn't recognise any of the plants – except just one; a small plant with long curled leaves and spines, and a deep red flower that looked to him like a long raspberry. He had seen this plant before, and he knew *exactly* what it was. It was called 'Seederum Quphoria', probably the best known plant in the whole of Amarly, because it's dried berries were used to make *Stroth-Brew*.

The recognition stabbed at his chest – this plant was definitely *not* of this world. Its berries were perfectly harmless when dried and ground into powder, but fresh off the plant they were potent enough to be used in many of the potions the Mage he thought was under his command regularly produced. There was no doubt – this was a *magical* plant, one of only two magical plants in existence.

But the question was, what was it doing *here*? He had been looking for Mitchel Elfee's house, hoping to track down Art, but instead he had found something that he just couldn't believe. He couldn't let it pass – he *had* to investigate. He silently hopped over the gate, and ventured up the pathway, pushing his way through thick foliage as he went. There were beams of light coming from little glass windows in the front door that lit his way. And when he reached it, he could see into the little porch; there were a couple of envelopes still lying on the floor. He could easily make out a name on one of them, and it shocked him to the core: Ms. D. T. Elfee. *Dorothy Elfee.*

'The Ainsworth Abductor!' he gasped.

And just then the door creaked open, and there she stood, in a blue dressing gown, staring down at him with piercing eyes.

Chapter Eight
a new student

Art stood facing the elusive figure, who he was now sure was the *same* figure that had followed him at the hospital. Art was ready to head it off should it try to run again, but it didn't move. After a while, it relaxed slightly, and pulled back a black hood, which Art hadn't noticed it was wearing. Art's eyes focussed slowly on the face, the last traces of shadow disappearing from the figure altogether. When Art realised who it was, his mouth fell open in disbelief.

It was the older version of Maga.

'Alright – how did you do it?' Maga said, looking slightly annoyed.

'MAGA!' Art cried, and his face broke out into a beaming smile. 'What are you doing here? And ... hang on – *why* have you been following me?' Art remembered he was still annoyed.

Maga's expression didn't falter. 'I asked you a question. *How* did you do it?'

'Do what?' Art asked.

'I am the best Field Agent there's ever been, and a Mage of *incredible* power. No one has ever spotted me – it's *never* been done. How did you do it?'

He was the same arrogant but likeable character Art always missed so much.

'I err, I don't know. What methods were you using?' Art said.

'A combination, actually. Anonymity Toffees, and Memory Bubbles when I thought it was getting too close. You saw through the Toffees, and the Bubbles only affected you for a few seconds at best. *You*, Mr. Elfee, are breaking the laws of magic. I want to know how you're doing it.'

'Never mind that,' Art nearly shouted. 'Why have you been following me? And why are you using that stuff on *me* anyway? I'm supposed to be your friend!'

Maga went to protest, but Art wasn't having any of it.

'NOW, PLEASE!' he shouted.

Maga looked slightly shocked. 'Okay okay. What do you want to know?' he said.

'Firstly, why were you following me at the hospital?'

Maga gasped. 'No *way* – you did *not* see me at the hospital!'

'That's kind of true,' Art said. 'I didn't *see* you as such, but I knew you were there. Every time I tried to look at you I lost concentration. But that's not the point! *Why* were you following me?'

Maga looked distraught. 'I ... you ... *how*?'

'Maga – *why were you following me*?' Art said, with no concern in his voice - he was still annoyed.

Maga sighed. 'You *can't* have seen me. It's simply not possible.' He folded his arms resolutely.

'MAGA! ANSWER ME!'

Maga straightened. 'Okay - calm down, Shouty-Boy.'

'Finally we're getting somewhere,' said Art. 'Now talk.'

Maga sighed again. 'I'm ... well *bored*. I'm supposed to be helping somebody with something, but the people who told me about it haven't told me who I'm supposed to be helping, or what I'm even supposed to be doing to help them. I'm at a loss. So I've been doing random Recon missions to try and figure it out. So far – zip. It's a bit hush-hush, so I can't tell you much about it.'

Art folded his arms. 'You mean, you've had a message from the Faculty telling you that you have a student Mage to instruct here somewhere, only you don't know who it is, where they are, or what you're supposed to be teaching them.'

Maga stumbled backwards in shock. 'Who told you ... what ... how on *Amarly* do you know that?'

'I have my sources. But why have you been following *me*?'

'I don't know, it's just something I do when nothing else works.'

Art's eyes widened. 'You mean you've done it *before*?'

Maga waved a hand. 'Oh, yeah. Years now. But ... it seems I can't even do *that* anymore!'

Then *his* eyes widened, as if he was figuring something out. 'Hey... ' he said, suspiciously, 'you haven't ... *been* ... anywhere recently have you?'

Art knew straight away that he was talking about his trip to the L-Shaped Village, and he was unable to stop a small smile from flickering across his face.

Maga's arms dropped to his sides. 'Whoa! When? And ... *how*?'

'That's not important ...'

'Of course it is!' he said, but then his face fell slightly. 'But it *still* doesn't answer the question of how you can see through my Recon magic. Unless ...' He began mumbling under his breath. '... *humans are more susceptible than us to all forms of Recon magic, that's been proven. But exposure to the realisation that it exists has never caused immunity before. The only case ever heard of ...*' Maga gasped. 'OF COURSE! The Unstable Hop-Yin Theory!'

Art gave him a puzzled look.

'You won't have heard of it,' Maga said, 'but Professor Hop-Yin from the Faculty, back when it was first established, theorized that humans only use a small part of their brain, and he proved his own theory right in a series of famous experiments. But in doing so he came across something else. One of the human subjects started to see *through* the methods used to hide the researchers, who were all recalled immediately it was discovered. The latter stages of the experiments were scrapped, so he never found out why it happened, but using the data he had already collected he theorized that in rare cases the unused parts of the human brain can become *unstable* if exposed to too much Recon magic. And in that situation it *may* manifest itself by means of immunity to being fooled by some kinds of Recon magic.'

Art stood with his arms folded, looking decidedly unimpressed.

'Brilliant. Really. But you're going off at a tangent again.' Art said.

'I'm a Sprite. It's my job.' Maga said, expressionless.

'No it's not ... I mean ... anyway, look, what's important is that I'm back, and you've appeared nearly a full year earlier than you usually do. That's not to say I'm not glad to see you though. It's ... well it's always good to see you, Maga.' He mini-punched Maga's small shoulder. 'But I wish you hadn't been spying on me. It's very rude you know.'

Maga looked mildly surprised. 'Is it? Why?' he said.

'Because it just is. DON'T do it, okay?'

Maga looked at the floor, and tutted. '... O-*kay*. But how am I going to find out who I'm supposed to be teaching if I can't snoop around?'

'Oh you can still do that,' Art said, 'just not around *me*.'

Maga cheered up a little, then looked inquisitive.

'Why? What do you know that you want to hide?' he said.

'Nothing,' Art lied. Maga saw straight through it, even though Art thought he had hidden it well.

'You *know* something, don't you? Of course you do, how else would you know about the Faculty and ...' Maga gasped. 'You know who it is! I can see it in your eyes! Come on – out with it!'

Art thought hard. He hadn't expected the conversation to get to this point so quickly. He wanted to make sure the two Magas stayed unaware of each other, but now he was faced with the exact question, he didn't know how to do it. His mind was blank.

'Art – come on - I *know* you know – tell me.'

Art couldn't think. Maga's eyes were boring into his, and he felt uncomfortable. He thought he might blurt it out at any moment uncontrollably.

'ART! I *NEED* TO KNOW THIS! IT'S IMPORTANT - WHO IS IT?'

Art was flustered. 'I ... well I *do* know, but ...'

Maga looked at him wide-eyed. 'Yes?'

'But I'm not supposed to ...'

'Art – we're the best of friends. You have to tell me. Who is it?'

Art was even more flustered now, and slightly panicky. It just came out without any warning, even to him.

'It's ... err it's ... *me*.'

There was stunned silence. Maga just stood there, gaping at him, for what seemed like an age. Art couldn't blame him; he'd be gaping at himself if he could. He had been so intent on keeping the secret, he had said the first thing that had come into his head – but he had said it before he had any time to think it through.

'No ... no no no. That's not possible.' Maga said, incredulously.

'Why not?' Art asked, slightly offended, though he hadn't a clue why.

'Well – for a start, you're a ... *human*.'

'And?'

Maga shifted, uncomfortably. 'Humans cannot *be* Mages. They just can't.'

'I'm the first then,' Art said.

'No no, you don't understand. Mage's have to learn to channel a very particular type of power. Humans simply aren't *capable*. It would be like trying to teach a squirrel to ... I don't know ... *fly*.'

Art raised a finger. 'There *are* flying squirrels, you know,' he said matter-of-factly.

'Really? Bad analogy then. But the fact remains.'

'Like I said, I'm the first,' Art said again.

Maga looked at him closely. 'I don't get it. Who told you that *you* were to be trained as a Mage?'

Art thought quickly. 'I ... er had a message from the Faculty, like I said.'

Maga narrowed his eyes. 'In English?' he said.

'No. EllShapyan,' Art countered.

Maga looked surprised again. He thought for a moment, looking Art square in the eyes, and then hopelessness filled his face.

'But – it *can't* be you,' Maga said. You're ...' he sighed, as if he had lost a battle with himself. 'You're ... already being trained as ... something else.'

This took Art by surprise. 'What do you mean?'

Maga sighed heavily. 'I've been a Shadow Instructor for over four years now. This is my first assignment as a Full Instructor.'

'A *Shadow Instructor*? What's that?' Art said.

'I'm a Field Agent, First Class. When Field Agents gain enough experience, they're allowed to put forward names of people they think are promising for training. If they're selected, the first part of Agent training is carried out *without* the knowledge of the potential recruit. The Agent who put his or her name forward is usually allowed to carry out the training, and it's *their* first stage to becoming a full Instructor. It's called *Shadow* Instructing.'

Art processed this new information. His eyes widened when he worked out what Maga was telling him. 'You don't mean ...'

'I'm afraid so,' said Maga.

'So ... every year you've appeared, you've been ...'

'That's right, Art; I put *your* name forward.' He sighed. 'I've been training you as an Agent for the past four years.'

Art's head was spinning. How had he not realised this before? All the times Maga had appeared just before the Drop every year suddenly came to the forefront of his mind. He remembered the elaborate way he presented the plan, how he had made Art memorise every one like the back of his hand, how he had shown him how to use the little stopper bottles for various amazing things, but interestingly, never how to *make* the strange liquids inside, or where they came from. He remembered how Maga had interrogated him after each Drop about how it had gone, and if there was any way he could make it better for the following year. Sure, it had been fun. Lots of fun. But Art felt a little hurt that Maga had always hung around afterwards not out of friendship, he now realised, but for little more than the need to *debrief* Art on how he had performed.

Maga looked deflated. 'I didn't want you to find out *this* way, Art. I'm sorry.'

Art looked at him. 'I thought you came because ... you were my friend.'

Now Maga looked hurt. He put his hands on Art's shoulders and looked at him squarely in the face.

'Arthur – I *AM* your friend. Of all the false things you have learnt of today, THAT is NOT one of them. You are *never* to forget that Art, do you hear me? We've known each other for a *very* long time – more than just the four years you hold in your memory. Trust me – our friendship has won *wars*, and will do for many years, I'm sure. *Never* doubt our friendship, Arthur.'

Art had known Maga for a long time now, and he didn't have any reason to believe Maga would lie to his face. He looked sincere, deadly serious, and it made Art feel better.

Art exhaled heavily. 'Whoa. Information overload – sorry, Maga.'

Maga waved a hand. 'Don't mention it. But really – what are we going to do about all this? Do you still think you could be my student Mage?'

Art focussed on his promise to himself, and to the younger Maga.

'As sure as I'm standing here. During my time in Amarly they must've seen something, I don't know what. But the message was very clear. Grandma Elfee read it to me – she still has it somewhere.'

Maga looked puzzled. 'Why would your *grandma* be relaying a message from the Faculty?'

Art raised his eyebrows. 'I was as surprised as you are when I found out that she's involved in all this somehow.'

Maga still looked puzzled. 'Hang on,' he said eventually. 'Which grandma are we talking about?'

'Well actually she's my great-grandma. I think her name's Dot or Dotty or something – I've only ever heard her actual name once or twice in my life.'

Maga's ears pricked up.

'*Dorothy* ... Elfee?'

'That's it!' Art exclaimed.

'You never told me she was called Dorothy.'

'Why? Is it important?'

Maga looked hesitant. 'Well ... yes. *Very*. If it came through her, then ... there's no question; you're my new student. How *you're* going to channel magic of any kind is beyond me, it really is. You simply don't have the physiology. But ... if they want me to instruct you, then I suppose I'll have to try. We'll start this time next month – I've got some *serious* planning to do. First lesson will be some of the methods I used today; we'll do Toffees and Chocolate. Bring a notepad.'

All of a sudden, a hundred questions filled Art's mind. Maga pulled his hood over his head as if to leave, but Art raised a hand.

'Wait. I've been meaning to ask you about some things since I spoke to Grandma just after I got back.'

'Back from the L-Shaped Village?' Maga said, pulling his hood down again.

'That's right,' Art said.

'Shoot.'

'She told me something,' Art began, 'Well, I'd sort of worked it out anyway, but ...'

Maga grinned from ear to ear. 'Took you a while,' he said. 'What gave it away – the snow? The Factory? Don't tell me you saw a guy in a red suit, because that's just silly.'

Art laughed. 'Stop – this is serious! I mean, I still feel silly saying it.'

'Saying what?' Maga asked. 'Santa Claus? That's what you lot call him, isn't it? That Jauger Clause, he's got a lot to answer for.'

'Have you met him?' Art asked.

Maga looked quizzical. 'She *did* explain it to you, didn't she?'

'Yes yes, I know there's not just one, and there's lots of different departments or whatever – I'm talking about the top guy, the man in charge of *everything* there.'

Maga looked relieved. 'The Boss. Yes of course – I have to communicate with him on an almost daily basis. And of course every year we have the Collection Awards. Is that a wild party or *what*? Well, you wouldn't know. Not yet, anyway.'

'What's he like?' Art asked.

Maga laughed behind a closed mouth. 'He's amazing. I mean, you sort of have to be to do a job like that – his predecessor was pretty amazing too so I hear. She was the most amazing Agent there ever was, the stories of her missions are legendary, and the Boss now is no different. You'll meet him someday and then you'll know what I mean – I can't really put it into words.'

'*She?*' Art asked, 'The Boss before him was a *woman?*'

Maga tutted. 'What's with you humans and your prejudices? Yes, she was a woman - what's that got to do with *anything?*'

'Sorry,' Art said. 'You're right – it's the human condition – I'm afraid I suffer from it just like every other human.'

Maga tilted his head. 'That's a staggeringly frank confession. I like it. How long were you away for?'

'Three days,' Art replied.

'It's rubbing off on you.' Maga pulled his hood up again. 'I have to go – I've got some lessons to plan. See you next month – get some rest – you'll need it. Oh – and have fun at the Ball.'

Art looked at his watch – he'd been away for far too long. 'Oh no! Evi!' he said, and darted towards the nearest exit to the science labs as fast as he could. The deluge of questions he had for Maga suddenly seemed unimportant – they could wait.

As he ran across the yard towards the sports hall in the distance, he couldn't stop his mind racing with all the things he had found out. It all seemed too much to handle at once, but he would have to, somehow. For a start, he couldn't believe he had put himself forward as Maga's student Mage. Firstly, he was sure this would cause bad Time ripples or whatever they were, and secondly, how would Maga cope with a student who wouldn't be able to do any of the things he was supposed to be being taught? Art supposed he would have to relay the information to the younger Maga somehow or he would get behind in his training. But all this was secondary to the revelation that his mind was really reeling from; for the last four years, Art had been in training as a Field Agent, and he had been totally unaware of it. As far as he had been concerned, he was just doing exactly what he had always done every year, but with a little extra help from his trusted friend Maga. Nothing had changed when Maga had turned up, except that it was a lot more fun – it certainly didn't resemble any sort of *training*. And try as he might, he couldn't think how *anything* he had been 'taught' by Maga could have any relevance to being a Field Agent. He didn't really understand what one was for a start. He didn't have a Mage's power, or a Warrior's power, or *any* type of power for that matter. How was he going to cut it as ... well as anything otherworldly? He didn't even know if he *wanted* to be trained as an Agent. He was totally dumbfounded by it all, but he couldn't stop thinking about it, however hard he tried. One thing was for certain – he would get as much information about it from Grandma as he could, as soon as he could.

He eventually reached the doors and crashed through into the main hall, nearly tripping over as he went. He skidded to a halt, and scanned the tables for Evi; she wasn't hard to spot. The dance floor was packed with students having a first attempt at a waltz before the meal; Evi was the *only* one not dancing. Art's chest stabbed in guilty pain, made worse by the looks he got from Tina as she waltzed past.

Evi was sitting at their table, looking around her worriedly, searching the hall. Art walked over to her with a feeling of dread in his stomach, adjusting his shirt and trousers as he went, but to his surprise Evi's face lit up when she spotted him.

'Oh Art – there you are. Where have you been?'

'I was err ...' he pointed towards the changing rooms. '... this shirt, I thought I was going to choke it's so tight around the throat.'

'Well undo the first button. Here,' She stood up and reached up to Art's collar. She unbuttoned it with her one good hand, and her perfume made Art feel giddy.

'There,' she said, and rested her hand on his chest.

'Erm, thanks,' he managed. 'So ... do you want to dance?'

'I'd love to, but my wrist is throbbing a little. I should have bought the sling, but it didn't go with this dress.'

'Oh no – are you okay? Have you got any tablets or anything?' Art fussed.

'No no I'm fine. But could we just ... go for a walk? The heating's a bit high in here.' She took his hand, and led him past the dance floor towards the door, but he stopped her halfway. He reached down to his waist, undid his belt and slid it from the beltloops; his trousers were uncomfortably tight – they weren't going to fall down anytime soon. The belt was the perfect colour of blue. He fashioned a sling from it, and fitted it around Evi's shoulder and under her cast. He adjusted the length until it was comfortable, and folded the loose end so it was out of sight. Art could see the relief in Evi's eyes, even more so when she kissed him on the cheek.

'Thank you,' she said softly.

'When you start to feel a bit better, we can dance, okay?' he said.

'Okay,' she said resolutely.

Art made to carry on across the floor, but Evi took his hand and stayed put.

'What's the matter?' Art said.

'I'm feeling better,' she said, with a smile on her face. 'I'm not quite up to waltzing, but I'm sure I could manage something.'

Art froze. He hadn't even *thought* about this scenario, and he turned white. She gently pulled him back towards her, and slipped her good arm around his neck. He didn't know what to do with his hands, even though he knew where they *should* go.

'Don't be shy, Arthur. That's not like you,' she chided.

It really *was* like him, and he felt awkward as he slipped his hands around her waist. He was careful not to hurt her bad arm as they started slow-dancing at the edge of the dance-floor, moving from side-to-side clumsily. Evi was smiling broadly, her eyes alight and sparkling. As Art stood there in the arms of Evi Wise, arguably the most beautiful girl St. David's Comprehensive had ever seen, he wondered *again* how on Earth he had found himself here.

'I ... I don't really understand this, Evi.' He said.

'What's not to understand?' she replied.

'Well, this. I mean you and ... *me*.'

'You don't have to understand it, Art. Just listen. Everyone else understands,' she said.

Art hadn't heard it start, he had been totally immersed in the absurdity of the situation he found himself in; every dancer on the floor had stopped and turned to look their way, and were cheering and applauding loudly. Although he heard it, he didn't turn and look.

'You see?' Evi said. 'Every now and again, the world turns out a truly *good* person. It took me a *long* time to put the pieces together and work out who you *really* are. And I, for one, will not let you get away.'

He looked at her, confused.

'So let's give them something to *really* cheer about,' she said, and the next thing Art knew, her lips were on his, and even though the sound of the crowd reached deafening levels, Art was even less aware of them, as he was lost in the most defining moment of his life.

Chapter Nine
THE UNEXPECTED WARRIOR

Danny stood looking up into the face of Dorothy Elfee. A moment ago, he thought he had found something *else*, something *other* than the extraordinary story of Art's great-grandmother; something from the other world he knew for so long. But now he realised that what he had researched, and what he had found *here*, were one and the *same thing*.

'Yes?' she said, coolly.

Danny glared at her, unshaken.

'Mrs. Elfee?' he said.

'*Ms* Elfee,' she corrected him.

'*Ms* ... Elfee then?' he said, slightly louder.

'Yes?'

'Ms *Dorothy* ... Elfee?'

She sighed. 'Yes. And you are?' she asked.

'My name is Daniel. But I suspect you know me by ... another name.'

'Oh?' she said, nonplussed.

'Before we continue, let me just say that since then, I have been given ... shall we say ... a stay of execution,' he said. 'And may I also say how remarkably young you are looking, considering.'

Her eyes locked onto his, with a sudden interest.

'And what exactly do you mean by that?' she enquired.

'For a few decades I went by the name of ... *YerDichh*.'

Grandma Elfee stared at him with a blank expression. But then her mouth fell open, and she adopted a certain readiness to her stance.

Danny held up a hand. 'Relax, Dorothy. I have been fully chastised, and even though I do not deserve it, I have been given another chance at life. I shall walk the correct path this time, I assure you.'

Grandma Elfee looked hestitant. 'And who exactly *gave* you this second chance, may I ask?'

Danny smiled. He leant closer, and spoke quietly but slowly. 'The grandson of one Jonathan Ainsworth, *the little boy you abducted in 1936.*' Danny maintained direct eye-contact with her, gauging her reaction. There was none that he could see.

But then she relaxed, and stood to one side. 'You had better come in then,' she said.

'Thank you,' he replied courteously, but was careful not to take his eyes off her. He filed past, and she closed the front door talking a quick glance left and right out of the doorway before she did. Danny turned and paused in the hallway, and Dorothy gestured towards the living room.

'After you,' she said.

Danny cleared his throat. 'If it's all the same, after *you*,' he replied.

Dorothy raised her eyebrows, and led the way into the huge living room. Danny noticed a fairly large fireplace in front of the sofa, and a small writing desk and chair to the left of it.

He smiled. 'So you keep in regular contact then,' he said.

'It's for emergencies,' she replied, as she continued past the sofa and into the kitchen.

'I'm sure it is,' Danny said under his breath.

She began banging pots and pans about as she searched for one to set on the boil. 'Stroth-Brew?' she called.

'Thank you,' he called back. 'I noticed you grow your *own*.'

Dorothy froze.

'You should be more careful,' he cautioned, 'you'll give yourself away ... *again*.'

She paused a while longer, then turned her attention back to her pots and pans, finding one and filling it with water.

'I'll sort it, so I will,' she chided.

Danny looked around the room. There were pictures in ornate little silver frames sitting on every conceivable surface. As he scanned them, he found lots of photos of Art and Walt with their parents, and lots of photos of Art's father Mitchel as a child, standing with a girl around the same age as him, presumably Maisie, his sister. He looked around for some pictures of what he had really been looking for, and to his surprise he found only one, in a small frame on the mantelpiece above the fireplace. It was a picture of Mitchel and Maisie standing with their parents, Jonathan Elfee, previously Ainsworth, and Alianor Elfee, previously Templar. But next to that, was the most telling picture of all; it was a photo of Grandma Elfee and her newly-adopted son, Jonathan, standing outside a courtroom. She had her arm around him and was clasping onto him for all she was worth. She was smiling broadly, but little Jonathan was wearing an expression of pure terror. The picture was old and faded, but it was unmistakably a clipping from a newspaper.

Eventually, Dorothy returned from the kitchen, carrying two mugs of Stroth-Brew. She set them down on the coffee table, and sat down on the sofa. Danny sat on one of the upright chairs opposite her. Danny picked up his mug, and tasted the contents warily, but then his face relaxed, and a hint of a smile appeared in the corners of his mouth.

Dorothy raised her eyebrows. 'You're aware of the recent additions then?' she said.

Danny turned his head to one side, keeping his eyes on her. 'You mean milk and honey?' he said.

She nodded.

Danny raised his eyebrows. 'But whose additions *were* they? His or – *yours*?'

'You needn't be so wary of me, Yer ... Danny. I have Arthur's best interests at heart,' she said.

'I'm sure you do,' Danny said, 'maybe ... a little too much.'

Dorothy sighed. 'How do you mean?' she said.

'Art has done a lot for me, unwittingly. I owe him everything. And if I really am going to make a go of my second chance, I need to help him. And to do that, I need to *protect* him. And to do *that*, I have to decide whether to make him aware of ... certain *facts*.'

Dorothy shifted uncomfortably. 'And by the word *facts*, you mean ...'

Danny smiled grimly. 'It's amazing what you can learn from the internet.'

'I really wouldn't believe everything you read online,' she said.

'ENOUGH!' he shouted, and Dorothy started slightly.

'*You* are the Ainsworth Abductor, are you not?' he demanded.

Dorothy's eyes widened. She was speechless for just a moment, then composed herself.

'I suppose I am,' she said, coolly.

'You abducted Jonathan from his house in 1936. Correct?'

'I did,' she said.

'And – you were charged with the murder of Ellie Ainsworth. Is that also true?'

'I was,' she said.

'So.' He said. 'I shouldn't believe everything I read on the internet then?'

'You shouldn't,' she confirmed.

They sat staring at each other.

'Exactly *what* are you attempting to discover?' Dorothy said eventually.

'Whether you are the sort of person who would be willing to commit murder,' he said, staring her straight in the eyes. 'And if so, and if you are truly from Amarly, then the consequences for Art's future may be very bleak indeed.'

She stared back, as if trying to analyse his glare. 'How do you mean?' she said.

'You know full well the damage that can be done by erasing someone from the Timeline before their end. I have to make sure that Art isn't exposed to that damage, even by association.'

'You have no idea what you are getting yourself into, young Danny.' She said.

Danny chuckled. 'Young! *You* ... have no idea.'

'That depends on your definition of *age*, Danny. Naivety has a lot to account for. Remember that.'

'What happened to Avarice Ainsworth?' he demanded.

Dorothy's face changed; she looked startled, yet again.

'That is *not* your business, Danny.' She said firmly.

'Art *is* my business – he *cannot* be around a murderer. I need to know if he is safe in your presence.'

'I can assure you of that ...'

'That is a matter of opinion!' Danny snapped.

'How so?' she enquired.

'We'll get to that later. What happened to Avarice?' he asked again.

'This won't do you any good, Danny. I would stop now if I were you.'

'*NO ONE* IS ME! ANSWER THE QUESTION!'

'Now why did you say that exactly? It's very telling, so it is ...'

Danny leant closer. 'ANSWER! Don't change the subject!'

'I won't go into this ...'

'TELL ME!'

'Stop this! I can't discuss it ...'

'DOROTHY – DID YOU KILL AVARICE?'

'YES!' She clapped her hand over her mouth, and her eyes bulged.

Danny sat stock still, staring her straight in the eyes again; neither of them moved a muscle. Dorothy's eyes glistened, and after a while a solitary tear rolled down her cheek.

'So,' Danny said eventually. 'You *are* willing to commit murder. You know the consequences of this, I presume?'

'Of course! It was calculated!' Dorothy said.

'It seems logical then,' he continued, 'that you also murdered Ellie. And all so *you* could be responsible for raising the descendant of Jonathan Ainsworth yourself.'

'NO!' she shouted. 'Ellie's murder was *never* proven! And for good reason!'

'Ah yes, your little tricks to fool the jury. No doubt the work of an accomplished Mage.'

'You don't understand – I'm *not* a Mage,' she said angrily. 'And like I said – the risks were calculated - it was necessary.'

Danny raised his eyebrows. '*Necessary*?' he said. 'Is Art aware of any of this?'

She glared at him, with poison in her eyes. 'He *can't* know. He has to discover his *own* importance.'

'I see. Deception *and* murder. It seems I was right to be wary, Dorothy. The mere matter of Jonathan's abduction seems insignificant now in comparison, yet I still find myself wondering ... *why*?'

Dorothy shook with anger. 'Why are you doing this?' she demanded.

'I must say,' he continued, 'your attempts to keep Art in the dark about all this are pretty lame. A few key strokes on any computer and literally *thousands* of entries appear, clear as day. What exactly are you doing to keep his history from him?'

Dorothy thought hard, choosing her words carefully. 'There are ... certain mechanisms in place.'

Danny leant forward. 'Well they don't work on *ME*,' he said.

'Clearly,' she countered.

They stared at each other some more.

'So,' he said, 'the golden question is ...'

'Why was it so important that *I* raise Jonathan?' she finished for him, picking her mug up from the table, attempting to calm herself. 'What do *you* think?' she said.

'*That* ... is another thing I am here to ascertain,' he said, matter-of-factly.

'And if you don't like what you hear?' she said.

'Then I must be careful,' he said. 'But one thing is for certain; Arthur will be made aware, despite your ... *mechanisms*.'

Danny continued drinking from his mug, while Dorothy watched him.

'How's your drink?' she said after a while, sitting back in her chair.

'Very good,' he said. He took another sip, and swallowed loudly.

'You asked earlier why I thought Art's safe being in your care was a matter of opinion,' he said. 'I believe I am about to find out.' He took another sip.

Dorothy looked at him through narrow eyes.

'This really is excellent,' he said. 'Of course, I took the liberty of ingesting a Quphoria leaf on the way in. Just in case you tried to ... *liven* up my drink in any way.'

Her face turned dark. She rose from her seat, and Danny rose with her, placing his mug down without spilling a drop as he did. They faced each other over the coffee table, and Dorothy's hand quivered next to her waist. Danny narrowed his eyes.

'So I was right,' he said. 'Arthur *is* in danger.' He looked to her hand hovering over her waist. 'I take it you are, among other things, a Warrior. Fascinating. More and more I learn.'

'You don't understand how important this is!' she said. 'And I wasn't going to kill you – just alter your memories.'

Danny tilted his head. 'Forgive me if I'm not *entirely* convinced of that.'

Dorothy drew her Sta'an from under her dressing gown with impressive speed, and in the blink of an eye she had made her strike against Danny. Without a second's hesitation he leapt over backwards and flipped over his chair, his hands clasping the back. He landed lightly on his feet just as the chair erupted forward with the force of the weapon intended for him, watching as it smashed the coffee table sending both mugs flying, their contents spilling in every direction. Dorothy's eyes widened in fright, but she took little time in readying herself for another strike.

Danny flipped over onto the dresser behind him on his hands as the second strike took hold, and the dresser was wrenched forwards, china and glass ornaments crashing to the floor. Danny landed running this time, and made for the small wicker chair by the writing desk. He grabbed it and swung it round, placing it in between himself and Dorothy, who was already preparing another strike. He didn't let go of the high back and sprang over the top, his feet high in the air as her strike yet again hit the wrong target, and the legs of the chair splintered forwards from under him. He landed right in front of her this time, and before she could see what was happening, her Sta'an was gone from her hands and Danny was on the other side of the room, threatening to snap the weapon.

'NOOO!' she cried, holding her hands out in panic. Danny remained still, placing a slight strain on the wood.

'Any more attempts on me, in any form, and you will be weapon-less forever, Elfee.'

'OKAY! Okay!' she begged, fear in her eyes. Danny slowly released the strain on the weapon, and held it with one hand, examining it. He sighed deeply.

'My Sta'an never found me,' he said. 'My physical form was too young, apparently.' Dorothy stood still, breathing heavily.

'But that doesn't mean I don't know how they work,' he continued.

She looked shocked and confused at the same time. 'But how ... how did you ... I mean there's *no* way to defend against a Fell. How on Amarly did you manage it?' she said, incredulous.

'The one thing about knowledge that *everyone* forgets,' he said coolly, 'is that it's endless. Con'tek, Jo'Sys, even the great Scem, will tell you they know *everything* there is to know about combat.' He locked eyes with her. 'They are *wrong*.'

'How so?' she enquired carefully.

'With enough downward force, and enough meditation, it's just a matter of momentarily projecting your own life force into another object.' He held the Sta'an up to his eyes. 'They are easily fooled. It seems ... naivety has a lot to account for. Remember that.' He tossed it over his shoulder, and it flew through the doorway into the hallway and thumped against a wall, before hitting the carpet with a dull thud.

Dorothy relaxed slightly.

'So,' he said accusingly, 'murder, abduction, deception, poison, and a one-sided duel. Your sense of honour is truly admirable.'

'Danny – Arthur *cannot* know about any of his past,' she pleaded. 'This is bigger than both of us.'

'That is apparent, in your eagerness to repel me,' Danny said caustically. 'You are far more dangerous than I thought, Dorothy, *and*, you're hiding a murderous past from the one person who has a right to know. Don't think this will end in any other way than Art knowing *everything*, even if just to warn him of the danger you pose to him and everyone around you.'

At that moment, Danny heard a sound from behind him. He turned, and the young Maga walked in from the hallway, carrying Dorothy's Sta'an.

'Grandma? Is everything ...' He stopped when he recognised Danny, and a smile broke out on his face.

'There you are! I was wondering when we'd see you!' he said. 'We didn't know where you'd been sent to. Are you okay?'

Danny's gaze remained on Dorothy, and hers on his. Maga looked at each of them in turn.

'Erm, what's going on? ..... Grandma?'

Chapter Ten

THE SUMMER

It had been nearly a month since the New Year's Ball, and the whole school was talking. Art had fully expected to be bullied as never before, now that they knew he was seeing Evi Wise, and Peter had taken to escorting him to all his lessons just in case. But actually, quite the reverse happened – he was treated totally differently. No one scowled at him as he entered a classroom, no one put signs on his back saying "kick me" or "ten points if you trip me up", and people only ever tackled him in rugby unless he actually *had* the ball, which made a nice change. Even Peter wasn't totally ignored any more – if he was walking with Art, he was still ignored on the whole, but no one would avoid looking into his eyes at any cost like they used to. Even Tina had completely forgiven Art for how he had treated Evi on the night of the ball. He could recall the conversation on the morning after the ball as if it was yesterday.

'Well. You came back from the dead good and proper last night.' Tina said.

'How do you mean?' Art answered.

'I thought you'd totally blown it when you left Evi on her own for all that time. I nearly punched you on the nose myself when you turned up again.'

'Oh. Yeah. It was that shirt – the collar nearly suffocated me,' he said shyly.

She raised her eyebrows. *'So you went all the way over to the science labs to sort out your collar, did you?'* she demanded.

Art started. *'How did you ...'*

'I went looking for you. Poor Evi, sat there all on her own. I saw you running out of

the science labs before I went back in. What were you doing in there?'

Art sighed. 'It's really complicated. You wouldn't believe me if I told you anyway.'

Tina narrowed her eyes. 'Well, Evi certainly forgave you – she must really like you. But I'm *not so forgiving,*' said Tina.

Art absentmindedly put his hand to his lips. 'Yeah - about that,' he said, and paused.

'Go on,' Tina said.

'Well – what is it? I mean, me and ... and her – really? I don't get it.'

Tina nearly smiled. 'You're such a klutz. She likes you.'

'Even if that's true – why?' Art had said.

Tina placed a hand on his shoulder. 'Just stop thinking, and accept it for what it is.'

Art frowned. 'Tina – you ... you would tell me if ... you know,'

'Oh, of course I would. You're both my best friends, and however much I like her, if I thought she was playing you I wouldn't let her. Even though you've got a lot *of making up to do.'*

But she forgave him eventually, which he was glad about, because it made the walks home from school every day much more bearable. Art would walk home hand in hand with Evi, and Tina would walk with Peter and Walt, who were becoming good friends. Walt's cool friends would avoid him whenever they saw him with Peter, but Walt seemed to care less and less.

One morning, Art sat in his form tutor room and bit into the slice of cake he had picked up on the way to school. As usual, Grandma had waved at him from the window as he walked past. She had been very secretive recently, and had avoided talking to Art. She had been out almost every day when he called to talk to her about his meeting with the older Maga at the ball – he wanted to ask her a lot of questions. But she still appeared every morning at the window, and every morning Art tried to signal something about coming in to talk to her, but she just smiled and put her thumb up, clearly misunderstanding Art's signal, and hurried off out of sight. So he took the box as usual every morning from the post box fixed to the gatepost, and put it into his bag.

He sat at his desk in his form tutor room waiting for Tina, chewing on the cake. He reached into his bag and brought out his EllShapyan diary, and a pen. He opened it to the page where he had written the symbols that he knew already, and practised them again, as he had every day. He figured he would have to be convincing if he was going to fool Maga that he was his student Mage, and he would start with learning this language, at all costs. He couldn't let the young Maga down, and he was willing to bet that most of the notes he was going to have to take would be in EllShapyan. He wrote them out once more, finding it slightly easier every time he did.

He turned the page and found the piece of paper that Tina had given him at the ball, still littered with crumple lines despite being pressed together in the pages of his diary for nearly a month. He could still remember the excitement he had felt when he wrote out the new letters he had learnt from it, and he felt excited that he still had more to learn – it was possibly the first time in his life he had been really interested in learning anything – it didn't feel like work at all. Tina couldn't start working on the rest until she had some more examples of it, and he hadn't seen Grandma to ask her. He carefully wrote out the ones he knew again, with the corresponding letters of the alphabet next to them. He was surprised at how easily they flowed from his pen as he copied them over and over.

Tina eventually slumped into her chair next to him, jarring the table and nearly making him score a huge clumsy line across the page.

She reached into her bag and pulled out a neatly folded piece of paper. 'Here,' she said, 'I've started an alphabet tree for you. It's got all the letters from the message you gave me, including your name at the top, and the dots – you know, those punctuation marks.'

Art chuckled. He still couldn't believe how quickly she had worked out the punctuation rules – he hadn't said anything to her about it. He unfolded the paper, and inspected the list. Surprisingly, her version of the EllShapyan letters were not as neat as his own. She had written them very carefully, but the ones in his diary seemed to have a certain flourish to them, as if they were from an ancient love letter. She noticed it too.

'You've been practising. I'm impressed,' she said. 'All we need now is some more examples of this dialect and we can start working out the missing letters.'

'I told you,' he said, 'I haven't seen Grandma to ask her. I'm going to try again tonight, though.'

'Okay then. I'm sure I can work the rest out if you do. I can't do a lot with just this though,' she said, holding up her exercise book. She had the alphabet tree copied into it too.

Art's form tutor walked in holding the register, and everyone settled down. At the same time, Art saw Evi walking past through the windows that ran the length of the classroom. She spotted him and waved, with a big grin on her face. Art waved back, but was unaware of what expression he wore.

'You haven't gotten used to that yet, have you?' Tina said.

'I know,' he replied. 'I should have got some accident insurance.'

Tina elbowed him playfully.

Art looked around the classroom.

'Where's Peter?' he said.

'Erm, how am I supposed to know?' Tina said, a little too innocently.

Art smirked. 'What do you mean, *how am I supposed to know*? The partner of the dance due that wowed everyone at the ball. I've seen you walking with him you know.'

'Shut up,' she said. 'He's a perfect gentleman.'

'You bet he is – that's my best buddy.'

Tina looked momentarily offended.

'Next to you, of course.' he corrected quickly. 'How did that happen anyway?'

'I told you at the ball,' she said, 'our families know each other. It's a long story.'

Art rested his chin in his hands and stared at her.

Tina tutted at him. 'Nosy.'

Art gaped. '*Me* nosy! Cheek!'

Tina smiled. 'Woman's prerogative. Now when do you think you can get some more of that code – I'm intrigued.'

'I *told* you already - tonight. I'm going to knock on her door and speak to her if it kills me. Then I'll pop over. Can I stay for tea – dad's cooking again.'

Tina smiled knowingly. 'That's if you've got *time* to pop in tonight. You might be busy.'

Art gave her a puzzled look.

Tina tutted again. 'You've got a *girlfriend*, Art. Remember? You've been round at hers every night since the Ball.'

Art's mind started wandering at the sound of the word "girlfriend", and he totally missed the bell for lessons to begin.

Tina clicked her fingers in front of his face. 'I don't know about you, but I'm going to science class. You coming?'

*

Walt clicked open the gate to Grandma's elaborate garden, and Art followed him through. He hadn't seen or heard from Evi all day apart from when she walked past that morning. She was in totally different classes to him, and she had started studying for her exams with her friends during breaks. So at the end of school he resigned himself to walking home with Walt and calling in on Grandma on the way, intent on talking to her.

To Art's surprise, Grandma opened the door even before he pressed the bell. She looked slightly dishevelled.

'Hello there, dears! Come in won't you. I'll fire up the Puu for you Walt just as soon as I've had a wee word with Arthur.'

She sounded just the same, despite her slightly haggard appearance.

'Grandma – are you okay?' Art enquired.

'Oh, I'm fine, so I am. I was up a few times in the night that's all. Come in come in.'

Art filed into the front room, but Walt peeled off into the study where the games console was. 'I can work it, Grandma – I'll get started, okay? Cakepleasethanks.' He disappeared around the corner out of sight.

Art looked around the room; it wasn't the same - he couldn't quite put his finger on it. It was still clean and tidy, but things were different. He looked at the dresser, and noticed gaps where some of the china cups and plates had been. Then he noticed that the writing desk was looking empty somehow.

'Grandma – didn't you have a wicker chair there?' he asked.

She looked a little flustered – Art wasn't used to her composure being anything other than perfect. He felt a little uneasy.

'Oh I've had a bit of a change around, so I have. Threw some things out. That old chair was close to breaking.'

Art had the unmistakable feeling she was lying, but he decided not to question her about it. He decided he'd give her some good news instead.

'I translated the message,' he said, 'some time ago now.'

Her face lit up. 'That's wonderful! What did it say?'

'You know what it said.'

'I know that *I* know – I want to know if *you* got it right, so I do.'

Art told her what was in the letter, then stood with his hands on his hips.

'Why are you looking at me like that, dear?' she said.

'I met Maga – the *older* Maga – only moments after I understood the message. Why did you let it get so close? I could have told him.'

'You wouldn't have told him,' she said.

'How can you be so sure?'

'Well – did he *ask* you?' she said.

Art shifted uncomfortably. 'Erm, well, not exactly. He sort of guessed I knew.'

Her face turned white. 'He knows you *know* who it is? Why on earth did you let that slip?'

'You see?' Art implored. 'Why didn't you tell me what was in the message before?'

Grandma sat down. 'I didn't think he'd just come out and *ask* you,' she said. 'Besides, the message wasn't from me.'

'Who sent it then?' he asked.

'It was from Pud and Jimma. And it was addressed to you,' she said.

'But you knew what was in it,' he countered.

'I had a sneaky peek, so I did.'

Art snorted. 'You'd like my friend Tina, you know.' He sat down opposite her with the coffee table between them. He noticed it was damaged, but he ignored it.

'You didn't tell him *who* it was, did you?' she said. 'What did you tell him?'

'The first thing that came into my head. That his new student is *me*.'

She laughed out loud, and clapped her hands together.

'And he believed it? Genius! Well done, Arthur dear!' she cried.

Art remained stony-faced. 'Only now, I need your help. He believes he's teaching me – and I've got to be believable or he'll guess something is wrong. I've got my first lesson any time now.'

'Oh, you don't need my help with that dear – just listen to him. And make sure you learn our written language – that's important.'

She made a temple with her hands, and spoke to herself.

'Oh, this is perfect – it'll move you on so much faster so it will!'

'Grandma!' Art snapped. She came back to herself.

'That's not all,' he said.

'What else is there, dear?' she asked.

'He told me something else that you probably know as well.'

She looked vacant. 'Go on,' she said.

'Apparently I've been in training. As a Field Agent. For the last *four years*.'

She went completely silent, and her eyes widened.

'Grandma?' he ventured.

She said nothing.

'Grandma? What's the matter?'

She rushed over and sat next to him, grabbing his shoulders firmly.

'Are you sure, dear? I mean are you absolutely *sure*?' she asked, still wide-eyed.

'Maga's been instructing me himself,' Art confirmed.

'Oh my gosh! This is amazing news! You're *so* much more involved in all this than I thought! Wait here – I want to show you something, so I do!' she enthused, and rushed off in the direction of the hallway. Art heard a cupboard opening, and a key being turned in a lock. Then he heard another door opening - it sounded like a heavy door, and Grandma returned holding something that Art recognised only too well. She handed her Sta'an to Art, and he took it, looking incredulous. He gaped.

'Whoa! Whose is this?' he asked.

'It's mine, Arthur. I've had it for many of your lifetimes now. She's served me well, as I have her.' She said, with genuine love in her voice.

Art looked at her. 'But that means ...'

'That's right Art. Maga's the best there's ever been – you'll be learning from a good'n, but *I'll* be on hand too, so I will. Anything you need to know, just ask.'

Art was dumbfounded. He had always thought of her as being a typical great-grandma – spoiling them whenever she could, and always there if they needed her, but nevertheless very old and frail. But recently he had seen another side to her that kind of suggested she didn't feel as old as she was, and this had confirmed it. There was one thing, however, that didn't add up; if she *was* from Amarly, why was she ... well, *tall*? But Art wanted so much to believe that she was, that he dismissed it. The question could wait for another time.

'So are you an Instructor too?' he asked.

'No, no, I told you before – nothing so grand. I was too busy in the field to have time for any of that nonsense. But I've been around a bit, so I have; you could do worse than take advice from me.'

'But ... Maga is a *Mage* ... why is he an Agent as well?' Art asked.

'He insisted. Someone had spotted his potential as an Agent long before he was identified as a Mage, and he got wind of it. When he finished his magical training, he sought out the Agent who had recommended him, and insisted on being trained as an Agent too. Caused quite a stir, so he did. Mages are meant for much grander things.'

Art stared at the Sta'an in his hand. It was clearly very old, and a chip of wood was missing from a part of the handle, but it was clean and shiny, very slender, and very well cared for. It was engraved with her surname on the latter end of the little round blade; a very quaint, incredibly well carved font spelling the word "Elfee". He had never seen engraving on a Sta'an before, but then he supposed he had seen very few Sta'ans in his limited experience.

'I can't believe it. Grandma, this is amazing!' he said.

'I know! And I'm actually going to be around for your training! I never thought anything so grand could happen to me!' She hugged him, and he hugged her back, with genuine affection. He finally had someone to talk about all this with; more than that – someone who could *help* him.

'So you're a Warrior then!' he said, inspecting the Sta'an. 'Are all Field Agents Warriors?'

'Oh no - we can be anything. I was just lucky. I expect your Sta'an will find you when you go back again.'

Art smiled weakly. 'Sorry Grandma – that's not going to happen.'

'What do you mean?' she said, surprised. Art told her all about little Maga's parents - Shay-la and Jonnoe - and how he had had breakfast with them one morning. He told her about the amazing wood-work shop Jonnoe had shown him, and how that had led to Jonnoe discovering Art's incredible skill as a carpenter.

'So you see,' he finished, 'I already know what I'm going to be. And it doesn't involve a Sta'an. Sorry Grandma.'

She looked slightly crestfallen, but then smiled knowingly. 'You forget – I'm in contact with Pud and Jimma on a regular basis - what do you think that fireplace is for?'

Art looked puzzled.

'I know about your *unique* talent with a Sta'an, Arthur. Hité wrote to me and told me herself. Forget what you *think* you know, and just ... well, go with the flow. You're talented – it's almost a legend already – Amarly has never seen *anyone* like you Art. Remember that. Don't limit yourself.'

Art still looked puzzled. He had no idea what she was talking about.

'Oh, I almost forgot. Hité sent you something. Here.' She stood up and walked into the kitchen, and returned with a small package wrapped in white paper. She handed it to Art. He opened it up, and inside were a dozen or so slightly browned Dough-Drops, nestled around a small tub of honey. The aroma took him right back to The Horn Keeper Inn for a moment, and he could almost feel the heat from the huge fireplace.

'I'll put a pan of water on. Milk and honey dear?' she said.

Art was smiling inside and out.

*

Art eventually left Grandma's house to take Walt home for tea. As they filed through the front garden, Art noticed that the plant he had always liked by the front gate had one of the leaves ripped from it, leaving an untidy stump. He was just bending down to inspect it more closely, when Walt cleared his throat, a little louder than necessary. Art looked up, and waiting for him by the fence was Evi, smiling slyly.

'See you, stinky!' Walt said as he walked briskly away, waving at Evi as he went. He clicked the gate shut behind him.

'Hi,' Art said.

'Hello, you,' she said, and placed a small kiss on his cheek as he approached.

'Oh, Tina has a message for you,' she said. She turned round and put her arms around herself like she was pretending to hug someone and made kissing noises.

'Very funny,' Art chuckled.

She turned back round and linked her arm in his, and they began walking back towards the direction of their houses.

'Sorry I couldn't see you today,' she said, 'I had revision sessions booked ages ago. You should come tomorrow.'

Art pictured himself with his books open amongst a crowd of Evi's friends, baffled at everything they went through. He shuddered.

'Erm, okay.' He said. At least he would be spending time with her.

'I'm having tea at Tina's tonight,' she said. 'You should come along – she said it would be okay. Apparently they're having gooseberry tart for pudding.'

Art thought for a second. '*Gooseberry* tart?' he said.

'That's what she said.'

Art chuckled.

'What?' Evi asked, elbowing him gently.

'That's probably a joke. Come on, this is *Tina* we're talking about.'

Evi smiled and sighed at the same time.

'You're supposed to be the smart one, too,' Art said.

They walked to Tina's house, rather more slowly than they usually walked, talking and laughing all the way.

Behind them, Danny appeared from behind the bush in Grandma's front garden; he had seen Art looking at the Quphoria plant from his hiding place. He narrowed his eyes as he watched Art and Evi walking into the distance, wondering when he would get the chance to talk with him alone.

Chapter Eleven
THE ELFEE FILES

Art popped into his house to make sure Walt had got home okay, and to tell his dad that he had been invited to tea at Tina's. Evi came in with him, and Art's dad kept grinning slightly as if he couldn't help it. In the end Art left just to get away from the smirks, but as they headed down the hallway, Evi made a point of holding Art's hand tightly, and that seemed to shut Art's dad up.

They arrived at Tina's house, and she opened the door before they rang the doorbell.

'It's my two best buddies!' she said, wearing her best-behaviour smile.

'Hello, Tina,' Art and Evi droned together.

Evi cleared her throat. 'I'm looking forward to that gooseberry tart, Tina.'

Tina laughed. 'You can have double helpings if you like,' she said.

Evi raised her eyebrows. 'No, *you* can,' she said, and kissed Art on the cheek.

'Yuhhchh! Okay, okay, no more "three's-a-crowd" jokes I promise! Just don't do that again!'

They all filed through the hall and headed for the stairs.

'Hello, you three,' called Tina's mum from the kitchen. 'Cuppa tea?'

'Thanks Mrs. Rosenbaum,' Art said. Tina's mum didn't seem in the slightest bit surprised to see Art and Evi together, even though it was the first time they had both been in Tina's house at the same time.

'I'll bring them up, okay?' said Mrs. Rosenbaum.

'Thanks, mum,' Tina called back.

Tina's room was surprisingly large, and very plain. Everything was tidy and clean, and the cream coloured walls were dotted with posters and pictures, and a huge cork board covered most of the wall above her bed. There was a desk with a laptop computer whirring away to one side, while the main work area was filled with a large pad of lined paper, with a pot of pens next to it. The whole room looked very business-like, and even her duvet cover had a huge bookshelf printed on it, showing leather volumes of classic novels. On the notice board, Art noticed some EllShapyan writing sticking out from behind a piece of paper – he made a mental note to see what it was as soon as Evi wasn't around.

Evi sat down on the bed, and Art went to sit next to her, but thought better of it and slumped into the bean-bag instead. Tina put some music on, and she sat down in her desk chair, and swivelled it around to face them both as if she was a therapist of some kind facing her patients.

'So,' she said, 'what shall we talk about?' She had a smug look on her face.

Evi leaned over and rested on her elbow, looking Tina square in the face.

'Peter,' she said.

Tina's face altered slightly, but she regained her composure just as quickly. 'Off limits,' she said quickly.

'Why?' said Art. 'You keep clamming up about that. This is top gossip, you can't just keep it to yourself!'

Evi looked at Art and laughed. 'He's right. Out with it – come on – the lot. Now please!'

Tina looked at them both. 'Is this how it's going to be from now on – the two of you teaming up on me like this?'

'You bet,' said Evi, and she high-fived Art, who nearly didn't get the signal, and then they waited for her to talk.

'Women's prerogative,' she said again, and turned her nose up at them both.

'You've used that excuse already. You can't use it more than once.' Art said.

'Here, here,' said Evi.

'Since when?'

'Since just now. Two against one,' said Evi, winking at Art.

Tina rolled her eyes. 'We're just friends. Honestly. He took me to the dance and we had fun – that's it.'

Art scoffed. 'He just took you to the dance? That's all?'

'That's all,' she said.

'And *at* the dance, you just happened to be the two best dancers there. By a mile.'

Tina said nothing.

Art carried on. 'And your face when everyone applauded – there's definitely more to it than that.'

A small hint of a smile appeared on Tina's face.

Evi's face lit up. 'I knew it!'

The door opened, and Mrs. Rosenbaum brought in three cups of tea.

'Dinner's ready in five, okay? You may as well come down now and lay the table, Tina.' she said.

'Thanks mum,' said Tina, sounding a little relieved. 'Come on guys – a little help please.' Tina and Evi got up and headed out of the room, and Art followed a little more slowly, giving himself time to lift up the paper hiding the EllShapyan writing on the notice board. It was another copy of the incomplete alphabet tree – probably the first one Tina had written out, as the symbols were untidy and some were rubbed out and re-written. He reached into his pocket, pulled out a slip of paper, and slid it under the top sheet of Tina's lined pad without anyone seeing; it was a sheet of examples of the EllShapyan language that he had asked Grandma for before he left with Walt. She had said that he should be learning it for himself, and he felt bad that he was asking for Tina's help, but he figured he only needed help with decoding it – once that was done, he would learn to use it himself, without her help. But as he walked away with the note safely stashed where she would find it, he felt an unexpected emotion; the flicker of *guilt*. He and Tina were working on something together, and Evi was not part of it, neither did he want her to be. For some reason he didn't want her to know about it – he was taking a risk getting Tina involved in case she found out exactly what it was, and letting Evi in on it as well felt like too much. So he stuck to his decision, hoping that Tina wasn't feeling guilty for keeping something from her best friend too.

As he closed the bedroom door behind him to follow Evi and Tina downstairs, his phone vibrated in his pocket. He fished it out, and waiting for him was a text message from Maga. Art wondered how he had got hold of his number, but immediately dismissed it – this was Maga after all, infinitely resourceful, and cunning as a fox. Even if he was annoying and slightly immature at times.

He scrolled down to his inbox and opened the message.

MEET T'MROW LNCHTME @ LBRY. BRNG NOTEPAD.

Art grinned to himself; finally his first lesson, and he was surprised to find he was looking forward to it. He made a note to ask Tina if she could decode the rest of the language before tomorrow – he had a feeling he would need as much of it as he could remember. He locked his phone, and joined the rest of them at the dinner table.

After dinner, Evi and Art left Tina's house and walked home together. Evi's house was just around the corner from Tina's, and it didn't take them long to get there. Standing outside the house, Evi clasped both his hands and looked into his eyes. The closeness made it seem all the more unreal to Art again, and he failed to hide it from her.

'What's the matter?' Evi said, looking concerned.

Art sighed. 'I'm sorry, it's just ... well, I mean ...'

'Yes ...' she said.

'It's just ... well you and me,' he said uncomfortably.

'What about you and me?' she answered.

'I don't really understand it. I mean, look at you, and then ... look at *me*.' He sighed again.

She let go of his hands and slipped her arms around his waist.

'What's to understand?' she said, and kissed him lightly on the lips. 'I'll see you tomorrow. Revision session's at lunchtime, okay?' And she slid out of his arms and through the front gate. *Oh no*, Art thought. *Tomorrow lunchtime.*

He was just trying to think what he was going to do when he heard a voice from behind him calling his name. It was a well controlled but fairly high-pitched voice, and Art recognised it before he believed it.

He turned round at breakneck speed, and standing not ten feet from him was Danny, looking sharp and in control, as he had been when Art first set eyes on him from opposite sides of the battlefield. For a split second he forgot their reconciliation, and a chill went through his body. But then Art broke into a smile, and walked over to him.

'Danny! How are you ... where have you been?'

Danny smiled back, and reached out his hand in welcome. 'I'm very good, thank you. I've been ... around.'

Art was slightly taken aback by Danny's mannerism, but only because his youthful looks seemed to have returned in full.

'Sorry, Danny - this is going to take some getting used to, shaking hands with a seven year-old.' He reached down and shook Danny's hand. 'Good to see you again. How have you been?'

Danny sighed. 'Very good at first. It's true what they say – ignorance really is bliss. But then it started coming back. Just glimpses at first, but then ...' he shuddered. 'All at once, the whole four decades knocked the breath out of me.'

Art frowned. 'Whoa. How did you cope?'

'I didn't to begin with. I thought I was going to tear the house apart. I nearly hurt ...' he paused. 'But anyway – I'm good. I really am. And I'm glad I found *you*, Arthur – I've been trying to find the right time to come to you with this. We need to talk.'

Art tilted his head. 'Oh?'

'Not here. And I haven't got much time – Michael can only cover for me for so long. Where can we go?'

Art looked around. 'Well, it's pretty dark. And you must be cold in those clothes.'

Danny waved a hand. 'I'm fine. The park behind the shop?'

'Lead on,' Art said, and they darted down the alleyway that led to the recreation ground behind the grocery shop owned by the old couple that Grandma took soup to on cold days.

They sat down on the old roundabout, probably the last of them in existence, and Danny reached into a bag he was carrying on his shoulder. He took out a brown envelope and handed it to Art.

'What's this?' Art said. He began to open it up, but Danny stayed his hand.

'Before you look at it, Art, I just want you to know that I'm just looking out for you.'

'How do you mean? What's this about?'

Danny sighed. I'm afraid this is about your grandmother. Or more to the point, your *great* grandmother.'

Art narrowed his eyes. 'Not many people know she's my great-grandma, Danny. How did *you* know that?'

'How well do you know her, Art?'

'She's my *grandmother*, Danny. I know her better than most.'

'Really? No ... surprises recently then?'

Art thought about how close to her he had felt recently, because of the discovery that she had been a Warrior from Amarly in her younger days. At the time, he had thought of nothing other than pride, and relief that he had someone to talk to about it, someone to ask questions and take advice from without being thought of as insane. But on the evening he had found out, when he was back in his room, he hadn't been able to help thinking about the implications of it all. The most obvious being that he was *related* to the people of that world by blood, but also that he was not necessarily the only member of his family to have been there. How many others had there been, if any? And what did it mean if they had? Did he have direct family members in the L-Shaped Village? And if so, how come they all looked different, smaller, and clearly a bit magical, when he wasn't?

All these thoughts surfaced at once, and Danny noticed the change in Art's expression.

'I see,' Danny said knowingly. 'I'm sorry to do this to you Art, but I'm afraid you might be in danger. You and anyone who associates with her.'

'That's silly. In what way?'

Danny raised his eyebrows. 'In the worst way.'

Art looked into Danny's eyes, searching for any hint of joviality, but he found none.

'No, that's silly ... I mean do you have any proof?' said Art, just as he remembered the envelope he was holding. He started opening it, eager to see the contents.

'I found it on the internet first,' Danny said while Art ripped open the seal, 'and I've carried out a lot of research since then – police records, newspaper articles, public records, everything I could find to try and explain it rationally, in the hope that it wasn't true. But every piece of evidence I found just seemed to back up the stories further. Some of the accounts differ, probably due to the limited powers of the human mind, but the facts remain, I'm afraid.'

Art pulled out a blue file, containing documents of all sorts, the first being a printout of the news article Danny had first come across on the computer. Art read in disbelief, turning the pages wildly as he read further. The second was a transcript of the court hearing that had explained the charges against her, and the subsequent collapse of the trial, and then a report of the adoption of Jonathan Ainsworth. Danny had even found a copy of the adoption papers confirming Jonathan's change of name to Elfee, and a very old photograph of the two of them, showing Jonathan with an expression that looked like fear. Art flicked through the rest of the file; there were eye witness reports, more newspaper cuttings, and fingerprint evidence. It was chilling reading, especially the description of the murder charges, and the fact that Avarice Ainsworth had disappeared, and was long since pronounced dead.

Art looked at Danny when he had reached the end of the file.

'What does ... I don't understand ...'

'I'm sorry Arthur – Dorothy Elfee is an abductor, *and* a murderer. Simple enough crimes to understand in human terms, and shocking on their own, but possibly disastrous for the Timeline and everyone associated with her.'

'NO!' Art shouted. 'You've got that wrong! Look, here – the murder case collapsed ...'

'She told me, Arthur.'

Art fell silent, staring at Danny.

'What?' he said eventually.

'I've spoken to her. I asked her outright about Avarice, and she confessed. I'm sorry, Arthur – she *did* kill Avarice, which makes it all the more likely that she killed Ellie too. And I'm afraid she's not your grandmother. Not biologically, anyway.'

Art's eyes unfocused, and he shook his head with the effort of processing it all. 'You ... you've *seen* her? When?'

'A few weeks ago. It wasn't hard to find her – she keeps Seederum Quphoria in her front garden. Well, she *did*.'

Art thought about the plant that he had seen ripped up in Grandma's front garden. 'What did she say?' Art asked.

Danny sighed again. 'It was quite an exchange. She certainly knows how to use a Sta'an – especially when she feels threatened.'

Art's mind wandered to the missing and damaged pieces of furniture in Grandma's front room. 'You fought with her?'

'No, no – *she* fought. I defended. Quite successfully, if I do say so myself. And before you ask, *she* started it. And nearly lost her Sta'an in the process. She should take more care of it, you know.'

'Yes, but what did she *say*?' Art asked again.

'We talked about everything. Jonathan, Ellie, Avarice – she confirmed it all, before trying to poison me.'

Art gaped. 'No way ... there's no way ...'

'But more importantly,' Danny continued, 'she confessed to Avarice's murder. She killed him, Art.'

Art sat on the roundabout, stunned into total silence. He was dumbfounded.

'I'm so sorry to do this to you, Art – but I believe you're in danger, and I had to protect you.'

Art still said nothing. Danny collected the contents of the file together and went about putting it back in his bag.

'No,' said Art, taking hold of the file. 'I'll ... keep this for a while if it's okay.'

'Of course. Be my guest,' Danny said. 'Hang on to it as long as you need. But be warned – Dorothy must *not* get hold of it – she doesn't handle confrontation well – take my word for it.'

Art sat there thinking, occasionally seeking something out of the file, then closing it again and pondering some more. He wore an expression of concentration, and his face had a tinge of green to it. All the while, Danny sat patiently, waiting for Art to fully digest what he had told him.

Eventually, Art sighed, as if he had exhausted his thought processes.

'What does this mean?' he said.

'It means that you are in danger. And the most appropriate course of action would be to ... not see her again.'

Art looked at him quizzically. 'You can't be serious?'

'Art – you read the file. I've tried to find evidence to disprove it, but all I found was more evidence that supports it ...'

'YOU'RE WRONG!' Art shouted.

'I'm sorry, Art – even *she* didn't deny it.'

'But why? Why would she do it?'

'That's the confusing bit. What I'm about to say next would probably make most people laugh, but not you. Not after the things you've experienced.'

'Go on,' Art said hopefully.

'I'm guessing, just *guessing* Art, that you have some importance in all this. For some reason *you* seemed to interest her all those years ago. This is not the first instance of "Time-Fame" that I've heard of.'

'"Time-Fame"? What's that?' Art asked.

'I heard a lot of fantastical things during my time in Amarly,' Danny answered, 'most of them I dismissed as nonsense. That was until Hité found me, and returned me home in the way that she did. All the stories I had heard about Time criminals suddenly didn't seem quite so silly.

'Imagine if you had the power to go back in Time and associate yourself with someone famous. Say for instance you could be one of Einstein's teachers at school or something, anything to get you close to your hero, and published in the history books even if not by name, which would give yourself away. I mean that's just an example – Einstein flunked most of his classes at school so there'd be no interest in becoming one of his teachers, but you get the idea.'

'Erm, sort of,' Art lied.

'The problem is, if you want to take someone's place in Time, you have to *do* something with that someone.' Danny paused.

'You don't mean ...'

'I'm afraid so, Art. Dorothy wanted to be a part of your rise in history, however remote. It could easily be one of your descendants, but I'm guessing it's you after what happened in Amarly recently.'

'But she wouldn't ... I mean she couldn't ...'

'Arthur – she *killed* your great grandmother and took her place. And when a relative turned up to claim you, she killed him too. What I don't understand is why she kept her own name, and changed the Timeline to include it. That still has me baffled ...'

'YOU ARE WRONG!' Art shouted again. 'SHE WOULD *NOT* DO THIS, DANNY.'

Danny sighed. 'Arthur I'm sorry. But you are associating with a murderer, and a

Temporal-Criminal. You cannot ...'

'NO!' Art shouted, and dropped the file, putting his head in his hands. 'It's ludicrous! She's helping me, she ... she's my *Grandma* ...' He stood up, and Danny stood too.

'Art, I have to protect you – *don't* go back there, okay? Is anyone else with her? ART!' he shouted.

'Just Maga ... he's staying with her.' Art said.

Danny's eyes widened. Shay-la's boy? He's *here*? Why?'

'He's in training, he's ... it's not important – Danny there's no danger. You've got this wrong, somehow, I'm sure of it.'

'Just promise me you won't go back there Art.'

'I CAN'T!'

They stood there looking at each other, Danny with a pleading look on his face, and Art's with a look of confusion and anger. Danny rubbed his eyes.

'Well then, I'm coming with you. Every time you go. If I have to camp out and wait for you I will, but you're not going in there alone.'

Art stared at him some more. 'Fine,' he said after a while, and sighed. 'But you don't have to camp out. I'll let you know. Maga will be glad to see you for a start. Do you have a mobile?'

'Of course. I can't believe they sell these in supermarkets.' He fished out a smart looking flip phone, and opened the contacts folder. They exchanged numbers, and started walking back towards the main road. Danny carried the file, and as they reached the main road, Art's phone rang. It was Danny's number on the screen.

'Just checking,' he grinned. Then he patted Art's shoulder.

'I won't forget what you did for me, Art. So I'm here to help whether you like it or not.' Danny sprinted back in the direction of his own street, and Art watched him go, wondering whether he liked Danny's particular brand of 'help', and wondering whether he would ever get rid of the slight sickening feeling he had in his stomach.

Chapter Twelve
THE FIRST LESSON

Art sat at his usual seat at school, waiting for his form tutor to arrive and take the attendance record. His head was still spinning from the conversation he had had the night before with Danny, and a lot of it still wasn't making sense. The only part that did make any sense was that he had discovered he was *not* related to Grandma Elfee by blood, which he was very sad about; he had always found it odd that his grandma spoke with an Irish accent when there had never been any mention of an Irish connection in his family history before. And of course, it also meant that he was not related to any of the inhabitants of the L-Shaped Village either, which actually saddened him almost as much.

But he was still having problems with the accusations against her. For a start, they were outrageous. Abduction? Murder? They simply couldn't be true, could they? If they were true, then according to the rules of engagement he had learnt during his time at the L-Shaped Village, she had committed crimes that were simply *unthinkable* to the villagers, not to mention the disastrous consequences to the Timeline that Maga had mentioned, whatever they could be.

He hadn't been able to think about anything else since the conversation, and the only conclusion he could even entertain without confusing himself again, was that if for some strange, bizarre, unfathomable reason it was true, then there had to be some sort of explanation, some reason for her to do it. And that was if he ever believed there could be any truth in it at all.

Despite his muddled brain, he had noticed that Tina wasn't as punctual as she usually was, and that Pete hadn't turned up to class either. But just as he thought they might miss the register, Tina waltzed in and sat at a desk directly behind Art. She normally sat next to him, but this morning she didn't. Pete lumbered in almost straight after her, looking slightly dishevelled, and he sat down too, somewhere near the back where the nearest free seat was. Art grinned. *They are seeing each other,* he thought.

'Nice of you to join us, Miss Rosenbaum.'

'Sorry sir,' she said, with as much enthusiasm as she could muster.

They sat listening to the names as they were read out, and when Art's and hers had both been called, Art felt a jab in his back.

'Oi - Elfee.'

Art turned around. 'What, Tina?' he said, as quietly as he could. She had her hand stretched out, and in it was a piece of paper, folded several times.

'Finished it,' she said.

'Oh, brilliant - thanks.' He took the piece of paper, and concealed it in the front pocket of his bag just as the bell rang, and everyone got up to leave for their various classes.

'I'm not doing all the work though,' she said, 'I've left three for you to do. Oh, and I've left you a message of my own as well. I'm off to Latin - you've got Maths - say hi to Pete for me'.

'Yeah - about that ...' Art grinned.

'Gottagobye...' Tina said, and disappeared out of the door.

Art picked up his bag and headed towards the back of the class to meet Peter, who hadn't made an attempt to get up yet. Art was just about to rib him about Tina and why he had been late when he noticed that one side of Peter's face was bright red, and his eyes were puffed and slightly wet. Everyone had already left, including their form teacher, and they were alone. Peter made no attempt to acknowledge Art's presence.

'Peter? What ... what's happened?'

Peter started to gather his things together to go to class, and stood up rather quickly.

'Pete - wait!' Art blocked his way, and he saw the mark on his face much clearer; it was slightly swollen and beginning to bruise.

'My God - what happened?' Art asked.

'Nothing. It's nothing,' he said quietly, trying desperately to avoid eye-contact.

'Peter this is me. Your best friend. It's clearly not nothing.' Art sighed. 'And it doesn't look ... accidental, either.'

Peter glared at him, but Art didn't move.

'Peter, please...' Art sat on the corner of the nearest desk, staring at him resolutely. Slowly, Peter lowered his head, and he sat down again.

'What happened?' Art asked again.

Peter put his head in his hands, and mumbled something unintelligible.

'It was what?' Art asked.

'IT WAS A 'D'! ANOTHER 'D', ALRIGHT?' Peter shouted.

Art's eyes widened as he realised what Peter was saying. 'It was ... your *dad*? Your dad did that because ...'

'BECAUSE I GOT ANOTHER DAMN 'D', OKAY?'

Art sat down in the nearest chair, looking incredulous. They both sat there in silence while Art tried to process what his best friend was telling him.

'I don't ... Peter that's terrible ...' he said eventually.

Peter said nothing. Art pulled his chair over so it was next to Peter's. They sat together for a while, Art sensing that his being there was helping, despite the silence. After what was probably a quarter of an hour, although Art couldn't really be sure, Peter sighed heavily. Art patted the big man's shoulder.

'I don't know what to say,' Art said, genuinely.

Peter just shrugged his shoulders, and Art felt that familiar pang of pain he always got when something happened to his best friend.

'I suppose we'd better get off to Maths,' he said.

'But we're late now,' Peter said quietly, and the pang of pain stabbed Art's chest again.

'You let me deal with that,' he answered, and he fished his mobile phone out of his pocket. He scrolled through his recent messages list, and found the one from Maga about his first lesson; he clicked 'reply', and typed a simple message asking for help. He clicked 'send', but a warning message came up on the screen telling him that there was no number attached to the original message. Art thought for a second, but then he grinned, and clicked 'continue' anyway. And sure enough, a 'message sent' box appeared, and Art clicked his phone shut.

'Come on Pete - let's go.'

Peter looked alarmed. 'But Mr. Phillips will go spare.'

'Help's on its way,' he said, and Peter stared back, confused.

And just then, Art felt the faintest wind of a whisper right next to him; *Help's already here*, he heard, almost in his head. Art smiled, knowing that Maga was concealed right next to him, and they left the classroom.

When they arrived at the door to their Maths class, it flew open, and Mr. Phillips marched out looking red-faced and angry. Peter cowered as Mr. Phillips opened his mouth to shout, but as he did, Art saw a small bubble float down and pop on his head, and Mr. Phillips' face slowly went blank.

I'd say you have about thirty seconds. Go! Art heard right in his ear, and he ushered in a totally bewildered-looking Peter to the back of the class where they both sat down and unpacked their exercise books. The rest of the class were looking similarly confused, no doubt wondering how the two late-comers had escaped Mr. Phillips's renowned temper.

After a while, the maths teacher walked back through the door. He looked totally confused, and said nothing for a minute or two. 'Erm, what was I … did anybody see …' He pointed back through the door as if he was trying to remember something, but after a while he closed the door and faced the class.

'Well, err .. are we all here? Good, good. If I could just …hmm. Okay then. If you'll look at the board …'

Peter nudged Art. 'What was that?' he said.

Art smiled again. 'Help,' he said simply. Peter shook his head, and they both went about trying to stay awake for the next hour.

*

Art met up with Evi at lunchtime. She smiled warmly when she saw him, and took his hand as he approached.

'Tina has another message for you. But it's the same as yesterday, so I won't bother relaying it.'

Art laughed.

'Come on then brain-box - off we go,' she said.

'Where to?' Art asked.

'Revision lesson, remember?' she said, and went to lead him off down the corridor, but Art resisted.

'Art?' she said.

'Evi, I'm sorry - I've got to help Peter with something. It's really important. He's had a hard time - his dad's being really strict with him. I've got to help.'

She looked at him, and after only a few seconds the corners of her mouth turned up, and she scowled mockingly. 'Anything to get out of revision, eh? You'll give me a complex.'

'Actually it's more revision. Our next biology assignment is due, and Pete needs to get more than a D. I said I'd help him plan,' said Art.

'We revised biology yesterday, otherwise I'd invite him along too,' Evi said.

'It's okay. I think we're slightly below your level anyway.'

'Will you walk home with me after school?' she asked.

'Of course I will,' he smiled. 'We won't be alone though, you know that.'

'We never are,' she answered, 'but there's always later. Have fun,' she said, and kissed him on the cheek before waltzing off down the corridor. Literally waltzing - it was clear she'd had some lessons from Tina. Art chuckled, still amazed at his luck.

He headed upstairs to the library, wondering where he would meet Maga, if he had even left his side at all. He wondered how Maga had concealed himself that morning, considering Art could see through all his usual methods of disguise, and there was no hint of a shadow or a shimmer around him in the classroom when Art realised he was there. He hadn't seen or heard from him since their maths lesson, but as soon as Art walked through the library door, he spotted Maga sitting at one of the small round reading tables in the far corner, bold as brass, wearing his usual black raincoat and black trousers, but now he also wore the black beret he always wore on missions.

Art rushed over and sat down. 'What are you doing Maga? People will see you!'

Maga waved a hand. 'Relax, Art - no one else can see me.'

'I saw through your 'methods' at the Ball!'

'Aha - but you didn't this morning, did you?'

'Well, no,' Art conceded.

'There we are then. I'm using the exact same methods now as I did at the Ball; *you* can see through them, as we discovered you could in the science labs, but no one else can. Before that, I was using a more ... vigorous method. By the way, nice excuse about having to help out with your friend Peter. She totally bought it ...'

'That wasn't an excuse,' Art cut in.

Maga stared at him. 'Say that again?' he said.

'It wasn't an excuse, Maga. I can't make the lesson. I really do have to help Peter out - you saw him this morning - I've got to help him.'

Maga stared at him some more. 'This is your first lesson as a trainee Mage, Art. Do you understand the importance of this? It doesn't sound like you do ...'

'Peter is in trouble. Not like being grounded, or going to bed without any supper, but *real* trouble. He needs my help ...'

'Your training is serious, Art ...'

'THIS IS SERIOUS!' Art shouted. A few people turned round and gave him strange looks. He whispered as loudly as he could. 'I can't waste any more time - I have to go. We'll have to do this another time, Maga.' He got up to leave.

'Art!' Maga whispered just as loudly. 'THIS is the time! You can't just leave!'

'Watch me!' Art said, and swept out of the library.

Maga watched him go, then smiled warmly. He flipped open his mobile and sent a message to the Faculty;

AS AN AGENT, ART IS FURTHER ON WITH HIS TRAINING THAN I THOUGHT. MAGE TRAINING WILL BE A LITTLE TRICKIER. REQUEST PERMISSION TO EMPLOY TIME-STOP TRAINING. PLEASE RESPOND IMMEDIATELY.

He flipped his phone closed, and casually walked out after Art.

Art leapt down the stairs two at a time and tore around the corner to the long corridor that led back to their tutor room. He ran down the corridor as fast as he could; he had left Peter sitting at his desk looking over his revision notes while he popped out to make his excuses, and he was worried he had left him for too long. Their tutor room was the very last room at the end of the corridor, but as he was half-way along it, his ears popped as he felt the air pressure changing around him, and heard the familiar low hum of Time being halted. He came to a stop, and out of the corridor window the sight of three birds frozen in Time as they were flapping away from the bird-table caught his eye. The last one had a stream of water glistening in a long icicle flowing from its back.

Art turned, and in the distance, walking towards him, was the familiar gait of Maga as he sauntered down the corridor.

'Very funny, Maga,' Art shouted.

'It's not meant to be. As an Agent, you were absolutely correct to put your friend first. You would have scored full marks if I was testing you. Not that you would have known. But this is not Agent training. This is Mage training, and as such you have a duty to the cause, not to people. Any people. But your situation is unique - certain allowances have to be made. This way you get to have your lesson *and* help your friend.'

Art narrowed his eyes. 'But how much time do we have? I mean Time still moves forward, right? Just much more slowly.'

'Not in this case, no - this is a FULL Time-stop. It's very powerful, and not something I can administer; it comes from the Faculty, and I had to get special permission from them. I bet Pud and Jimma are frantically trying to work out where it's coming from as we speak - I wish I could see their faces! Now if you please - the lesson?'

Art got his breath back, and dropped his hands to his sides. He thought about arguing with him, but he knew it wouldn't make any difference. It didn't matter if he walked away the way he did in the library either - Time wouldn't restart until Maga did ... whatever it was he did, and Peter wasn't going anywhere. In fact no one was, himself included. So he resigned himself to the fact that the lesson was going to happen. He had been looking forward to it after all, and this way he got to help Peter just as quickly.

'Okay, okay. Where shall we go?'

Maga indicated the classroom he had stopped outside of, and they both filed in.

It was an empty English room, the tables arranged in a huge U-shape, and the walls plastered with quotes from all the literary greats from the last two centuries. Most of them were illustrated with posters of modern-day film adaptations starring famous actors dressed in period costumes. Art sat down at the nearest table, and went to get out the notebook with the newest translations written in it, that he had done sneakily during an English lesson. But then he remembered that he had left his bag in his tutor room with Peter. Luckily there was a spare piece of paper folded up on one of the chairs next to him, and he always carried a Biro in his pocket, so he flattened the paper out in front of him and sat ready to take notes.

Maga planted himself firmly in front of the whiteboard, fiddled with his mobile phone for a minute, then pointed it at the projector hanging from the ceiling. It immediately sprang to life, and a flashing title appeared on the whiteboard:
RECON METHODS 101.

Then he pulled out a small black box and placed it on the desk. He pressed a button on the top, and a red light started flashing.

'What's that?'

'It's an audio-visual recorder. The Faculty aren't too hot on not knowing what's happened during a full Time-stop – they need real-time recordings of everything that happens during a Temporal Blackout. Now, as I said the other day - this lesson will cover two methods – Reconnaissance Chocolate and Anonymity Toffees.'

Art wrote down the heading, and looked up. Maga was smiling at him.

'Good start,' he said, looking at Art's notes.

Art looked down at the page, and was amazed to see that he had written it down in perfect EllShapyan, all except the numbers, which were the usual Hindu-Arabic Western-adopted symbols. 'Whoa,' Art said under his breath. Even he was surprised that he had assimilated the new symbols so quickly – he had only got them that morning after all.

Maga carried on. 'Can you tell me the difference between the two methods?'

Art paused briefly. 'Erm, no.'

'I'll tell you.' Maga said. 'Recon Chocolate allows you to walk wherever you like, in the busiest of places, and not be seen. It's quite powerful, so the squares are much smaller than ordinary chocolate. It's not that people can't see you - the human brain is almost impossible to fool completely - you simply won't be noticed. People will hold the door for you, even step aside to get out of your way, but when asked, they will have no knowledge that you were ever there - even if you're standing right in front of them, they'll swear blind they see nothing. But if you throw an object for them to catch, like a ball or something, even whilst they're denying there's anything there, they'll catch it. Ask them who threw it - they won't know what you're talking about.

'Anonymity Toffees work differently. You'll be in plain sight, no cover whatsoever, but no one will recognize you. Not even your own mother will know who you are - you'll be just another random citizen in the street. It works if someone is trying to spot you on CCTV, any other type of video, and on any picture that was taken while you were using it. Got all that?'

Art finished scribbling down the main points from Maga's little speech in a mixture of English and EllShapyan, still missing the three symbols that Tina had left for *him* to translate, and put his pen down.

'Good.' Maga said. 'Now - can you tell me the advantages and disadvantages of the two compared to each other ...'

'Maga,' Art interrupted.

Maga sighed. 'Yes?' he said, rolling his eyes.

'This is all very interesting, but aren't these things that an Agent would use?'

Maga cleared his throat. 'Well, yes. What's your point?'

'Well this is Mage training, isn't it? Shouldn't we be learning about magic and stuff?'

'Ah, I see where you're coming from. But don't forget we're starting from the very beginning here. An Agent would just be given this stuff to use, with a few quick words of instruction, nothing more; you have already, remember? How he or she then uses it would be up to them; my point is that *anyone* can use it. But we're thinking on a different level here. Now ask yourself this: where does it *come* from?'

'How do you mean?' Art asked.

'I mean, how does it come into existence?'

'You mean who makes it?' Art said.

Maga rolled his eyes again. 'Exactly. But "making" isn't really the right word. It's difficult to explain - these aren't the kind of things you can just reverse-engineer and find out what's in them; there's something special that makes them work, that can't be identified by any scientist, or academic of any kind.'

Art's eyes lit up. 'Magic,' he said.

'Hmm. That's not *really* the right word either,' Maga said. 'The ability to will something into existence can't just come from confidence alone, although you do need that. It's something more. The word "magic" is misused so often, and usually just used because of a misunderstanding of what's really been seen.'

'So what is it?' Art asked.

'It's a combination of things really. Physiology, energy, the ability to believe that nothing else is possible other than what you are trying to achieve. A certain credence, a unique type of conviction that ...'

'Belief,' Art said.

Maga looked at him, and tilted his head. He said nothing for a while.

'I've never heard it described as that before,' he said, 'but - well I can't exactly disagree with that use of the word, so ... yes. In a way.'

Art thought for a minute. 'Wow,' he said eventually.

'Wow, exactly. So in order to teach you what it takes to produce something like Recon Chocolate, which in turn will identify what you are trying to learn, we have to start at the very beginning, the basics – uses, advantages and disadvantages, and the like. And when we eventually get on to how it happens, you'll learn that this is just the tip of the iceberg. And when we've discussed the whole iceberg, we may, just may, start teaching you the basics of the energy itself. Which is where I envisage there being problems. But mine is not to reason why – I have my orders - so let's get on, shall we?'

Art sat back and listened as Maga went on in great detail about how Recon Chocolate and Anon Toffees were used, and when to use them; all the while Art was scribbling down notes about each part. He only stopped when he ran out of paper, at which point Maga grabbed a sheet from the top of the filing cabinet, folded it into a perfect jet fighter, and threw it to him; it landed gently on his desk.

Art was genuinely interested in everything Maga talked about, and he even got Art up for a demonstration. Maga popped half a cube of toffee into his mouth, and for a while Art became totally confused as to who he was talking to. He knew that someone else was in the room with him, someone he trusted with his life, but he couldn't work out who it was, even though he had moved to within inches of Maga's face – he was a total stranger. Then slowly the features started to look familiar, and after a few minutes Art wondered how on Earth he hadn't recognised his other-worldly friend.

'Usually that would be a very dangerous thing to do,' Maga had said, 'but the fact that you already know me, and hopefully trust me, *and* that it doesn't work very well on you anyway, should have stopped you totally freaking out. And I'm glad it did. I'm guessing now though, just like the Chocolate and the Bubbles, it won't work on you anymore.'

Maga carried on with the lesson, and eventually finished talking about an hour later. He turned the projector off with his phone again.

'Homework,' he said. For once, Art wasn't filled with dread upon hearing the word. 'I want an essay on the advantages and disadvantages of using both methods. I want you to write it in the form of a plan, detailing how *you* would go about concealing *yourself* if you ever met yourself in the past or the future. Outline which method you would use and why, along with why you wouldn't use the other. Our next lesson is in a week's time - have it ready for then. In the meantime, do you want to watch me slap all the school bullies in the face without them knowing?'

Art laughed. 'How do you know who they are?' he asked.

'Oh come on Art - there's a List – I've seen it. Didn't you learn anything while you were at the Village?'

'You're kidding me, right?' Art said incredulously.

'Course not. Come on - its fun. You can have a go if you like!'

Maga was out of his boring-teacher mode and back to his usual impish self. Not that Art found the lesson boring, far from it, but Art loved it when Maga was in one of his playful moods.

Art sighed. 'I'd love to, I really would. But I have to get back to Peter.'

Maga cleared his throat and straghtened up. 'Of course, of course. I'll err ... sort it out.'

He tapped a few words into his mobile, and almost immediately Art felt his ears pop, and heard the bass crunch that went with it, and the clock on the wall started ticking again, although Art hadn't noticed that it had stopped.

Maga casually popped a cube of Chocolate in his mouth. He momentarily vanished, but reappeared just as clearly an instant later, owing to Art's immunity.

'I'll send you a message about the next lesson. Oh - I've got to go - Jed McCready is just about to come round the corner and he needs a slap ...' And with that, Maga ran out of the door.

A moment later Art heard an angry shout, and he laughed hard as he made his way back to his form tutor room to help Peter with his planning.

Dialogue Five

'Jimma – Stasis alarm's going off!'

'What? The Stasis alarm? Really? I don't think that's ever gone off before.'

'I've checked the logs Jimma, and you're right. This is the first time we've ever had one. Is there even a protocol that covers it?'

'That's a good point. I'll look into it. First things first, though – why is it going off?'

'I'll punch it up. Are you logged onto your screen?'

'I am now, Pud. Fire it up.'

'Okay ... cancelling the alarm ... bringing up the dialogue box ... let's see now ... here it is. Oh my. Are you seeing this Jimma?'

'I'm not sure I believe it, but yes. An unauthorized full Time-stop?'

'It looks that way.'

'Can you locate the source?'

'I can try ... I'll need to bring up the Virtual Location software. Here it is ... okay, we're in. Scanning the logs ... nearly there ... oh. There doesn't seem to be anything to latch on to. I can't see anything that's relevant really ... just a few mobile phone signals a tad stronger than they shou ...'

'Pud? What is it?'

'I can't be certain, but I think I've found a Trans-world phone signal.'

'A Trans-world signal? But – we're the only ones even close to developing that kind of technology. How can that be?'

'I have no idea Jimma, but it's here alright. There's a few traces of the afterglow left, concentrating around this area here ...'

'That's a building, isn't it Pud?'

'It's a school, yes. Why would there be a signal like that in a school?'

'I have no idea. And anyway, tech of that kind is strictly forbidden - we're the only ones who have been granted permission to even study it – we need to get to the bottom of this. Can you scan the pupil records? Cross-check with any journeys through the Portal?'

'That's a good idea, Jimma.'

'That's why I have Four Gold Stars, Pud.'

'Have you? I hadn't noticed.'

'That's another reason right there. Perception, Pud. Got the records up yet?'

'Yes. Cross-checking ... oh. Well, well, – our Mr. Elfee is a pupil there.'

'Are you sure?'

'You should be seeing this at the same time as I do – it's there on the screen. Perception, Jimma.'

'Careful, Pud.'

'Okay, okay. What does it mean though?'

'I have no idea. I'm actually more confused now than when the alarm went off. There's no way tech like that could be in the hands of a human - this makes no sense whatsoever. Pud - what else can you do with that signal? Can you trace the owner of the phone? That might give us an insight into something.'

'Well I can, but ...'

'But what?'

'It's not exactly legitimate. I'm not sure I want to be caught using the trace program I'll have to use to find out.'

'What about backdoor programs within the console? Any more of those I should know about?'

'............................'

'Pud ...'

'Well, there's always ...'

'YOU SAID THERE WAS NOTHING MORE I SHOULD KNOW!'

'That's right. You shouldn't know. I'm thinking about your commission here.'

'Like Swarvikkz you are! Out with it!'

'Language, Jimma!'

'OUT WITH IT!'

'Okay – easy on the volume, Plus-One.'

'I've told you not to call me that! Besides, you'll have your fourth Star soon, so I won't be a "plus-one" for much longer. Make the most of it. Now tell me about this program.'

'You remember the one we used last time that enabled us to bypass the Faculty and send a signal to the Boss?'

'Yes. Go on.'

'That was a sneaky little algorithm, thought up by your Uncle. Well, I analysed it, and it turns out that if you take its base-code and insert it into any program, it gives it a little more ... "punch", shall we say. And it works especially well on Tracer programs. The only problem is, that if the base-code is left unguarded within any system, it latches onto any program it can find, and all manner of devastation can occur. Your Uncle's more elaborate experiments were banned for a reason after all, Jimma.'

'I'm aware of that, Pud.'

'The base-code signature is imprinted onto every server of every law-establishment there is, and if we're caught using it they'll close us down before we can say "early-retirement".'

'But we used it last time and it was okay.'

'Yes, but that was a tiny little program, it was like whispering in space. This one is more like shouting in a broom-cupboard.'

'They'll spot it?'

'A toddler drawing his first circuits with a metallic pen could spot it. I'll need your permission to do something very sneaky indeed.'

'I don't like the sound of this, Pud.'

'It's funny you should say that Jimma, because that's what I intend to use.'

'What?'

'Sound. What's your history of early Earth computers like?'

'Ahem. Well it's a little rusty to tell the truth.'

'I'll elaborate then. Earth computers in the eighties were extremely simple, with virtually no memory, which wasn't actually a disadvantage. It meant that you could load programs onto them with sound using a tape-recorder.'

'What's a tape-recorder?'

'It used two reels of magnetic tape to record the inverted imprints of sound waves on, which were fed through a magnetic pickup which sent signals through an amplifier and out through speakers.'

'I wish I hadn't asked. What's your point?'

'Well, I have a feeling the Faculty are somehow involved in this. If you can think of an excuse to call them about something, I could play some high-frequency sound waves in the background that upload a simplified version of the tracer program onto their servers through their own hard-line.'

'But won't it be spotted?'

'Sound wave program loading is such an antiquated method no one would ever think of looking for it. And anyway - they're tracking all outgoing digital transmissions – they won't be looking for something incoming, and especially not an analogue signal.'

'Okay then. How soon can you have it ready?'

'Well actually ...'

'It's ready now, isn't it? You've been sitting on this for a while, haven't you?'

'Ever since the Faculty tried to intercept our message to the Boss, yes. It really got to me. This is one of the things I've been working on, and I've been dying to try it!'

'I bet you have. Well – we'll give it a go. What can I call them about without sounding suspicious?'

'That's the clever part. There's nothing like the truth to steer someone away from the truth. Call up your counter-part and ask her if she knows anything about the illegal Time-stop.'

'Are you serious?'

'Of course I am. She'll be furious that you even asked if the Faculty had anything to do with it – it's the perfect cover.'

'I hadn't thought of it like that. Okay – I'll do it. Are you good to go right now?'

'Ready when you are, Jimma.'

'Okay – go.'

'Right - punching up the connection ... bringing it online ... placing the call ...waiting for a response ...'

'Faculty here. Where can I direct you, please?'

'Yadra Salveary please.'

'Connecting. Go ahead, please.'

'Salveary here.'

'Ah, Yadra. It's Jimma from the Complex. Nice to talk to you again.'

'Jimma? You've got a nerve, calling me out of the blue like this.'

'Now, now, Yadra. Let's play nice, shall we? We're both in the same business after all ...'

'Ha! How do you figure that?'

'Listen, I couldn't help what happened last time ...'

'The Faculty's use of what you call "contraband" is essential – you didn't have to report that any further up the chain than is normally required ...'

'I was just doing my job ...'

'Your job? Two trainees nearly flunked their finals because of your job. And what's more - I'll have you know that all of those substances have now been cleared for use by any Agent in the field.'

'I know – I had the memo. But I'm not calling about that.'

'Oh really? What is it this time, then? Did our last quarterly report have too many full-stops in it for you? That's a favourite of yours. Cost us a fortune in re-printing last time ...'

'No, it's not that either. Though it's interesting that you mention full-stops.'

'I beg your pardon?'

'We've detected an illegal Time-stop – a full Time-stop.'

'And?'

'And – I wondered if you knew anything about it?'

'And I suppose we're the first people you called.'

'Naturally.'

'This is OUTRAGEOUS – I'm not discussing anything of the sort with you! How DARE you suggest such a thing!'

'Come on now Yadra – it's not exactly beyond you ...'

'THIS IS ... HOW DARE YOU, HOW ... THIS CONVERSATION IS OVER! ....'

'Connection's dead, Jimma.'

'Did you have enough time Pud?'

'And some. I had it uploaded before she mentioned the contraband. It's just a waiting game now.'

'How will we get the results?'

'Well you'll have to ring again, but a call to the reception should do it this time – it'll download itself in a couple of seconds the moment someone answers, and remove all traces of itself from the system. They'll never know they've been hacked. An hour or so should do it. Time for a Stroth-Brew. Dough-Drops Jimma?'

Chapter Thirteen
THE GOLDEN THREE

Art walked home with Evi again that evening after school, although this time Tina, Peter and Walt were in tow, and they all walked in a big group. They had all decided to walk home together with Peter, as they were all still dumbstruck about how his father had treated him. No one said anything about it of course, because Peter had asked that they keep it just between him and Art, but everyone had noticed the mark on Peter's face. Tina was upset that he wouldn't tell her how he had got it, but when Art had seen how upset she was, he couldn't help himself, and he told her about it, swearing her to secrecy. She was furious with Peter's dad, and had been unable to stop herself telling Evi, who was equally horrified, and also sworn to secrecy. Walt had overheard them in the corridor, but was pretending he didn't know. So they all walked home together in a big group, laughing and joking, trying to cheer Peter up, although it was hard to tell if they had or not – his face looked just as angry when he was happy as when he was sad.

Evi insisted on holding Art's hand, which induced a small fit of giggling from Walt, and Tina held Peter's hand, fussing about the mark on his face, but without asking too many questions. He was secretly glad of the attention, especially as Tina had insisted on going over to his house to help him with more of his revision, though secretly she just wanted to look Peter's dad in the eye and fume. The revision session Peter had had with Art at lunchtime had gone well, and he was feeling better about the next essay, but with Tina on board he was even happier.

All the while, Art's head was buzzing from the lesson he had had with Maga. He had read the notes through again, surprised by his ability to read his own EllShapyan writing, and he already had the essay planned out in his head. This had been the biggest shock to him; he felt that when he got home, he would be able to quickly jot down his ideas, like Tina had taught him, and write the essay just like that. He had *never* felt like that before. But then he remembered, with disappointment, that the young Maga was the one who'd have to write the essay, *not* himself, so during a particularly boring moment in Home Economics class, he'd rewritten all the notes out again neatly, underlining a few things he thought the young Maga would need for the essay, and explaining some things in a less complicated way, and then written the essay instructions at the bottom. All he'd have to do was hand the notes over to Maga at Grandma's house, and his part was done, which made him feel slightly cheated. He *wanted* to do the essay, so he decided that he would anyway, in his own time. But right at that particular moment, he was there for his friend Peter, just like everyone else was; he would have to put it all out of his head for now. Which was difficult, because as they passed Grandma's house, the upstairs window flew open, and she shouted out to them.

'Art dear, I need to speak with you, so I do. Can you pop in now?'

Art looked at Evi, who squeezed his hand a little tighter. He was desperate to talk to Grandma about the lesson, and even more desperate to ask her about this silly abduction nonsense, but his chest was still aching with the need to help out his best friend.

'Not really, Grandma. Can I call back in an hour?'

Grandma looked taken aback. Art had never refused her anything, especially the chance to taste her delightful baking.

'Arthur dear, I wouldn't ask if it wasn't important. Your friends can wait, so they can. I have a ... *message*.'

Art looked at Peter, and couldn't help focusing on the mark on his face.

'No. My friends can't wait. I'll call back in an hour.'

She looked almost annoyed, but just as she was about to slam the window shut, Walt shouted up to her.

'I'm coming, Grandma. Cakepleasethanks!' And he darted up the drive and waited for her to open the front door.

The four of them carried on walking, Evi smiling broadly at Art as they went. They reached Peter's house, and they waved Tina and Peter off as they padded up the pathway, Tina clearly aching for a fight; Art chuckled in admiration for her.

Evi took the opportunity to put both arms around her boyfriend's waist, and she kissed him on the cheek.

Art was flustered. 'Would you like to come round for, I dunno, a cuppatea or something?' he said clumsily.

'I wish I could,' she replied, 'but Nathan's having his cast removed at the hospital today. I said I'd go. Walk home with me though?'

'Course I will. I suppose I'd better go see what Grandma wants, too, afterwards. How's your wrist doing by the way?'

'Nearly all better. Apparently bones heal faster when you're happy.' She planted another kiss on his cheek, and they turned and walked the rest of the way to her house.

Nathan was watching from the window when they arrived, and giggled when he saw they were holding hands. The front door burst open, and Jack and Jackie Wise stumbled out in their usual state of disarray. They noticed Evi and Art standing by the front gate, and Jack sort of straightened up slightly at the sight of him, and cleared his throat. Jackie looked relieved to see her daughter.

'Oh, Evi dear ... hello Art ... give us a hand Evi, would you?' Jackie said.

Evi rolled her eyes. 'See you tomorrow,' she said to Art, kissed him on the cheek, and casually strolled down the driveway to help them with Nathan's car seat, which they hadn't a clue how to fit. Art watched as Evi took it from her father with her good hand, and placed it exactly in position in a few seconds, securing the seat belt in the correct loops for when Nathan was ready. Art waved goodbye, and strolled back towards Grandma's house.

Art remembered the promise he had made to Danny, fished out his mobile phone, and sent him a quick text. For some reason that he couldn't fathom, he felt somehow responsible for Danny, and actually *wanted* to include him whenever he could. He also wanted to clear up the misunderstanding hanging over Grandma's head regarding her possible criminal past; he was sure that if he just got them in the same room at the same time, some sort of explanation would emerge that would exonerate her. It was firmly planted in his head that this was the only possible outcome, because the alternative was just too horrible to comprehend.

He passed Peter's house, and couldn't help looking through the front window to see if anything was happening, but it all looked quiet. Then he arrived at Grandma's, and he clicked open the front gate. The empty patch of soil where a plant had been ripped out was now filled with another plant, boasting a full bloom of metallic blue flowers. Just as he reached the front door, he heard the gate click open, and Danny walked through, looking out of breath and red in the face.

'Whoa, that was quick!' Art said.

'I've been running the route over and over to find the quickest way. Like I said, I don't want you going in there alone,' he answered.

'Thanks for your concern,' Art said, 'but really – I'm sure there's a perfectly rational explanation for all that. I'll be fine. I'm glad you're here though.'

Danny gave Art a grateful look.

Art knocked on the front door, and Grandma answered it almost immediately, clearly not expecting Danny to be there too.

'Oh,' she said. 'Nice of you to drop by, but … it's not necessary that you're here, Daniel.'

He opened his mouth to protest, but Art got there before him.

'I've asked him to come. I want him here.'

Grandma looked at Art, looking slightly sullen.

'Whatever for, dear?' she asked.

'Erm, he's my … *advisor*.'

Grandma raised her eyebrows, and then sighed. She moved to one side wordlessly. They both filed in, and sat down in the living room as she shut the door, with her customary glance left and right out of the doorway before she did.

Grandma swept past them into the kitchen, and went about readying four mugs of Stroth-Brew and a plate of Dough-Drops and honey, and as she brought them out, she shouted for little Maga to come and join them. Art heard little footsteps padding overhead, then down the stairs, and the young Maga emerged, wearing clothes that would fit a toddler, and looking snug on him.

'Hey Maga,' said Art.

'Hello Maga,' Danny said somewhat more formally.

'Hey guys,' Maga said, pretending to be up-beat, but Art could see the sorrow in his eyes. He was clearly missing his family. Art's chest began to ache in sympathy.

'It's good to see you,' Art said. 'And I have something for you.' He fished out his hand-written set of notes, with the first assignment, and handed them to Maga.

'What's this?' He said.

'It's your first lesson.'

Maga opened it, and looked it over briefly. He looked confused. 'But why are *you* giving it to me? Are you …'

'Maga - I'm not your Instructor, I'm just the messenger. I have a fireplace too you know.'

Maga's eyes widened in surprise.

Grandma smiled at Art, the first he'd seen on her face for a while. She was clearly impressed with his improvisation. Art, however, was still uncomfortable with the concept of giving someone a set of notes from a lesson given by their older self.

'There you go,' Grandma said to Maga reassuringly, 'something to take your mind off it.'

'Off what? Art asked.

Grandma looked pained. 'We had a message from the Faculty late last night. It seems Maga is not cleared to go back to the exact point in Time he left from when this part of his training's over.'

Now Art's eyes widened. 'Why not? That's not fair – Shay-la must be going out of her mind with worry …'

Maga's head drooped.

'Oh, sorry Maga,' Art said quickly. 'Erm, I don't know what to say. That's really not fair. Did they give a reason?'

'Not a good one,' Grandma said, 'something about a limited number of Temporal Energy bursts.'

Art felt as if he had been hit with an articulated lorry square in the chest. His immediate thought was that the full Time-Stop that the older version of Maga had had to use so he could teach Art that afternoon had something to do with it. Maybe the Faculty had a limited number of times they could do something like that, and doing so that afternoon meant that the younger version of Maga would have to allow whatever time he spent here to actually pass back in the L-Shaped Village as a result. Maga was homesick enough without knowing that his family would have to feel the same – they had been told that wouldn't happen. He wasn't sure that Maga's little brother Fallow could cope without him for a year.

'Maga, I'm so sorry. Really.' Art pleaded.

'It's okay. It's not your fault.' Maga said.

Art knew this wasn't exactly true, and he winced as the pang of guilt stabbed him again.

'Not to worry,' Grandma said. 'We got another message from them just this morning. Plenty to take his mind off of it. The year'll pass in no time, so it will.'

'What's it about?' Art asked.

Grandma smiled. 'It's Maga's *final* assignment – the one he has to pass at the end of this year. If he can pull it off, he can go back and start his second year's training. And the best thing is, it involves *you*, Arthur.'

'Whoa, whoa, what do you mean *it involves me*?' Art said, raising his palms.

'Just that, Arthur. Here, take a look.' Grandma handed Art a piece of paper, with what he supposed was the Faculty's logo at the top. He read it through, and after a while he had to sit down.

Danny sat next to him, looking concerned. 'Art – what's the matter?' He reached for the paper. 'May I?' he said, but Grandma rose and went to stop him.

'That's okay Danny dear, it's really only for Art's eyes …' she said with urgency in her voice.

'Gran – like I said – he's my advisor,' said Art, and handed Danny the sheet. Grandma sat down again looking disgruntled.

Danny studied the sheet. 'Well according to this, it's just dropping off some presents to a hospital. A … children's ward, by the looks of it. It looks fairly straight forward … oh - it gets harder. Your identities are to be concealed at all times, and no traces are to be left - no one must know you were even there. And hang on … there's a *deadline* – no more than plus-or-minus ten seconds either side of midnight. "Standard Recon methods are allowed" – whatever that means. The plan is to be submitted no later than the sixth of November for evaluation.'

Danny handed the sheet back to Art. 'You look like you've seen a ghost. Whatever is the matter?' he asked.

Art looked puzzled. 'This is something *I* usually do,' he said, 'every year.'

'You do?' Danny said.

'Have done since I was nine.'

'Whatever for?' Danny asked.

'It's a long story. And anyway, it looks like it won't be me this year,' he said, looking slightly disappointed.

'That's not how I see it,' Grandma said.

'Oh?' said Art.

'I'd say your mission is just the same Arthur – but it looks like this time, *you're* the help, in your role as –how did you put it – the *advisor*.'

'What does that mean?' Art asked.

'You've always had help, haven't you? The last four years for sure. The way I see it your objective now is the same, only it looks like this time you're more ... *managerial*.'

Art thought for a moment, but he didn't look satisfied. 'But why is *this* the assignment anyway - isn't this something an *Agent* should do? Maga's training as a Mage, isn't he? But *I'm* ...' He stopped in mid-sentence, unsure whether young Maga or Danny should know about his training as an Agent.

Grandma smiled. 'It looks as though the Faculty are trying to kill two birds with one stone. This is only first-year Mage training – it makes sense to pair it up with fourth-year Agent training – there's not a lot of difference.'

Maga and Danny stared at Art, and his face flushed furiously. 'I didn't even know,' Art said, trying to defend himself. 'Honestly. I only found out a couple of days ago myself. It's no big deal.'

'No big deal?' Danny said, clearly impressed. 'You're being trained as an Agent!'

'He's right,' said Maga, 'this is huge! Why didn't you say anything? Mum and Dad'll love this! You've got to tell them ... I'll get some paper ...'

'All in good time Maga,' Grandma cut in. 'We'll write to your family this evening, don't you worry. You can tell them everything.'

Maga cheered up at this. Art supposed that was an advantage of Maga's situation –

he could actually contact his parents now – it wasn't *all* bad.

'What *you* have to work out, Art,' Grandma started, 'is how you're going to do this. We can't have Maga here bumping into his ... *Instructor* ... on the day. You're going to have to plan this carefully. And Maga – you're going to have to study hard. Very hard. This isn't going to be easy.'

Art smiled at Danny. 'I'm glad I bought my advisor along then. I'll need you, Danny. You up for it?'

Danny smiled back. 'Of course. Anything you need, I'll be here.' He looked at Grandma. '*Every step of the way.*'

Art narrowed his eyes. 'O…kay then.' He raised his mug for a toast. 'The ... the Golden Three! We should all meet here tomorrow at the same time. Agreed?'

Maga and Danny agreed, and Grandma looked slightly offended at the unwelcome addition to their number.

*

And as it turned out, Grandma was right – it wasn't easy. The rest of the school year was the busiest of Art's life so far. He had so many things to deal with at once, he barely coped.

For one, Grandma was still on at him to become more fluent in EllShapyan so he could start working on his Lithogrics, even though he thought he was doing remarkably well. He had even worked out the last three symbols by himself, which he had been immensely proud of. But she kept telling him that "learning the language is just the first part – Lithogrics is all about what you can *do* with the language if it's properly manipulated". He had forgotten all about his homework – the sheet of paper Grandma had turned transparent right before his eyes, that he was supposed to be returning to its normal state. Try as he might, he couldn't work out how she had done it, and even though he had enlisted Tina's help to learn the language, he couldn't ask her about this. He supposed Grandma had written some sort of magic word on the paper, but he had no idea where he was supposed to find out about magic words, and

Grandma wouldn't tell him. She was beginning to get a little impatient with him about it, and it was becoming slightly stressful.

On top of that, Evi had been hinting continually that she would like to help him with the Drop at the hospital that year, and it was becoming hard to ignore. He had tried to think of some excuses, but he always got lost in the beauty of her eyes before he could say them.

On top of *that*, his Mage training with the older Maga had become a lot more intense, and he had got through nearly a whole A4 pad of lined paper with all the notes he had had to take, on top of all his school work, which was suffering. And then, after every lesson with the older Maga, he had to sit down with the younger Maga and explain what he had been taught in the lesson, as it wasn't straight-forward enough to be just explained with a set of notes, and even then Art didn't fully understand it all himself. But Maga looked as if he was understanding – he was learning frighteningly quickly and was starting to do amazing things that Art couldn't comprehend, but at the same time he was becoming more and more suspicious of Art, who was running out of lies as to where his real Instructor was.

And then there were the meetings. He had one almost every day with Grandma, young Maga, and Danny, planning how they were going to do the Drop with *three* of them. Art thought that would make it easier, but as they started the planning, he realized it would actually be much harder if they were to obey the rules to the letter. For a start, Art had to figure out how to keep young Maga concealed from his older self, who would be observing the whole thing. He had to incorporate Danny into the plan, not really because he had to, but because he *wanted* to. He felt a certain kinship with him, as Danny had spent many decades among magicians, but had never been able to do any himself, just like Art.

The plans were constantly changing, because just as they thought they had got it right, Art would learn something else in the lessons with the older Maga that would make the plan a whole lot easier, so they had to incorporate it somehow, or worse, start again.

The only thing that had got easier was the situation with Peter. Tina was helping him with his essays and revision now, and his grades were slowly improving (Art's were actually getting worse, but he was so busy he hardly noticed). There had been a big argument the day Tina went home with Peter, and Peter's dad was now living in one of the downstairs rooms on his own. Apparently, Tina's *whole family* had turned up at Peter's house, and were so annoyed with Peter's dad, and gave so much support to Peter's mum, that she had found the courage to stand up to him and kicked him out of the house completely. Since then, Peter's relationship with his dad had improved, and his parent's relationship was beginning to mend, and his dad had been allowed to move back into the house, but not into the main bedroom. All this had been news to Art – he still didn't understand the relationship between Tina and Peter's families, but somehow they had all pulled together and sorted it out. Both Tina and Peter were much happier, and spent a lot of time together, though they still denied anything was going on.

They all found time to revise together periodically though as their exams approached, and Art found that he was slowly improving too, but still firmly the least clever of the lot. He convinced himself it was because his head was full of all the lessons the older Maga was teaching him, and all the planning the "Golden Three" were doing every day. So when their exams arrived, and went, and they all paraded at school for their results, Art wasn't the least bit surprised to find out that he had passed only four of the eight qualifications he had studied for. He was actually quite happy with this, but as his parents pointed out, he'd need a minimum of five for any kind of decent job, and especially if he wanted to go on to college. So he had reluctantly decided to stay on at the school's sixth form to retake some of his exams, much to Evi's delight, as she was also staying on to take the higher level of exams, as was Tina. Peter, who had scraped through most of his exams thanks to Tina, had decided to go to the posh culinary college around the corner to study as a chef. At first they were all sad he was going, especially Tina, but when he pointed out that they shared lunchtimes together and could meet every day at the school cafeteria, they were all much happier.

The unusually long summer holiday between school and sixth-form was magical for Art. Most of the daytimes were spent at one-another's houses talking and drinking coffee (except Peter's house, where the atmosphere was still a little frosty), and Art spent every evening, after his meetings with the Golden Three, in his dad's workshop making toys for the Drop, with Evi. She would sit and chat to him, and he would chip-in answers where he could, while she handed him bits of wood and tools while he worked. She seemed to love spending time with him in this way, and Art loved it too. She made suggestions about the types of toys to make, especially for the girls, an area Art was not that familiar with, and he was glad of her guidance. She catalogued every toy he made with a photo and the exact date and time it was finished.

By the time the summer holidays were finally over, they had a huge stack of toys, and a beautifully kept record book, charting every toy in the pile. She had been so happy to chronicle all of the toy-making that she seemed to have forgotten about helping Art with the Drop. He had told her that Danny was now helping out from afar as sort of a communications expert, which seemed the best way he could help, and that she could help him with that. She seemed happy to do it, especially as when she finally met Danny, she was intrigued by his mannerisms. He was the perfect gentleman, and made her feel totally at ease whenever she was with him. Tina just thought he was weird, but she kind of liked him too. After all, he was extremely hard to dislike, if you were on the right side of him.

While they were all sad when the holidays came to an end, Art soon settled into a routine of sixth form life, intense Mage training, insanely complicated meetings of the Golden Three, and pointless studying of Lithogrics, which had still yielded no results. That was, however, until he got a rather panicked telephone call from Tina.

Chapter Fourteen
DOROTHY'S TALE

Art was walking home from a particularly gruelling meeting of the Golden Three, where they had had a disastrous evening planning another part of the operation again due to some restoration work they had just found out was happening at the hospital on a vital corridor, when his phone vibrated in his pocket. He looked at the screen – it was Tina. He flipped it open.

'Hi Tina. What's up?'

'Get over here *now*!' she shouted down the phone.

'Whoa there – calm down. What's happened?'

'I'll tell you when you get here – just hurry!'

'Okay, okay,' Art said, 'I'll turn around. I was on my way home anyway, I'm not far from yours. Hold on.'

He flipped his phone shut, turned round, and walked a bit faster down the road to Tina's house.

When he got there, she was waiting with the front door open. 'Come on! Upstairs!' she whispered as loudly as she could. They darted up to her room, and Art saw straight away what she had been frantic about. Sitting on her desk was a rectangular slab of rock, like a stone tablet. The flimsy desk was buckling under its weight.

'Look!' she said, and pointed to it.

Art raised his eyebrows. 'Wow. Are you re-doing the Ten Commandments?'

'*Not* funny! How did it happen?' she snapped.

'How did what happen?' Art asked.

'ARTHUR! LOOK AT IT!'

Art moved closer to it, and could just make out some lines just visible on the surface, that looked like the type of lines you get on a pad of notepaper, and when he narrowed his eyes, he noticed what looked like some EllShapyan writing that appeared to be *engraved* onto it, between some of the lines.

'What is it?' he said.

She tutted angrily. '"*What is it*" he says! Really! What does it LOOK like?'

'Erm, well I'm not sure ...'

'It's my notepad, that's what it is!' she screamed as quietly as she could.

Art pointed to it gingerly. 'Erm, it's really not ...'

'WELL IT WAS!' she shouted. 'I was practicing that code you gave me – I was just copying out a random page of a book, and ... *that* happened.'

Art gasped. 'Really? What, it just ...'

'YES! IT JUST!'

He looked at it even more closely, hardly believing his eyes. The book she had copied from was lying open next to it – it was some old fairytale about a creature who could turn people to stone just by looking at them. He looked at the tablet again. 'That's amazing! How did you do it?' he said, looking impressed.

'I didn't *do* anything – I was just translating from that page and ... Art – *what* is going on? What *is* that language?'

The smile on his face vanished. 'Erm, well that's a bit more tricky to explain. There's not a lot I can tell you about it. I don't really know much myself to be honest ...'

'Well, I know where it came from!' Tina said angrily. 'Shall we just go and ask her, shall we? Your Grandma is in, isn't she?'

Art panicked. 'No, no – don't do that – Tina please ...'

She stood fuming at him with her arms crossed. 'This has got something to do with *that*, hasn't it?' She pointed to the Fragment on his wrist, still snugly secured with the leather twine, where it had been all year.

'What do you mean by that ...'

'Don't try and fool me – it's got the same kind of symbols on it!'

Art looked at it, and was genuinely surprised when he realized she was right. He hadn't noticed, in all the time he was wearing it, that the outside edge was engraved with EllShapyan words. But he didn't have time to look at them properly.

'That's it – we're going to see her. She all but threw me out last time - well not *this* time! Come on!' Tina commanded.

She heaved the stone slab off the table, which seemed to almost sigh with relief, then she grabbed his hand, and before Art knew what was happening he had been dragged downstairs, out onto the pavement, and up to his Grandma's house.

Tina knocked hard on the door, ignoring the doorbell, and waited. Before long, the door opened, and Grandma appeared, with an empty pan in her hand. 'Oh, hello dears ...' she said.

Tina barged past before Grandma had a chance to say anything else, dragging Art with her. Art gave Grandma an apologetic look as he was yanked through the door, and they paraded in the front room waiting for her.

'So erm, to what do I owe ...' Grandma started.

'That language you've been teaching Art - it did *this*.' Tina let the slab flop onto the sofa where it bounced clumsily, and a cloud of dust enveloped it. 'What is it?'

Grandma narrowed her eyes, looking at the slab and then at Tina.

'Did ... did *you* do this?' she said.

'Of course not,' Tina said irritably. 'I mean, well the language did it ... erm ... I don't know.' She put her hands on her hips as if she had explained herself perfectly well, and was waiting for an answer.

Grandma thought for a while, then she smiled broadly and looked at Art. 'I think *you* can tell her how this happened Art. Go on, don't be shy.'

Art looked confused. 'Don't look at me,' he said, holding his hands up.

'Come on now, Art,' Grandma said, 'Join the dots. You're virtually fluent in the language now – it's time you looked beyond what it is, and saw what it can *do*. Come on now, think.'

'Grandma – I have no idea ...'

'ART! COME ON!' she shouted. 'IF YOU'RE TO HAVE ANY CHANCE OF HELPING MAGA PROPERLY, *WORK THIS OUT!*'

Art stared at her, wide-eyed.

Grandma took a few deep breaths. 'Remember what I told you,' she continued, a little more subdued. 'If you apply the symbols to our letters of the alphabet, it will translate *itself*. Come on now! Think!'

Art stood there, looking from Grandma to Tina and back again, totally at a loss. To his relief, Tina was looking just as bewildered, but she still had an unmistakable spark of anger in her eyes. He remembered the look from the day she confronted Peter's dad about the bruises on his face.

'This is not helping,' Tina said quietly, but with venom, staring at Grandma.

'COME ON NOW ART, THINK!' Grandma shouted again, more aggressively, ignoring Tina completely.

Tina stepped in between them. 'DON'T SPEAK TO HIM LIKE THAT!' she shouted back.

Grandma's face flashed with anger. 'OUT OF THE WAY, GIRL! THIS IS MORE IMPORTANT THAN YOU KNOW!'

'I WILL NOT!' Tina spat, 'AND DON'T CALL ME "GIRL"!'

Grandma flew towards Tina, and before Art knew what was happening, he had grabbed Tina and dragged her round behind him in a protective embrace.

'TINA, NO! SHE'S DANGEROUS!' he shouted.

Grandma froze, a look of pure shock on her face. She stood there for what seemed like an age, panting and looking around herself in confusion. Art had his eyes closed, and was waiting for something to happen, anything. But nothing did. He had even surprised himself at what he had cried out as she lunged at Tina. Eventually he opened his eyes, feeling slightly foolish.

Grandma stood up straight, and Art noticed a look of sadness in her eyes. She looked at him. 'So Danny told you,' she said. She stared into the middle distance, and spoke quietly, seemingly to no one in particular. 'It's not true. I wish someone would believe me … I … oh my goodness …'

She sat down next to the stone slab, looking totally deflated.

'Art what did you think I was going to *do*?' she pleaded, looking into her hands.

Art let go of Tina, who was looking as shocked as Grandma had a moment ago. She edged around the room and stood opposite Grandma, never taking her eyes off her.

Art walked over and sat down on the comfy chair next to Grandma. 'I … I don't know. The things Danny showed me … I didn't *think* I believed any of it, but … I'm sorry,' he said.

'What did he tell you?' she said quietly, tears forming in her eyes.

Art cleared his throat, thinking carefully before he spoke.

'He showed me the file. The ... Ainsworth file.'

Grandma winced at the mention of the name.

'He ... told me about Avarice. And that you ...' he paused, before lowering his voice and saying slowly, 'you ... you didn't, did you? Look at me and tell me you didn't, Grandma.'

She said nothing.

'Grandma?' Art said again.

She sighed heavily. 'Who do you mean?' she said. 'Ellie or ... or Avarice?'

Art's eyes widened. 'Em ... Ellie ...'

'NO – I DID NOT KILL ELLIE! I WOULDN'T!' Grandma shouted.

'Avarice then,' Art said.

Grandma fell silent again.

'Grandma? Tell me you didn't. Grandma!'

She sighed again, and Art noticed the faintest nod of her head.

He gasped, and he heard Tina do the same.

'What are you two talking about, Art? Who's Avarice? And Ellie?' said Tina, looking slightly panicked, and keeping her eyes on Grandma.

Art sat down in the comfy chair, but Tina remained rooted to her spot across the room.

'Ellie was my great-grandmother. Avarice was her brother-in-law,' Art explained.

'But ... *she's* your great grandmother ...' Tina said, pointing to Grandma.

Art sighed. 'Apparently not.'

Grandma looked up at him. 'I am every bit as much your great-grandma as Ellie is, so I am! Don't you *ever* think otherwise!'

Art was starting to get a little agitated. 'But you ... I can't believe this ... you *killed* my great uncle!'

'THERE WAS NO OTHER WAY!' she pleaded. 'He was rotten to the core, so he was. He ... Arthur you don't need to know this. Please just trust me.'

'You've just admitted to murder and you want him to TRUST you?' Tina said, looking annoyed and still very anxious.

Grandma stood up again. 'Will you please LEAVE!' She spat at Tina.

'GRANDMA!' Art shouted, and she jumped in surprise. 'Tina is my best friend. We know everything about each other, and that's never been truer than now!' he pointed to the slab.

Grandma looked shocked. 'Art – *why* did you tell her about that ...' she stammered.

'She helped me with the translation. She knows as much as I do. In fact if I know her as well as I think I do, she knows more. So she stays, you understand?'

Grandma looked at Tina, but Art couldn't tell what she was thinking from her expression. Then she looked at the stone slab and closed her eyes briefly before she slumped back down on the sofa.

'Why did you kill Art's uncle?' Tina said strongly, though clearly still very wary.

Grandma sighed and sank further into her chair. She rubbed her eyes, then she spoke with a tiny, hopeless voice. 'Okay. I'll explain as much as I can ...'

'You'll explain *everything*, Grandma.'

'Arthur, please ...' She nodded towards Tina.

'Everything, Grandma.' He picked up the stone slab and held it up to her. 'I think it's a bit late to pretend there's a rational explanation to *this*.'

Grandma looked at Tina and sighed heavily again.

'Okay, okay. Just ... give me a minute.'

Tina gingerly walked over to the other comfy chair and sat down, keeping her eyes on Grandma, who was composing herself.

'I don't know where to begin,' she said.

'We can wait,' Art replied, and he settled himself into his chair, more to make a point than anything else. Eventually, Grandma resigned herself to the fact that she was going to have to tell Art what had happened.

'The Prophecy had been read and reread, decoded by so many people, but no one could truly understand every detail,' Grandma began, her eyes unfocused.

'What's the Prophecy?' Tina asked.

'Tina – I'll fill you in on anything you don't understand afterwards,' Art said, 'and I think you'd better be holding that slab when I do – it's going to be pretty hard to believe.'

Grandma carried on. 'There was one particular section that warned us of someone who *had* to be protected at all costs, though there was no mention as to why. We argued and argued about what we should do, or if we should do anything at all, as we didn't even know who the Prophecy was referring to. In the end, all we could agree on was that the Prophecy was pointing very strongly to one particular family line. The … *Ainsworth* family line.

'I was sent as a Guardian to watch over the family and see that nothing happened to it, and for a long time nothing did – I could check up on them from afar – the kind of 'afar' Art knows about. But then Albert Ainsworth was sent to war, and Ellie suddenly became very vulnerable.'

Art interrupted. 'In what way vulnerable?' he asked.

'Well, for a start, rumours were starting to spread about the Ainsworth's considerable fortune.'

'What?' Art said. 'The Ainsworths were rich?'

'Absolutely they were. Albert went to war as a Private – but he'd have been an officer if they'd have known about his money. But they kept it quiet - no one quite knows why to this day. Ellie didn't take Albert's leaving very well either. She became reclusive and very private, and everyone thought that little Jonathan was being neglected. So I was sent into the field to intervene and keep things straight, but it didn't go according to plan.'

'In what way?' Tina asked. Grandma looked up as if she had forgotten Tina was there.

'Ellie was ill. Very ill, and no one could work out why. They put it down to the stress of it all, but I knew something wasn't right.'

'Was Jonathan okay?' Art asked.

'Oh yes – Ellie put *everything* into looking after him, even though her own health was failing. So I moved into a house a few streets away and made it my business to get to know her.'

'The papers said you moved next door to her,' Art said.

'I know they did,' she answered. 'The reporters said a lot of things – they made up whatever they thought would sell papers. But the truth was far more grim.

'I knocked on her door, and when she answered she was so ill she couldn't be sure if she knew me or not. I took advantage of that and introduced myself as her auntie on Albert's side. I'll never forget the look of relief on her face to have a relative around. And then ...' Grandma shuddered as she recalled the next part.

'The knock on the door, and the little yellow telegram. Albert had been badly injured, and they couldn't save him when they eventually got him to a field hospital. Ellie was heartbroken. On top of her illness, I thought it would kill her.'

Tina and Art stared. 'Is *that* how she died?' Art asked reticently. 'Not ...'

'That's *not* what killed her no,' Grandma said quickly, before Art could say any more. 'She was stronger than that. I should have given her more credit.'

'So what happened?' Tina asked. 'Did she cope?'

'She coped. She had to for Jonathan's sake. I helped her with little things at first, the shopping and some of the cleaning, but mostly just someone to lean on. I was becoming quite fond of the both of them – little Jonathan was an angel. And then I started bringing meals round for them, and that's when I met ... Avarice. The moment Ellie started eating the food I had cooked for her, she started to feel better, and that's when I found out that Albert's brother had been 'helping' out as well. He was furious when he found out about me.'

Art and Tina looked aghast. 'He was ... poisoning them?' Tina said.

'With arsenic-trioxide, yes. But not both of them – only Ellie. You see he had found out about his brother's money. And he had also found out that the only way to get his hands on it was if something happened to Ellie. If something happened to her *and* her son, the money would be dissolved, but if he became Jonathan's appointed guardian, he could control the fortune in his favour.'

Art looked confused. 'But ... Ellie was ill before she got the telegram about Albert. Was Avarice poisoning them even before Albert died?'

'It was a grim war, Art. Especially for the infantry, as Albert was. It was almost a given that he wasn't coming back – that's why it broke her heart so when he left, so yes – Avarice started to interfere almost immediately. But he was sneaky – he went to great lengths to make sure no one knew he was involved at all. And that's when I realized her condition was no illness. Avarice was an animal. Ruthless and cruel. Every time I went to see them after that, he was there, and I knew Ellie was in danger. He became aggressive, and I wasn't allowed in. So I had to resort to 'other' methods.'

'What do you mean by that?' Tina said, darkly.

'Recon magic,' Art breathed.

'What are you talking about Art?' Tina said.

'I'll explain it all to you, I promise. But I want to find out what happened first,' Art said. 'Go on, Grandma.'

'I did my fair share of espionage Art, don't get me wrong, but I had to go beyond Recon magic - Ellie was in terrible danger. It was clear what I had to do - I had to get them out of there – I had to get them *away* from Avarice.'

'What did you do?' Art asked.

'It was hard – Avarice was aggressive and very strong. Even using Recon Chocolate I couldn't get close - it was like he was guarding her, waiting for her to die. I could stand in the room and watch and he was none the wiser that I was there, but he *wouldn't* leave her alone, even for a second. In the end I had to resort to giving him some of his own medicine – quite literally.

'I bought three tickets to the coast and packed a few things, and went round to Ellie's house. Avarice let me in – he had no idea he had done so. I rooted around in his things and found some of the powder he was using to poison her, and I spiked his drink with a near fatal dose. And that's when the plan went wrong.

'I'd forgotten the effect of poison on humans – it lessens the effect of Recon magic – and before I could realise my mistake, he *saw* me.'

Art gasped. 'But ... Ellie had been poisoned well before that – couldn't she see you when you started spying?'

'She was too far gone to notice anything – she could hardly stand most of the time.'

'What happened when Avarice saw you?' Tina asked.

'He flew at me – there was rage in his eyes and the poison hadn't affected his strength yet. He knocked me to the floor, but I was prepared. I was ... *armed*.' She looked knowingly at Art. 'That was how she got damaged – my poor Sta'an. But she put Avarice to the floor several times, and when he looked like he wasn't getting up again I rushed upstairs for Jonathan. To my surprise Jonathan *saw* me coming, and he rushed downstairs with me. But when we got there, Avarice had got to her first – I couldn't get close.

'He saw me and lashed out with the coal shovel and caught me on the side of the head, but I managed to pull Jonathan out of the door, screaming and flailing for his mother. I got him to safety, but something was wrong. I don't know how, but Jonathan had been poisoned too. He was confused and dazed, and the look in his eyes. I'm sure he thought *I* had …' Grandma put her head in her hands.

'Why had Jonathan been poisoned as well?' Art asked.

'I don't know *what* Avarice was doing. I'm not sure he even cared at that point,' she said.

'Did you go back for Ellie?' Tina said.

'I called for backup, but they kept insisting that what I had done had protected the family line enough – nobody came to help. I couldn't go back myself – I had to get Jonathan to a hospital – he'd been poisoned far more than I thought; I thought I was going to lose him. And his eyes … the way he *looked* at me …'

'So what did you do?' Art asked.

'I got Jonathan to a hospital, but I was constantly on edge in case Avarice came for us. I had to keep moving him. In the end we made it to the coast, but it took a while for Jonathan to recover – he was so young, he was lucky he survived.

'Jonathan pleaded with me to go back for his mother, and eventually we did. He was still very weak and the fever was still strong in him. But when we got to the house, Ellie was lying on the kitchen floor with terrible head injuries. I tried to revive her, but she died right there in my arms. Jonathan saw me standing over his mother, my hands red with blood, and he screamed for what seemed like hours.

'Eventually the neighbours called the police, but I had to protect Jonathan. I couldn't think of anything better than to let the police take him for the time being, but I didn't expect to be arrested myself – for murder and kidnapping!

'The next thing I knew, I was in a police cell and Avarice turned up at the *same station*, staking his claim on the boy. I had to act.

'Thankfully, backup finally arrived. They saw to it that I was released, and we started planning how we would fight the court case to keep Jonathan out of Avarice's clutches.'

'How did you do that?' Art asked. 'Wasn't Avarice *entitled* to take Jonathan – he was his uncle after all.'

'That's right,' Grandma sighed. 'and that's when things got complicated. For a start,

Jonathan was only three, and he hadn't understood what he had seen. He was frightened of me, and he'd cry whenever I came near him. The police told me Jonathan had said he'd seen *me* kill his mother – I didn't know what to do. But we *had* to protect him.'

'Why was that? Because the family line was at risk?' Art said.

'No! Because he was a dear little boy in danger of being murdered by a greedy uncle!' she exclaimed. 'The police were starting to trust Avarice, and so was Jonathan – I had to get the two apart. That's all I could think of then.'

Art looked slightly ashamed. 'Sorry,' he muttered.

'We couldn't let Jonathan into Avarice's hands for a second, so we had to … use 'other' types of magic. There's only so far Recon magic can take you – when you need to take action, you have to pull out all the stops.'

'What did you do?' Art asked.

'I'm not proud of it, Arthur. We had to sway the jury, and we used a lot of deception, a lot of dangerous methods. We weren't sure how much damage it would do to the humans involved but we *had* to protect Jonathan.

'In the end, after months of hard work, it looked as if we were winning the court case. And Avarice knew it. The night before the verdict should have been reached, he tracked me down. He was wild with anger, and he was carrying a shotgun. He knocked down the door and damn near killed the both of us, but we got away. Jonathan was slowly starting to trust me by then, and we raced down the road to the Parson's house. The Parson was away and the house was empty, and somehow Avarice knew where we had gone, and he followed us inside. He'd used up all the cartridges for his shotgun, so he picked up the poker from the fireplace and found us in the cellar. I Felled him several times, but he kept coming, and somehow the poker found its way into my hands and …' Grandma closed her eyes tightly.

'Grandma?' Art said. She sat there looking drained and exhausted.

'Grandma?' he said again, tentatively.

'I don't know how it happened,' she said quietly. 'I just … I …'

They all sat in silence, Art only then noticing the soft hiss of the embers in the fireplace.

'Jonathan saw the whole thing, and he started screaming again,' Grandma continued in a whisper. 'Seeing that made him think I *had* killed his mother after all, just as we were getting somewhere. If I'd only have ...'

Art looked at Tina, who was white as a sheet, then back at Grandma, who had slumped back into the sofa staring into space.

'It's okay, Grandma. I'll er ... make us a drink.' Art rose from the chair, and Tina rose with him. They walked slowly out into the kitchen, still trying to fully take in what they had heard. Art boiled the kettle, which looked as if it hadn't been used for years in favour of a boiling pan of water, and made a Stroth-Brew from the two little bottles of powder he found in the cupboard.

'What's that?' asked Tina.

'It's er ... Grandma's herbal tea,' Art said.

'It smells good,' she said blankly, as Art added honey and a little milk. 'Can I have one too?'

Art supposed it didn't matter if she did. So he made two more mugs for him and Tina, and they sat down again in the sitting room.

Art handed Grandma hers, and she took it without saying anything. She sipped at it, and Tina sipped hers too, and looked surprised at how good it was.

Art spoke first. 'Grandma – there's just one thing that I don't understand.'

'Go on, dear,' she said quietly.

'Well, you're a Warrior, and an Agent. But ... where did you *come* from? Here or ... or Amarly?'

Grandma answered, her face drained of all emotion. 'When I gave you the picture, I told you that was my home. So what do you think?' she said.

Art thought for a moment. 'But if that's true, why are you so ... well, *human* sized?'

She paused momentarily. 'It's my punishment, so it is.'

'What? Punishment? What do you mean?' Tina said.

'Oh not *being* a human dear. No no, it's just that ... I ... I *killed* someone. Now whether for good or for bad, that affects the Timeline – ending a life before it should – there are certain consequences that just *happen* – no one is quite sure why. You know how Time doesn't seem to affect us in this world or you in that world? Well *I'm* the exception now, because of what I did. I'm *stuck* here – I'm not able to go back. I'm to stay here and grow and age like a human. And ... die like a human – just as quickly. Well, maybe a smidge more slowly.'

Art sat thinking about everything he had heard. Tina looked just as confused as when they first arrived, but she was enjoying her Stroth-Brew too much to say anything. In any case, Art had promised he would tell her everything as soon as he could, so she was content to wait.

Art stood up and went to sit next to Grandma on the sofa – he had to heave the huge slab of rock out of the way first.

'I'm ... sorry I thought that ... well, you know. I'm really sorry, Grandma.' he said.

She looked at him with sorrow in her eyes. 'That's okay dear. I'm sorry you had to find out anything at all of that nature.'

'Why is it so secret, anyway?' he asked.

'It's an altered past. The family line was obviously meant to disappear, and we intervened. It's never good to know more than you should about an altered Timeline – all sorts of things can happen. And thanks to Danny, *they just might.*'

Chapter Fifteen
THE PLAN

The next day was a Saturday. After Grandma's confession of the evening before, Tina had been itching for Art to explain everything to her. But after a long whispered discussion, they had decided to leave Grandma's house as soon as they could, to let her be by herself, and Art was less than keen to discuss it anywhere else in case they were overheard. Evi was meeting Art at midday at his workshop, as she now called it, to sit with him and help him make more toys for the hospital Drop, so Art had agreed to meet back at Grandma's house at eight o'clock the next day for breakfast and to explain it all to Tina.

Grandma had cheered up considerably after Art and Tina had both apologized for thinking she could do such a thing in cold blood, and she had actually warmed to Tina quite a lot, once she had accepted that Tina was now a part of it all too. It was her idea that they both come back the next morning for breakfast to talk about it, and Tina was actually looking forward to it, despite the fact that she *still* hadn't found out how her notepad had been transformed into a lump of rock.

Art's alarm clock buzzed next to his ear at seven o'clock sharp, and he ran to the bathroom to shower, and hot-footed it over to Grandma's house as quickly as he could, still munching on a slice of toast. He trudged up the pathway to Grandma's house, and before he got there the door opened and Tina poked her head out. 'Where have you been?' she said smiling.

'You're here early,' he said.

'We're having herbal tea,' she beamed, and Art caught a whiff of Stroth-Brew on the air.

'Ooo,' he said, 'two drops of honey in mine please,' happy that she and Grandma seemed to be getting on well.

'Already done. Come on – we've got so much to talk about!'

Tina ushered him in, and the three of them sat round the kitchen table with Stroth-Brew, Dough-Drops and honey.

'Morning Grandma,' Art said reticently. 'I'm sorry about yesterday, I really am.'

'Oh, it's forgotten, dear. Dough-Drops?'

'Two please.'

'So,' Tina said, placing her hands on the table. 'Let's talk about … well everything I didn't understand yesterday.'

'Okay,' Art chuckled. 'What didn't you get first?'

'We'll start with … *everything*,' she said.

Art smiled at Grandma, and she smiled back at him. 'I'll get the picture dear. By the way – you still haven't taken that home yet,' she said, rising from her seat.

'What picture?' Tina said.

'Grandma's right – it all starts with that. Well, almost.'

Tina sat and listened intently as Art recalled everything that had happened to him since Grandma had given him the painting, which Tina was now marvelling over. He explained about the Fragment, falling asleep in his room, his extraordinary trip to The L-Shaped Village; his first disastrous battle with Dabellar; finding the infamous YerDichh who turned out to be the lost little boy called Danny, whom Art had been sent to retrieve, and that Danny was now in *this* world. Tina gasped when she heard this, but then admitted that it explained a few things about him.

Art told her of his own discovery of exactly where he had been all this time, and how he had arrived back in this world just a moment after Tina had seen him fall asleep on his bed. Tina's belief in the story started to falter slightly when he mentioned Santa Claus, but Grandma stepped in and explained it in such a way that it made perfect sense to her, as she had to Art. And she explained how proud of Art she was when she found out that he was in training to be an Agent, and that she had once been an Agent too (one of the best in fact, Art added with similar pride).

The conversation moved onto Grandma's house guest Maga, although they left out the bit about him being trained as a Mage by his older self, thinking it might be one step too far for her belief in the story. They talked animatedly about the meetings of the Golden Three, who were trying to figure out how to carry out Maga's end-of-year assignment without his instructor seeing him, which they told Tina was one of the conditions of the test. They briefly touched on the information Danny had so 'helpfully' provided, before finally leaning back in their chairs and sighing with contentment. Art always felt good after he had offloaded, and Grandma looked more relaxed too.

Tina looked remarkably calm despite everything she had heard. Grandma placed another batch of Stroth-Brew and Dough-Drops in front of them, and Tina ate two more before she spoke again.

'So what's Maga's assignment?' she said.

'That's it? *That's* your first question?' Art said incredulously.

'Hey – I'm a geek – I *deal* in assignments,' she said.

'You don't have *anything* to say about ... well everything else we just explained to you?' Art said.

'Well, to be honest,' she said tentatively, 'I'm still having a slight problem with one thing.'

'What's that?' he answered.

'Well the err, the *Santa* thing,' she said.

'What's the problem dear?' Grandma said.

'For a start, I'm Jewish. I mean, isn't it a Christian thing?' Tina said, with as much delicacy as she could muster.

'My dear. Have you ever read any Dickens?' Grandma said.

'Of course. Remember the geek thing I just said?'

'Dickens is *not* for geeks, dear – don't put yourself down.'

'What's your point?' Tina said.

'Dickens once wrote "There are some upon this earth of ours who lay claim to know us, and who do their deeds of passion, pride, ill-will, hatred, envy, bigotry, and selfishness in our name, who are as strange to us and all our kith and kin, as if they had never lived. Remember that, and charge their doings on themselves, not us."'

'A Christmas Carol?' Tina said.

Grandma nodded. 'Remember the very last sentence, and you'll understand.'

'*Charge their doings on themselves, not us,*' Tina recited.

'Exactly. Everyone understands it as a Christian thing, but only because we've *made* it that way. It's not exclusive.'

Tina slowly grinned as she understood.

'And anyway,' Art scoffed, 'don't go thinking about a guy in a red suit, because *that* would just be …' He stopped mid-sentence, and his eyes widened.

'What's the matter, Art?' Tina said.

Grandma looked at him pensively. 'Hang on Tina dear – let him think,' she said.

'I've got it!' Art exclaimed.

'Got what, dear?' Grandma said.

'I've worked out how we can do it!'

'Do what?' Tina said.

'Maga's assignment! I've worked out how we can do it without little Maga being spotted at all! Quick – we need to call a meeting of the Golden Three right now! The Golden Three plus Tina!'

Art whipped out his phone and sent a text to Danny, then he sprinted into the hallway and shouted upstairs for Maga.

'Grandma – some more herbal tea … oh, it doesn't matter if you know now Tina – some more Stroth-Brews please! Tina – find yourself another notepad and a pen – I'll need your help on this! Where's Maga got to? I hope Danny won't be long!'

Grandma looked on proudly as Art took proper charge of the meeting for the first time. She opened a drawer and found a pad of paper for Tina, then she rushed off to put some more water on to boil.

*

Doctor Dawn Levvy finished her rounds quite conveniently next to the café, and she joined the queue of people waiting.

'Evening, Dawn,' said the lady behind the counter.

'Evening, Ethell. Just a coffee please. Oh, and a mince pie if there's one going.'

'Just in they are,' Ethell said. 'Gets earlier every year it does. Five weeks yet 'till Christmas 'n' all. Milk in yer coffee?'

'Please.'

'There yer go love. Two sixty.'

'Thanks, Ethell.'

She headed back to her office clutching her coffee, and her mince pie wrapped in a serviette, but when she got there, she stopped. Her door was ajar. She was sure she had locked it. She knocked gingerly. 'Hello? Anyone there?' she called. No answer. She pushed open the door, and scanned the office. It was deserted, and nothing looked missing. But straight away her eyes were led to her desk, where a red envelope was resting against her pot of pens. She smiled in recognition.

He's early this year, she thought. She walked over and picked it up. It was addressed to her, but the writing was different from how she remembered it; it was less tidy, and in blue ballpoint, not elegant fountain-pen ink. She opened it. It was a very short message; *Your office, half-past four*.

She looked at her wall clock – it was twenty eight minutes past. She shrugged her shoulders, and sat down at her desk. She ate her mince pie and drank most of her coffee, and watched as the clock turned half-past four exactly. She waited for a knock at the door, but instead she heard a voice from the other side of the room.

'Hello again, Doctor Levvy,' said Art, sitting at one of the comfy chairs around the small coffee table.

She jumped out of her skin, almost spilling the rest of her coffee.

'Art! How did you ...' She pointed to the door and then at him, trying to work it out.

'Oh, it's just something someone taught me. Like it? It'll make my job a bit easier this year I can tell you.'

Art heard a faint whisper next to his ear. *'Nicely done,'* it said.

He whispered back, 'I thought you'd be watching.'

'What was that?' Dawn asked.

'Nothing. You got my letter then?' Art said quickly, pointing to the envelope on her desk.

'Oh. Oh, yes. Same envelope as last year and everything,' she answered.

'I told you then – I didn't send you a letter last year.'

Dawn looked again at the writing on the envelope. 'Well, somebody did.' She shrugged it off. 'Anyway – you're early this year – and you're here in person too. To what do I owe the pleasure?' she smiled.

'I need your help.' He said.

'More than usual?' she asked.

'Yes and no.'

'Hmm. Go on.'

'Is there a Christmas party this year?' Art asked.

'I think so.' She flicked through her desktop diary. 'Yes – yes there is - one of the new nurses is organizing it. Why?' she said.

'I kind of need you to become involved in it. Well, one aspect at least.'

'As well as the usual help with the delivery?'

'No, not this year,' Art said. 'It's all taken care of. It's all planned and ready. But thanks for the offer.'

'O...kay,' she said hesitantly. 'I take it you're aware of all the building work that's affecting the main corridor?' she said.

'Oh yes.'

'And what do you propose to do about it?'

'Not use the main corridor,' he said simply.

She narrowed her eyes. 'And how do you propose to do that?'

He smiled. 'Well, you know how a few minutes ago I wasn't here, and then I was?'

'Yes,' she said suspiciously.

'Something involving that. Like I said – it's sorted.'

Art heard the faint voice in his ear again. *'Careful now Elfee. You're revealing too much.'* It said.

'Shh!' Art whispered back irritably.

'Hmm,' Dawn said, eyeing Art up and down. 'And you're sure about this?'

Art held his hands up. 'Trust me – all I need this year is your help with the party.'

She relaxed a little. 'And what exactly do you need me to do?'

'Oh you don't need to *do* anything – just change an aspect of the organization that's all. I need the party to be a little more … shall we say … 'festively themed' this year.'

'Oh?' she said.

'I can't say any more right now – these walls have ears you know.' He nudged his elbow into what he hoped would be the older Maga's ribs as inconspicuously as possible. He reached into his pocket and pulled out another envelope, and handed it to her. 'It's all in here.'

'*What are you up to, Elfee?*' the voice whispered again.

Dawn took the envelope from him, and placed it on her desk.

'For my eyes only?' she said with a smile.

'Strictly,' Art replied curtly. 'I have to go now,' he said.

'Won't you stay for a chat? We haven't done that in a while,' she said.

'I'm sorry, Doctor Levvy – I've got so much to do. I promise I'll pop in after the New Year.'

He stood up and hugged her briefly before exiting through the door.

Dawn smiled after him. 'He's so grown up now,' she mused.

Just before he reached the doors at the main entrance, Art heard the voice again, right in his ear. '*You know I'll read that letter when she's gone, don't you?*' it said.

Art smiled broadly. 'Good luck with that, Maga,' he said, and walked out into the cold.

'*What do you mean good luck? Art? Come back here!*'

Dialogue Six

'Faculty here. Where can I direct you?'

'Yadra Salveary please.'

'Connecting ... connecting ... please hold ...'

'Is there something wrong?'

'Please hold, sir. Connecting ...'

'Are you having problems?'

'Yes sir. The number you are calling from is disallowed a connection to Salveary.'

'Oh. I see. Well that's quite convenient actually. Thank you. Goodbye.'

'Line's dead Jimma.'

'Did you get it, Pud?'

'I sure did. The tracer program was waiting for me like a little lap dog.'

'And they have no idea it was ever in their system?'

'Not a clue. Want a look?'

'Absolutely - this mystery's been going on far too long. We still haven't had a response from the Boss yet regarding what we should do about the Paradox.'

'We got the clearance through for the instructor's transfer though, Jimma.'

'Yes, but we didn't get an explanation, which means we still don't know any more about it than we did in the first place. Anything we can glean from the Faculty about the illegal Trans-world phone signal AND the illegal Time-stop is a plus. Let's have a look.'

'Okay. Bringing it up. Opening the program ... oops careful now ... stop that you little ... hold still ... good. Now open. OPEN!'

'Having problems, Pud?'

'Yes. It's a feisty little algorithm this – it keeps trying to latch on to my surveillance programs. Your uncle has a lot to answer for.'

'Can you manage it?'

'Yes, but I'll have to disable it the moment it yields. Shame - I was hoping to use it again. Okay - the package should be out any second ... and ... deleted. Bye little pal.'

'I'm touched. Really. Can we get back to the problem at hand?'

'Sorry, Jimma. Okay, reading ... scrolling ... ah! Here it is - the owner of the phone is ... hmm. That's odd.'

'Pud - I've got this on my screen, but I'm not sure I understand it. It says the illegal phone doesn't have an owner as such, but the registered user is ... Calsow. Maga Calsow.'

'I know. It's odd though ...'

'What is, Pud? Well, apart from the fact that someone who clearly shouldn't even be in the field has a piece of highly illegal tech.'

'That's just it though - the gene ID of Calsow is all wrong. It's like little Maga Calsow is ... well older than he should be. Quite a lot older, in fact – nearly a century.'

'How do you mean?'

'Well take a look - his gene ID has twelve figures. Little Maga Calsow is just a youngster - his ID shouldn't have more than seven ... unless ... OH! OH MY! I'VE GOT IT!'

'Got what?'

'Can't you see Jimma? The illegal Trans-world signal showed up at a school, right?'

'Right ...'

'The school Art Elfee goes to at the moment, right?'

'Right ...'

'And we know little Maga is with him, right?'

'Ri ... oh – yes I'd forgotten about that.'

'Well? The Paradox! Think!'

'I still don't see, Pud.'

'The phone belongs to Maga Calsow!'

'Yes you told me that already, but how did he get his hands on that kind of technology? It doesn't even exist yet.'

'Not THAT Maga Calsow - the other one! The Paradox, remember? His older self!'

'Oh my word. So not only is little Maga being taught by his older self, but his older self has brought some tech back with him that hasn't been invented yet.'

'Exactly. And if he's using tech like that, then ...'

'Oh.'

'That's right - Jimma. You owe Yadra an apology. It can't have been the Faculty who ordered the illegal Time-Stop. Well, not a version of the Faculty in this Time anyway. It must have come from further in the future, just like Maga's older self – should have guessed really - and we have no jurisdiction in that area.'

'Swarvikkz! Advice Pud?'

'Well I suggest flowers. Possibly some chocolates ...'

'Not that! What does it mean for the Paradox? We're still none the wiser as to who set it up and what damage it might do.'

'Oh that. Well there's nothing for it. We'll need to place a call to the Boss, Jimma.'

'But won't the Faculty be looking for it?'

'Yes, but now we know it's not them, they can listen all they like. They might even be able to help. Shall I use my access codes again?'

'Yes, they'll do.'

'Okay - patching. Please hold ...'

'No mickey-taking, please Pud.'

'Please hold ...'

'PUD!'

'Boss here. Is that Pud and Jimma?'

'Why yes it is. Hello Sir - I trust you are well?'

'Hey Boss.'

'Hello you two. I'm glad you called - I have a lot to discuss with you. I hadn't forgotten about your ... ahem ... secret communication asking about the Paradox.'

'That's right, Sir - I'm quite keen to find out what's going on with that.'

'Of course you are, Jimma - and you're right to. But I'm surprised you haven't *worked it out for yourselves yet.'*

'Worked out what, Sir?'

'The Paradox, Jimma. If I know you two like I think I do, you'll have done a bit of digging. What have you worked out so far?'

'Well, we've worked out three main areas of illegal activity, one of which is potentially existence-threatening: the Paradox, the illegal Time-stop and the illegal Trans-world phone signal.'

'Go on, Jimma.'

'Erm, well that's as far as we've got, Sir.'

'Really, you two. You know what might cause the Paradox, but have you worked out the source of the Time-stop and the phone signal yet?'

'Well, actually yes, Sir. We're ninety-nine percent sure they originated from the future.'

'Correct. And we all know that laws change over time, so what may be illegal now may not be when they were sent back, so I think you can safely put those to rest. Now – what about the Paradox? Pud – explain to me how you see it, as if I know nothing about it.'

'Okay, Sir. Well, we know there is a Paradox, the alarms went off and we have it on record. And when the communication came through from the Faculty, Jimma spotted the actual event. It concerns The L-Shaped Village's new Mage, little Maga Calsow. More importantly, it named his Instructor.'

'The Founder, Pud.'

'That's right – I keep forgetting that bit. Anyway, his Instructor was named as Maga Calsow, Sir. It didn't make sense at first, and when we worked it out it made even less sense, but it explained why the alarm went off. The Faculty created a blatant Paradox – being taught by an older version of yourself is simply not possible, Sir – it would mean the information came from nowhere, which would cause existence to fold in on itself.'

'Well put, Pud. Jimma – your uncle programmed the Paradox alarm, right?'

'Er, yes Sir.'

'Can you tell me under what circumstances it is programmed to go off?'

'If the discovery, implication, or possibility of a Paradox is detected within the Timeline.'

'Exactly. In this case, I think it went off purely because of an implication of a Paradox. If the implication is strong enough, it'll go off even if there's no chance it will actually happen. And if you scan the pupil records for recent Mage training, you'll see that it hasn't happened.'

'You mean it's happened already?'

'Or rather hasn't happened already Jimma. Pud – bring up the records – you'll see what I mean.'

'Okay, Sir. Bringing it up; Public Faculty records ... recent training ... exam times ... ah, here it is - Instructor Records. "Student: Calsow, Maga. Instructor ..." oh my! Oh my word Jimma look at this!'

'What does it say, Pud?'

'You're not going to believe it ...'

'I don't even know yet, Pud – what is it?'

'I can't believe it myself ...'

'PUD!'

'It says "Elfee". Arthur Elfee.'

'..............'

'Come on, you two – is that so hard to understand?'

'Erm, well, yes, Sir. I mean why did the communication say it was his older self for a start? And how can Art Elfee be any kind of Instructor – he's a human for a start, and barely out of Agent training at that.'

'All good points, Pud. And the answer to the latter is both complicated and incredibly simple. You see Art is a very special teenager. The effects of Time seem to dwell around him, and guide him for some reason. He can almost detect when something has to be done to protect a Timeline, if he has enough information about it. Now there's a part about all this that even I don't understand – someone made sure he did have enough information, and once he had, he did something remarkable: he made sure the two versions of the same person never met, and he convinced the future Maga that he, himself, was the Mage in training. He attended all the lessons himself, and passed the information on, but he did so in his own special way – he put his own angles and viewpoints on everything as he passed it on to the real student Mage, so much so that the Timeline recognized Art as Maga's Instructor, completely invalidating the Paradox. The Paradox was set up alright, but Art prevented it.

'The only question left is why Maga was put forward as his own Instructor. The Faculty deny all knowledge. They say they have an infiltrator, as yet unidentified. Gentlemen - someone is trying to destroy Time around Art, and they seem happy to threaten all of existence to do it. This is something we need to get to the bottom of, and quickly. You'll be working with Yadra closely on this from now on - cooperation is essential.'

'Oh. Erm, of course, Sir.'

'Is there a problem, Jimma?'

'Sir – Jimma and Yadra have ... history.'

'PUD! I'll thank you to hold your tongue! I'm so sorry, Sir. It won't be a problem. We'll get on it right away.'

'Now, Pud. About your promotion.'

'Yes, Sir?'

'I've decided to give it to you early. Congratulations, Four Gold-Star General - I salute you.'

'Wow – thank you, Sir! That's very generous of you!'

'Not at all, Pud – you've earned it. Mind you, there is a reason for your early promotion.'

'Oh? What's that, Sir?'

'Well, actually it concerns you, Jimma.'

'Sir?'

'The board has sat, and we all agree. You are to be promoted to full, Five-Star General. Congratulations!'

'Oh my! Sir, thank you! Thank you very much!'

'Again, not at all Jimma. But Pud – I'm afraid this has certain consequences for you.'

'I know, Sir. Jimma will be able to lord it over me for another decade or so. I can't wait.'

'I thought you might say something like that, Pud. So you'll be happy to hear that's not going to happen.'

'Sir?'

'Jimma's new role as a full General will take him away from the Complex of Temporal Protection and Border Control – leaving you in sole charge.'

'Whoa! Really? Me in charge? I don't believe it! I'll be on my own?'

'Oh no. Someone has to take your place – someone to work with you, and I have the perfect candidate.'

'You do? It's not Sheelandra is it? I mean she was a promising student, but she'd never ...'

'No, it's not Sheelandra.'

'Johnstone? It can't be ...'

'Not Johnstone either. It's the Lost Soul, Pud.'

'It's ... you don't mean ... really?'

'Absolutely, Pud. He's young by our standards, but his mind is remarkable - the vitality of youth, but the wisdom of human middle-age. The reports regarding him make interesting reading. Of course we'll have to wait until he's finished his human education, so you'll be on your own for a decade or so. The only problem is – convincing him and his family that this is best for him when the time comes.'

'I'm sure that won't be a problem, Sir.'

'That's the spirit Pud. Now – if the two of you can get your reports written up and submitted as soon as you can, we'll have a celebration lunch for both of you sharp at two. Then you must get started on investigating the Paradox – Jimma – your promotion should help with that. That's all for now – Boss out.'

'Thank you, Sir – goodbye!'

'Bye, Boss! I mean, er ... goodbye, Sir!'

Chapter Sixteen
The Drop

December 24th, 2011.

Tradition was what had led Art to this point. Again. Making new traditions, an ironic statement in itself, was the main reason he now stood facing St. David's Hospital, on a cold December night. Again. But this time, he was flanked by the young Maga, and Danny. Gone was the huge heavy sack he usually carried, replaced by a small dark back-pack (he would have felt naked without *something* to carry). Maga was dressed for the occasion, and both Art and Danny were dressed in black from head to foot.

They all stood looking up at the tall building, waiting for the signal from Doctor Levvy - her only other role in the plan, added at the last minute. The party a few floors up was in full swing, and the rapidly-changing disco lights were dancing in their eyes as they watched.

'You all know what to do?' Art asked.

'Of course,' Danny replied confidently. 'As soon as you get the signal, I'm to run back to Tina's house and liaise with her and Evi that the plan is a go. From then on you'll have me on radio comms only.'

'Good. And you, Maga?' Art said.

Maga cleared his throat nervously. 'Erm, I have to ... erm ...'

Art patted Maga's little shoulder. 'Maga - you CAN do this. We've all seen the things you can do - you're amazing. Don't forget I'll be in there with you, keeping your Instructor off the scent. I won't be right next to you, but you can talk to me or Danny whenever you like - he assures me the comms are secure. You can do this, okay?'

Maga breathed in and out nervously. 'Okay,' he said shakily.

'Good man,' Art said. 'Now don't forget - I'll locate the sack and get it so far towards the Children's Ward. When I'm happy that your Instructor is on my tail, I'll leave it at the rendezvous, and *you* take it the rest of the way.'

'I still think that's a sticking point,' Danny said. 'We should have used a decoy sack - the plan would be far simpler without a rendezvous point in my opinion.'

'We went over that, Danny. Maga's Instructor would notice two of us in there for sure. The whole plan rests on him tracking one person, one sack - that's what we submitted to him, and he accepted it.'

'Except that there'll be two of you in there,' Danny added.

'Yes, but he'll only be tracking one of us,' Art answered.

'You seem awfully certain about that, Art. Are you absolutely sure?' Danny said.

Art smiled. 'Nope,' he said, noticing a flashing light coming from the building five floors up. 'Too late now - there's the signal. Good luck, everyone. Go go go!'

Little Maga watched Danny turn round and run back towards the houses, and hardly noticed Art running around the back of the hospital. He sighed, and casually strolled up to the big hospital doors, pushed through them with some effort, and strolled into the reception area, in plain sight.

*

Art found a seat in the crowded cafe area, and placed two mugs of hot chocolate down on the table. He sipped at his drink, and before long the seat opposite him at the table was occupied.

'Evening, Art,' the older Maga said, looking awkwardly at the drink in front of him. 'Erm ... what's this?'

'Hot chocolate,' said Art. 'Try some.'

Maga took a sip, and was surprised that he didn't want to spit it out immediately.

'That's not half bad. I mean it's not ...'

'Yes I know that, but they don't sell Stroth-Brew at human cafés, Maga. Here,' Art handed Maga a couple of Dough-Drops he had brought from Grandma's house, and he took them gratefully.

'Teacher's pet. This won't get you any extra marks you know. But thanks.' He leaned back as far as the plastic chair would allow him, and bit into one of them. 'So. Are you ready?'

Art nodded. 'All set.'

Maga narrowed his eyes. 'Hmm. We'll see. Remember - your task is to deliver as you always do, but I need to be as surprised as the rest of the nursing staff, and I'll be right there, watching. Standard Recon magic is allowed, and if I see you using it I'll assume you're well enough hidden, but you'll need more than that to fool me when it comes to the actual Drop, which I *mustn't* see. Oh, and I'll be keeping an eye on all the corridors around the Children's Ward too.' He leaned forward and tapped the side of his head, grinning. 'I am *not* easily fooled, Elfee.'

'Oh no?' Art said, mirroring his grin. 'So what did you glean from Doctor Levvy's letter? Let me guess - a blank page, am I right?'

Maga's smile vanished. 'I don't know how you did that Elfee, but I will find out. Mark my words.' He sipped his chocolate again. 'However, I *suppose* I must commend you on that.'

Art drained his mug, and placed it down on the table. 'Okay. One hour till midnight. I'll go and prepare. You'll be waiting for me here when it's all over, I presume?'

'I will. That's if you succeed,' Maga said. He placed his mug down on the table, and suddenly looked sincere. 'Good luck, Arthur - and I mean that. I've taught you everything you should know as an Agent over the last four years, and it's been a genuine pleasure. But I've also taught you everything I think you should know as a first year Mage, and you've taken it all on board; I can't fault your enthusiasm, but ... I just don't know how you're meant to actually *do* any of it. It's beyond me, it really is, but I wish you luck - I really do. Remember - I'm trying to fail you on this assignment, but don't take it personally, okay - it's just my job.'

'I know. And thanks, Maga.' Art held out his hand, and Maga shook it. 'See you later.'

Art walked away leaving Maga to finish his drink, but as he glanced back he saw that Maga was already gone. He thought about what he had told him, and couldn't help feeling guilt at the deceit. Part of the plan was based on the fact that Maga thought *Art* was his student Mage, and *not* his younger self. It gave him an unfair advantage, but Art couldn't shift the feeling that if he found out Maga had been teaching his younger self through Art, or worse bumped into him, all manner of bad things would happen. He didn't know what, but whenever he thought about it, it gave him a sickening feeling that he didn't understand.

*

'Danny - are you there?'

'Absolutely, Art - with you all the way,' crackled the response in his ear. The tiny wireless receiver that Danny had cobbled together from a mobile phone headset was working well.

'Okay, Art - it's time for phase one. Proceed to the first stop.'

'Are you sure I won't need Recon magic for this?' Art whispered back.

'Of course. I've checked all the cameras - the coast is clear.'

Art opened the fire door and walked into a small corridor, and he winced at the strong smell of disinfectant.

'Keep us updated please, Art.'

'Sorry - emerging just behind the Emergency Department now. All clear. I'm proceeding towards the service lift.'

Art walked as casually as he could along past the slightly mirrored windows, listening out for footsteps as he went. At this point, it didn't matter too much if he was seen, which was just as well because the E.D. was busy all year round, but it was good practice for when it did matter.

Art reached the end of the corridor and hid in a recess next to the elevator. 'Danny - what's the situation with the lift?' he whispered.

His earpiece crackled. 'Camera looks clear. Bring it down,' came the reply.

Art pressed the summon button and waited. The usual mechanical whirring sound sang from the gap in the doors, and the arrival light pinged on. The doors slid open, but the lift *wasn't* empty.

'Oh, hello again. Weren't you in earlier this year?' said nurse Jenny Hopkins.

'Oh. Erm, yes - hello.' Art said nervously.

'Are you lost?' said Jenny.

'No, no, just ... err ... took a wrong turn is all. Do you know where the cafe is, please?' Art stammered.

'Oh dear - you're way off. There's one on the ground floor - follow the corridor behind you and take a left - you can't miss it. Though I doubt it'll be open at this hour – you'll have to use the vending machines.'

'Thanks,' he said, and reluctantly turned round and walked away.

'That's okay dear - bye bye now,' she called after him.

'What do I do now?' he whispered as loudly as he could into his earpiece.

There was a crackling and rustling sound, and Danny's voice returned. '*Who* was that? The camera was clear!'

'That was Jenny – the staff nurse from the Children's Ward! What was she doing down *here*?' Art said.

'Art – the lift was clear, I swear to you. Listen, just keep going – there's a set of stairs up ahead. Sharp left, blue doors.' said Danny.

Art darted around the corner, and headed up the stairs.

'Where does this bring me out?' he said.

'Hold on,' Danny said, and Art heard several key-presses before an answer came back. 'Okay - just go one floor up, and find the lift again. Then you can carry on with the plan with minimal disturbance, hopefully.'

Art made his way up the stairs, and summoned the lift again. This time it was empty, and he hopped inside and pressed the button for level three. The lift obediently carried him up.

'Okay, I'm on the third floor – right next to CCU. I'm making my way to the Atrium to rendezvous with the package.'

The voice that answered in his earpiece was distinctly feminine. 'Erm, okay, Art.'

'Tina?' he said.

'Hellooo!' she chimed. 'Danny's just checking something out, so you're stuck with me for a bit.'

'Is Evi there too?' he asked.

'Yes – but you haven't got time! Get going!' she said hurriedly.

'Okay, okay.'

He dashed down the corridor, and up ahead the sounds of muffled disco music grew louder and louder.

'Sounds like the party is in full swing. Is the corridor round there clear?'

'Hold on,' said Tina. There was a lot of rustling and crackling before she answered again. 'Yes – Danny says it's all clear.'

'Tina – what's going on?' Art said.

'It's okay, Art – Danny is monitoring Grandma's house as well for some reason. He says ... oh, hold on he's ...'

There was a lot of rustling again, and Danny's voice returned. 'Art – Dorothy is *not* part of the plan, am I right?'

'That's right – what's going on, Danny?' Art asked.

'She has just left the house. Can you think why she would do that at this hour?' Danny said.

'What – you ... you've got a camera there too?' Art said. 'Danny – I've told you – we can trust her, okay?'

'I understand, Art. Nevertheless, I thought you should know,' he replied.

'Well, thanks. Maybe she's gone for a walk. Can we get on now, please?' Art said irritably.

'Of course. The corridor, as I just told Tina, is clear. You can proceed.' Danny replied coolly.

'Thank you,' said Art. 'Right - Doctor Levvy said the rear door to the Atrium would be unlocked, and that's where we can get in to retrieve the package. I'll need to deploy Recon magic from pouch number one. Half a cube should do it.'

Art noiselessly drew his back pack round to his front, and took out a brown leather pouch from the top pocket. Inside were three cubes of Reconnaissance Chocolate. Art broke one of the cubes in half, and popped it into his mouth, replacing the rest and returning the pack round to his back. He had forgotten that Recon Chocolate was just about the most *amazing* thing he had ever tasted, despite its odd side-effect on humans, and he had to stop himself from savouring the moment – he had a job to do.

'I hope I don't have to use any more of this,' Art whispered.

'Why?' Danny asked.

'Amazing as it is, I found out to my peril during Maga's lessons that it has a slightly … well, *laxative* effect on me. Still, I get a lot of reading done.'

'Arthur, that's too much information,' Danny said.

'Sorry. Moving in.'

Art crept forward keeping close to the wall, and peeked round the corner. It looked clear, so he dashed out and headed for the glass back door to the large room that was the Atrium, which was housing a special themed Christmas Eve party for the staff and their partners. But when he was halfway there, a voice startled him.

'Oh hello again. Weren't you in earlier this year?'

It was nurse Jenny Hopkins again. Art skidded to a halt.

'Err, y … yes,' Art said slowly, narrowing his eyes. 'I … told you earlier …'

'Are you lost?' she said.

'No,' said Art, with an odd feeling of déjà-vu. 'Just looking for the Atrium, is all.' He pointed to it. 'Found it …'

'Oh dear – you're way off. There's one on the ground floor – follow the corridor behind you and take a left – you can't miss it. Though I doubt it'll be open at this hour – you'll have to use the vending machines.'

Art paused, confused. 'Erm,'

'That's okay dear – bye bye now,' she said, and turned on her heels and walked off.

'Danny – did you hear that?' Art said, when she was out of sight.

'I did. Who was it?' he asked.

'It was her again – Jenny from the Children's Ward,' Art said.

'Yes,' Danny answered, 'and it sounded like *she* was having the same conversation as last time.'

'But that's not the weird thing,' Art said.

'*That* wasn't the weird thing?' said Danny.

'No,' Art answered, 'she saw *through* the Recon magic!'

There was a pause.

'Danny?' Art whispered loudly.

'Hang on, Art – I just need to check something. Did the Instructor mention anything about curve-balls to you?'

'What?' Art said.

'You know – putting things in your way to try and put you off the scent? To try and trip you up?' Danny said.

'Erm, not that I know of, no. Why?'

'I think our Mage friend is playing with us. Only he's not being consistent with his magical programming.'

Art gasped. 'You mean that *wasn't* Nurse Hopkins?'

'More than that; I don't think it was a *person* at all – I think it was a magical algorithm. Let me check it out. Carry on with the mission – I'll hand you over to Tina.'

'Oh – is Evi there?' Art said hopefully.

'Hello again!' Tina's voice chimed in his ear.

Art sighed. 'Moving in. Again.'

He walked over to the glass door, and as promised, it was unlocked. The noise of the music system blared as the door opened, and he realized he wouldn't be able to hear anyone in his earpiece until he was out of the Atrium – something he hadn't figured on.

The party was in full swing, and Art smiled at the sight – eighty, maybe a hundred people, were dancing under a huge glitter ball. And every single one of them, young and old, tall and short, male and female, was dressed as Santa Claus.

Art had to walk right through the middle of them to the other side of the room and back again to retrieve the sack, but his recent run-in with Jenny made him question whether he was properly disguised or not. He walked over to the edge of the dance floor, and gingerly stepped onto it. Immediately, two Santas stepped aside to let him pass, and Art froze, shutting his eyes.

Remember your training, he thought to himself. *What am I talking about? It was MAGA's training!*

He opened his eyes slowly, but no one was looking at him. He looked at one of them and waved his hand in front of their face. No reaction.

Wow – it really does work! He thought, and walked forward with more confidence. The whole crowd parted to let him through, but no one acknowledged him. He was invisible in the most perfect way.

He walked through the crowd to the other side of the dance floor, and sitting under the tree was the huge sack of toys he had spent all year making.

He chuckled to himself. 'This is going to be easy,' he said.

*

'Maga – can you hear me? Come in!'

'Yes, I can hear you Danny. What's the matter?' the young Maga said.

'I'm not sure yet, but we've lost communication with Art. There's huge audible interference blocking the signal. And … something else isn't right either.'

'Wh … what is it?' Maga said nervously.

'I can't quite put my finger on it, but I think your Instructor is … trying to trip Art up. He's seen someone he knows twice already.'

'Well, that's alright, isn't it? I mean he's been here before, hasn't he? He's bound to bump into someone he knows.' Maga replied.

'Yes, but … I don't know - something isn't right – can you check up on Arthur for me?'

'Erm, I'm … I'm still on my way to the first way-point,' Maga said nervously.

'Maga – we need you to check this out.'

'O … okay, erm, where is it? I mean he?'

'The Atrium. Be careful though – that's one of the places I think the Instructor was trying to trip Arthur up. And hurry – time is running out – use special measures if you have to.'

'Okay. Are you going to monitor me on the way round?'

'I'll be with you all the way. I know we couldn't find an earpiece small enough for you, but make sure that old radio is turned completely down - you could give yourself away. Remember to check in periodically, though. Now go!'

Maga stowed the cumbersome CB radio handset in his tunic, and took a deep breath. He stood up from the plastic chair he had been sitting on outside the padlocked

Pharmacy, and hurried towards the main corridor. He took another deep breath.

Okay, remember your training, remember your training, he thought to himself. He reached the doors to the lift, and pressed the summon button. The little box above the doors showed it was on the fifth floor, and it didn't budge. He pressed the button again. Nothing. He reached for his radio again.

'Danny? The lift isn't working. I'll have to take the stairs.'

'There isn't time, Maga,' came the hurried reply. 'I still can't contact Arthur – you'll have to be quick! Oh, and anyway – stay away from the lifts – I can't trust the cameras at the moment.'

Maga sighed heavily, and put the radio away. *Okay. Showtime,* he thought.

He concentrated on his own form momentarily, and slipped his molecular structure out of solid state just enough to dodge matter, and he slid his head through the closed doors and looked up. The lift was right at the top of the shaft.

He slid the rest of the way through and flung himself effortlessly onto the far wall of the lift shaft, with enough momentum to allow just enough time to ease gravity around him sideways, keeping him fixed to the wall. He stood up and sprinted up the shaft towards the motionless lift. When he reached it he got on his hands and knees and edged in between the internal and external lift doors, thinned his molecular structure again, and allowed the sideways gravity to ease him through the doors and into the corridor before he returned it to normal. He landed in a crouching position, and looked up to see where he had to go next. There was one corridor straight ahead of him, and another off to his right. The one straight ahead was the huge connecting tunnel-like corridor that joined the two buildings together, and he sprinted for it, looking around him as he went. Despite his size, he was surprisingly fast, and just before he reached the lip of the corridor, a door opened and a doctor wheeling a television and DVD player on a stand strolled out right into his path. Quick as a flash he vaulted into the air, over the top of the TV, and turned a full sideways circle before landing on his feet again. The doctor's face was a picture as she saw a small red blur flash past her eyes at a seemingly impossible speed.

Maga sped through the tunnel, and out into the big open space just before the Atrium. Up ahead, he could see a figure emerging from a frosted glass door with flashing lights behind it – it was Art, and he was dragging the huge sack behind him.

But just as Maga recognized who it was, his feet seemed to tie themselves together and he fell, crashing head over heels again and again, and as he came to rest, he saw the huge figure of Grandma standing over him, her Sta'an clenched firmly in her hand. Maga had hit his head on the way down, and as he tried to figure out what had just happened, he saw Art running towards him almost in slow motion, his eyes wide with fear, shouting something that Maga couldn't hear before he blacked out.

Chapter Seventeen
THE MAGE'S ASSISTANT

Art hauled the huge sack across the dance floor, the crowd parting to let him through without an inkling he was there. He pushed open the glass door and dragged the sack out into the open space outside the Atrium. He reached into his backpack and was rummaging around for the little stopper bottle that would make the sack temporarily light as a feather, when he noticed something out of the corner of his eye. He turned, and what he saw made him drop his pack. Little Maga was running through the corridor that came from the second building, and standing to the side, just out of his sight, was *Grandma* – he couldn't believe his eyes – with her Sta'an ready for an attack.

Art rubbed his eyes and looked again – it was definitely her, and as Maga emerged from the tunnel, she went into a battle-ready stance that Art had never seen before, and before his eyes she violently Felled the little running figure. Maga crumpled as his legs went from under him, and he fell crashing to the ground, rolling over several times.

'NOOOO! WHAT ARE YOU DOING?' Art cried as he rushed over to help up little Maga, who wasn't moving.

'ARTHUR! NO!' Grandma cried, and before Art was even close, he had been felled too, though he fell far less heavily.

'Stay there!' Grandma cried. 'Do you hear me? Don't move forward another inch!'

Art's head was reeling. He couldn't believe what was happening – he *wouldn't* believe it. He wrenched himself up onto his elbows and glared at her, just as his earpiece crackled to life.

'Arthur – do as she says. I'm right here, look behind you.' Art looked round, and Danny was standing some way behind him panting heavily, glaring at Grandma.

'Danny, what's happening? Grandma? What's …' Art managed.

'Dorothy Elfee,' Danny spat, staring at her with venom, in a voice that reminded Art of Danny's less glorious days.

She raised her Sta'an again. 'Danny – stay put …'

'I tried to warn you, Arthur. I understand she's family – it's not your fault – but do you see *now*?' Danny said slowly.

'Danny please – just stay there!' she cried out again.

'Yes, you'd like that, wouldn't you? Well, remember who you are facing, Dorothy.' He pointed to her Sta'an. '*That* … is not, and never will be, a match for me.'

'Grandma – what are you *doing*?' Art said.

'Arthur – let me explain …'

'You've done all the explaining you ever will, Dorothy. Now stand aside!' Danny said.

Little Maga was starting to stir; he rubbed his head and moaned.

'Grandma – let me check on Maga – please!' Art called out.

'I can't let you do that just now – trust me Arthur,' she said.

'Ha! *Trust*!' Danny laughed. 'You've had enough of that. The talk is over.'

He walked briskly past Art, who was still lying on the floor, keeping his eyes firmly on Grandma but heading for Maga.

'Danny – don't do that – stop where you are – please! DANNY!' Grandma called. But Danny ignored her and carried on. He was nearly at Maga's side when his body stiffened, his eyes widened, and his outline became blurred, like heat rising from a hot road.

'DANNY!' Grandma called, as his body became rigidly still and was lifted several feet off the ground. He was encompassed in a sphere of heat, and he was slowly spinning in the centre of it. Art rose to his feet and ran towards it, but Grandma called out again.

'ARTHUR – NO! Stay there! You can't help him now!'

There was an ear-splitting roar as the sphere turned red, and then it hardened and fell silent, save for a low almost inaudible rumbling. Danny was frozen in the middle of the now solid transparent sphere, his eyes wide. Art looked at it, and felt sick to his stomach.

'Grandma – what are you doing? Get him out of there!' he said.

'Arthur – that's not me – I was an Agent, *not* a Mage! I'm not *capable* of that!'

'Then who did it? Who did … whatever *that* is? And why did you …'

Maga moaned, and sat up slowly, rubbing his head. He caught sight of the sphere, and he gasped.

'Art – what's that … is … is that *Danny* in there?' he said.

And then a voice spoke from the other side of the Atrium, an angry, deep, gravelly voice that Art had never heard before.

'I have him! I have him! And what's this – DOROTHY! Dorothy is here too! How lovely!'

Art turned, and although he had never heard the voice before, he had met it's owner several times already. During the battle Art had been involved in just outside the L-Shaped Village on the last day of his stay there, a Mage by the name of Dabellar had led the opposing army. And standing to his right had been a stout little man with a balding head, whom Art had never heard speak. He had now.

The stout little man walked over to them, his shoes clacking on the floor like the sound of a bouncing billiard ball.

'Well, well, well. I never thought I would see you again, Dorothy. And to see you *here*, just as I've caught the heir of the Ainsworth fortune! All gone now, of course, but revenge is a dish best served cold and all that,' he said.

Art looked at Grandma. Her face was stricken with terror. Art stood up, walked over to her side and took her hand. 'It's okay Grandma. I know this man. And he's no match for Maga.'

Maga had pulled himself upright too, and was edging towards Art. He had a nervous look on his face.

The man smiled. 'Allow me to introduce myself. My name is Avarice.'

Art's eyes widened. '*Avarice*?' He thought for a moment. 'You're … *Avarice*? Avarice *Ainsworth*?'

'The very same. And you are? You will have to forgive me – my eyesight is not what it was,' he said to Art.

'Don't tell him!' Grandma barked as quietly as she could, grabbing Art's shoulder. She had her Sta'an up and ready again, though this time Art was glad she had.

'But ... you said you'd ... *killed* him, Grandma,' Art said.

'I ... I thought I had,' she said. 'He was lying there, covered in blood. I banished his body to the Burning Plains just south of Amarly.'

Avarice still wore his sickening smile, and it reminded Art of Dabellar. 'Ah yes. The Burning Plains. How could I forget. Not quite dead Dorothy, but very nearly. If not by your hand, then by the heat of that place. But still, limping along trying to avoid death, I found I was able, somehow, to *talk* to the remarkably vicious creatures that manage to live there. Just by thinking aloud they would do anything I asked, even transport me to safety. Just as well really, otherwise *they* would have been the end of me. And just think – I never would have found out about my 'talent' if it wasn't for you, Dorothy. Speaking of which, if you won't *tell* me who your friends are, it's a small matter to find out.'

He put two fingers to his temple and narrowed his eyes, but it wasn't long before his sickening grin disappeared. 'I seem to be being blocked by something. Or some*one*.' His eyebrows raised slightly, and he turned to face Maga, who was still edging towards Grandma, and was much closer to Avarice than Art was.

'And who, may I ask, are you, Sir?' he said.

Maga was sure Avarice would recognise him, but he had completely forgotten that as part of the plan for the Drop, he was dressed in a fancy-dress Santa Claus outfit, complete with big clumsy boots and huge false white beard, which was far too big and covered almost all of his face. His hat was nearly falling off after his fall, but thankfully everything else had stayed put.

Grandma squeezed his little shoulder, and he said nothing.

'No matter,' Avarice said. 'I got what I came for.' He looked up at the sphere, spinning almost too slowly to notice.

'Let him go – now!' Art said forcefully.

'I don't think so. Not after the years I have waited. Do you know how *many* years, Dorothy? Do you?'

'I'm not at all interested,' she said flatly.

Avarice's eyes glinted with anger, but he controlled himself. 'Again, no matter,' he said.

'What are you going to do with him?' Art said.

'Do? I'm not going to *do* anything. It's done. How long do you suppose one can survive with no air in *there*?' He pointed to the sphere, grinning his sickly grin again.

'Let him down!' Art shouted. 'You've got the wrong person! I'm Arthur!'

'NO!' Grandma shouted, and she grabbed hold of him protectively.

Avarice looked at Art in confusion. He took out a pair of glasses with very thick lenses and put them on, then he squinted at the sphere. He blinked a couple of times, then frowned. He looked directly at Art, and his eyes flashed with recognition. 'YOU!' he shouted. 'IT'S YOU!'

'ARTHUR – RUN!' Grandma shouted, and she pushed him away and raised her Sta'an menacingly.

'No, Grandma!' Art said.

'ARTHUR! GO!' she shouted in surprise.

'NO! DANNY'S UP THERE!' he shouted back.

Avarice's face was contorted with rage, but somehow he was controlling himself. 'Very … *admirable*, young Arthur,' he said. 'You certainly don't get that from *her*. But then there's a reason for that.'

'Get Danny out of there – you can take me – I'll let you. Just let him down!' Art pleaded.

Avarice glared at him. He breathed loudly in and out several times, then he reached into his top pocket and threw a handful of red dust at the sphere. It roared again, turned red, and slowly vanished. Danny fell to the floor unmoving, but to Art's relief, his chest was moving up and down. He was still alive.

Avarice stared at Danny in disbelief. He moved closer, unable to believe his eyes. Then a big grin spread across his face. 'This is a lucky day indeed! I have no less than *three* people who appear on the Blue Triangle Army's *most-wanted* list! Not only do I get my revenge on Dorothy *and* her ward, but I have the perfect excuse for being here! I, Avarice Ainsworth, will bring in YerDichh! Ha!'

Then Avarice turned to Art, like a child in a sweet shop. 'But first to *you*, Arthur,' he said menacingly. 'Arthur Elfee. *The* Arthur Elfee. This is better actually – I get to look you in the eyes before I kill you.'

'How did you find me?' Art said.

'Oh I have my spies inside the Helm *and* the Faculty. That's how I became aware of the Paradox. More to the point, to *whom* the Paradox related to. When I heard that *you* would be taking little Maga's place in your foolish attempt to heal the Timeline, it was like all my Christmasses had come at once. Quite ironic, really, isn't it? And of course seeing Pud and Jimma sweat like that is all part of the fun. But nothing compared to *this*. Never in my wildest dreams did I *ever* think I would meet a line-up like this!'

'Arthur – please step away,' Grandma said.

'It's okay,' he answered.

'He's right,' Avarice said casually. 'It's all okay now. I get to finish the Ainsworth line once and for all. Well, the important member anyway.'

'Art – step away!' Grandma said. Avarice reached into his inside pocket, his grin widening. He pulled out a little bottle of bright red bubbling liquid, and was just about to uncork it when Art felt a familiar, low bass rumble. He was sure any second that everything would grind to a halt around him as it usually did whenever he heard that very distinctive sound, but instead, a great white flash erupted between him and Avarice, and they were both flung off their feet with the force of it. A small figure dressed completely in black, covering even his face, landed in a crouching position where the flash had been, brandishing a staff made of a clear, hard material Art didn't recognize.

The figure was facing the fallen Avarice, and his free arm was held out to the side as if protecting Art behind him. A loud slow voice boomed from behind his mask. '*THIS MAGE ... IS PROTECTED.*'

Avarice scrambled back from the figure in fear, dropping the bottle in his hand. He looked down at it, smashed to bits on the floor, and he yelped. 'NO! THE WHOLE BOTTLE!'

The red liquid was rising up and forming a shell around Avarice, who was scrambling to get away. The shell grew and grew, rising up further and further, roaring as it formed a huge sphere in the air, turning various shades of red. Avarice was trapped in the middle, struggling violently. The sphere was growing rapidly, losing it's shape periodically, and getting very large. It was much larger than the one that had encapsulated Danny, but Art supposed Avarice had used just one drop of the red bubbling liquid for that – but now the whole bottle was loose, and the roaring sound was deafening.

'Art – get away from it!' Grandma shouted, and she grabbed Maga and ran towards the Atrium. Art managed to scramble away from under it, but the figure stayed where it was.

'You … whoever you are – get away from that! Quick!'

It turned around and waved its hand, causing an inexplicable wave of air that pushed Art sliding along the floor until the wall on the far side of the open space stopped him. Art watched as the figure was dwarfed by the huge red sphere. It put both its hands in the air, and was buffeted about like it was in the centre of a hurricane. It threw its staff on the floor and concentrated on using its hands, as if trying to control the sphere somehow. Art noticed that the sphere wasn't getting any bigger any more, but it wasn't getting any smaller either, and the roaring sound was still increasing. It pulsed as it tried to grow, but the figure kept forcing its hands together and it receded. It pulsed several more times, then it flashed bright white, and the roaring sound turned into an explosion. The figure shouted so loud as it concentrated that Art could hear it above the roar, and he was afraid that the sphere would get the better of it, and then Art noticed something else that chilled his blood; he could also hear another voice coming from inside the sphere, a scream rather than a shout of force. It was Avarice's voice. It rose higher and higher, and then stopped abruptly. Art could guess why, and the finality of it made Art's heart jump.

The explosion continued as one long sound, and the walls shook with the force. The figure was bellowing in the middle of it all, its arms open much wider now as it struggled with the strength of the blow. Its whole little body was shaking, but its arms vibrated the most, and Art noticed to his horror that they were getting further and further apart – it was losing the battle. It took a huge breath and shouted in concentration again, but its arms were still getting wider.

Just as Art was about to turn away in anticipation of what was about to happen, Grandma ran over and stood next to the figure. She pulled out her Sta'an and carried out a sort of reverse manoeuvre – she was pushing, rather than pulling, with her

Sta'an – something Art had never seen before. It didn't seem to have much of a visible effect on the sphere, but Art noticed that the figure's arms were now steady. It was just enough to contain the force of the continual explosion.

Art watched as the two of them, one tall and one small, battled against the rogue magic, and slowly, the sound of the explosion began to die away. The sphere turned orange, then white, and as the sound disappeared completely, it sunk in on itself and vanished with a final loud thud that shook the air. There was nothing of Avarice left, not even a shred of his clothing.

The little figure collapsed on the floor, and Grandma knelt over it. She turned it over onto its back, and slowly it began to recover. It was breathing heavily, with what looked like smoke rising from its arms.

Art rushed over to see who the mysterious figure was, but its face was still covered; Danny was lying on the floor some yards away, still breathing but not stirring; and little Maga was still over by the far wall, looking on nervously. Grandma was the only one who kept her composure, as she cradled the little figure who had saved them all in her arms.

'Thank you,' she whispered.

'Art?' came a gentle voice from behind him. Art turned around, and in one of the many doorways leading into the Atrium stood Evi and Tina, both wearing expressions of pure fear.

'What ... what was ...' Evi managed, before her eyes rolled up inside her eyelids and she fainted.

Chapter Eighteen
THE AGENT

Tina helped Art drag Evi carefully into a side room off the Atrium. Grandma picked up Danny and brought him in too, and laid him beside Evi. The mysterious figure had recovered enough to walk in by himself, and sat down in one of the more comfortable chairs by the doorway. By now, Art had a fairly good idea who the figure was; he could tell by the way he walked, but mostly because of the amazing feat they had all just witnessed, that it was the older Maga. But Art didn't say anything, just in case; he had that peculiar feeling in his stomach again whenever he thought of talking to him.

What happened next was something Art would remember always. Part of the plan for the Drop, which they had all forgotten about completely in the confrontation with Avarice, played itself out more perfectly than Art had ever intended. The young Maga, who Art had nearly forgotten about, gingerly walked up to the doorway and poked his head round nervously. It almost made Art laugh as the tiny person dressed as Santa Claus appeared, but it had the opposite effect on the young trainee Mage's *older* self, who was still completely covered from head to foot in dark clothing, including his face.

'I don't *believe* it,' said the older Maga when he saw the tiny, falsely hirsute person peering in. 'The "Santa" party is *that* way!' he said, jabbing his thumb in the direction of the party. 'And take off that *ridiculous* costume – it's not even *remotely* accurate!'

The little Maga looked at Art, searching his face for a clue as to what to do. Art looked at his watch – it was a little before midnight – he couldn't have timed it better if he had tried. He looked up at little Maga, and tilted his head as discreetly as possible in the direction of the alcove where the sack was still resting. Little Maga looked a bit confused, but then he tilted his head towards the sack too, and Art nodded. The tiny Santa disappeared back around the door frame, and Art heard his little footsteps as he hurried away.

Art could not believe what had just happened. He had prevented the older Maga from recognizing his younger self by using his innate arrogance against him; Art knew he would be angry at the sight of someone wearing a red Santa suit, as both he and Grandma had displayed their distaste at the costume, and Art had banked on that being enough to blind him to what was right in front of his eyes. And it had worked. What he hadn't banked on was that the older Maga would be wearing a face mask. That was just blind luck.

As soon as the younger Maga had gone, the older Maga slumped back in his chair and sighed, totally oblivious to who he had been talking to. Grandma came over to him and sat in the chair next to him.

'Come on, now,' she said, 'let's take a look at you.' Maga removed his face mask, and rolled up his sleeves. He watched as Grandma tended to the bruising that was starting to appear on his arms. He was smiling slightly, like he was in the presence of an old school teacher.

'Devilishly difficult to treat, magic-induced wounds,' she said. 'Take an age to heal. You were lucky.'

'It would have been worse if you hadn't stepped in,' he added.

'It's no trouble, dear. Really.'

She pulled a vial of thick dark cream from her pocket and started gently rubbing some into the swollen areas, as Maga winced every now and then with the pain. She noticed the proud way he was looking at her in between winces. 'What's the matter, dear?' she asked him.

'I just ... I didn't think I'd see you *here* is all. Not after ...'

'After what, dear?'

Maga looked at her quizzically. 'After ... *you know*,' he said.

'No, I don't dear.'

Maga narrowed his eyes. 'Do you ... *know* me?' he asked.

'Of course, dear. You're Maga Calsow. Shay-la's boy. A little further up the Timeline than I'm used to maybe, but aye, it's you alright. Why – do you know me? Apart from the year you spent with me as a boy that is?' Art could tell she was being careful with what she said to him – in case she endangered the Paradox too.

Maga smiled, still looking quizzical. 'Well, of course. *Everyone* knows you. I mean how can they not? You …'

'That's enough, now,' she interrupted quickly, and nodded towards Art, who thought better than to ask questions and let the matter go, even though his curiosity was peaking higher than ever before.

Danny started to stir, and he let out a loud moan. Grandma rushed over to him and started checking him over, telling him to stay lying down for the time being. Evi was still out for the count, and Tina was fussing over her. Grandma put a cold compress on Danny's head, and came back over to sit next to Maga again.

'He'll be fine,' she said. 'he just needs to rest. He had a lucky escape against magic like that. We could have used *your* help back there, too, Arthur,' she said.

'What do you mean?' he said.

'That was powerful rogue magic. We could have done with you, so we could.'

'What could I have done?'

'More than you know. Come on now, Arthur – think.'

He sighed. 'This again. Lithogrics.'

Maga's ears pricked up. 'What? You've been teaching him paper magic?'

'Just giving him a head start on year two is all,' she said. 'He's a natural.'

Art chuckled. 'Yeah, right. I'm completely useless at it. I can write it, that's about it.'

'It's just a step, Arthur. Just one little step and you'll have got it. Then the possibilities are *limitless*. You just need to think a little.' She nodded towards Tina, who was still fussing over Evi. 'Your friend nearly had it, so she did. Turned paper to rock – that's not half bad.'

Art looked confused. 'That was *Lithogrics*?'

'It was,' she said. 'And quite advanced stuff too.'

Art went very quiet. He was deep in thought, with an odd expression on his face, and after a while he began mumbling under his breath. 'No, no, it can't be. It just … it *can't* be.'

'What are you thinking, dear?' Grandma said.

'It ... it *can't* be as simple as that,' he said.

'As simple as what?' she said, hopefully.

'Well, when Tina showed me the stone slab, she had been practicing translating English from a book into EllShapyan. I saw the page she'd been copying from, and I also noticed the last thing she'd written on her notepad before it changed, but ... I didn't think anything of it.'

'What was it, dear?' Grandma said, like a kid in a sweet shop.

'The last part of the sentence she was translating was ... "*turn to stone*". She'd written "*turn to stone*" in EllShapyan on her notepad. And that's when it changed.'

Grandma looked at him expectantly. 'And?' she said.

'So that's it - that's what you do? You just write ... *instructions*? It's *that* simple?' he asked.

'It's *that* simple,' she said.

'But ... that would mean *anyone* could do it. You could even do it *by accident*, I mean that's what Tina did.'

'Oh no, dear,' Grandma chuckled. 'Not just anyone can do it.'

'Hang on a minute,' Maga interrupted. 'Are you saying one of your friends managed to perform Lithogrics?'

'Apparently,' Art answered.

Maga leaned closer. 'Who?' He asked.

'Me!' Tina called from across the room. 'And don't think I can't hear you from over here.'

'You?' Maga said in surprise. 'Really?'

'That's right, Maga,' Grandma said. 'But like I said, not just anyone can do it. Sure, anyone can learn the language, but it takes a spark to perform Lithogrics. Tina obviously has it – rather surprisingly – but the question is – do *you*, Arthur?'

'What do you mean by a spark?' Art asked.

Grandma smiled. 'Remember the set of notes you took from your first ever lesson with Maga? Remember the particular way *you* described magic?'

'Yes. Yes I do. I called it *belief*,' Art recalled.

'That's right. Lithogrics requires a tad of that, but not the kind that your Mage friend here uses. And you'd be surprised how rare it is, *real* belief.'

Maga sighed. 'As interesting as this conversation is, I'm afraid it's immaterial. At least for now.'

'What do you mean, Maga?' Art said. Maga showed Art his wristwatch.

'It's midnight. The Drop needed to be complete by now. And as you're *here*, and not up *there*,' he pointed to the top floor. 'I'm afraid that means you've failed your final assessment. So you won't be progressing to year two anyway. I know it wasn't your fault, but the rules are the rules.'

Art's top pocket vibrated – it was his mobile phone; he smiled from ear to ear. He took it out, flipped it open and held it up so Maga could see it. A picture message was there on the screen showing the huge sack, in place, on the floor of the Children's Ward. The phone showed that the message was sent dead on midnight, not a second more, not a second less.

The Mage sitting next to him immediately went on the defensive. 'What is it? What are you looking so pleased with yourself about?' He snatched the phone from Art and glared at it. He squinted his eyes in disbelief, then shrugged and handed it back to him in disgust.

'Ha. Tricks. That's just a picture.'

The sound of loud music came blaring into the corridor as the door to the party swung open and several Santa Clauses ran out heading for the stairs, talking to each other excitedly. 'He's done it again!' one said to another. 'Look! Someone sent me a picture message! How on *Earth* did he do it?'

'I know!' said the other. 'I got one too! I think everyone got one! I need to see this!' And they disappeared through the doors and up the stairs, just as Tina's phone went off, and so did Evi's in her pocket.

All this was clearly audible from where they were sitting in the side room. Maga sat looking at Art, clearly very confused. And then *his* phone went off. He ignored it.

'You know I'll check that out,' he said hotly.

'Be my guest,' said Art, gesturing towards the doorway.

Maga sat there bubbling away, until he could sit still no more. He rose from his seat.

'How did you do that? Not that I'm not pleased, sort of, but ... no one's ever fooled me ... HOW DID YOU DO THAT?'

Art smiled in sympathy. 'I'm afraid we've not been entirely honest with you, Maga.'

'What do you mean?' he spat back.

'You know how you thought it odd that a human was being trained as a Mage? Well, that's because I'm not. I'm *not* your student Mage. I never was.'

Maga's eyes widened as he listened to Art. 'WHAT?' he screamed. 'YOU CONNIVING LITTLE …THEN WHO IS?'

'Ah. I can't tell you that, Maga. More than my life's worth – I'm just the middle man.'

'WHY ON AMARLY CAN'T YOU TELL ME?'

'Pointers Maga, pointers,' Art said smugly, then he clapped his hands in the air. 'I always wanted to be the one who says that!'

'Oh, for Heaven's sake!' snapped Maga, and he went to sit down, but then he sprang up again and faced Grandma. 'If he's not the student Mage, then why have you been teaching him paper magic?'

'Ah. I thought we might get to this,' she said coolly. 'Every Agent has to have a basic understanding of Lithogrics as you know, and as you were going to be busy with your new student, the Faculty thought it would be best if someone else finished off Art's initial Agent training. I was given the job. I could see that he was way ahead – he'd covered everything already, thanks to you, so I was confident that if I could check just one last thing, then I could give him a pass.'

'And what was that?' Art asked her.

'A spark. I had to see if you had one. Lithogrics was the perfect way to test you.'

Art's face fell. 'So I've failed, then,' he said.

'The curtain hasn't fallen yet, dear,' she said. 'Remember the homework I set you?'

Art fished around in his pocket, and pulled out the sheet of perfectly transparent paper. 'I keep it with me,' he said.

'Well then. Here,' and she handed him a pencil. 'give the paper back to me as it was. Remember, as long as you think deeply about what you're writing, one word will do it. Choose carefully.'

Art took the pencil. He nervously smoothed out the paper on the unoccupied seat next to him, closed his eyes, and thought hard about what he should do. The pencil hovered over the paper as Grandma and Maga both looked on, intrigued. He thought about how shocked he had been when he saw Grandma turn the paper transparent, and what had happened when Tina had accidentally turned her notepad into a slab of stone. One was intentional, the other accidental, but both had something in common – an uncanny understanding of language – Grandma was a master of EllShapyan, Tina was a master of English, as well as every other subject at school. And then he had it. One word. As long as *he* understood what it should mean, it would work, he was sure of it. He put pencil to paper, and wrote six letters in perfect EllShapyan. R, E, T, U, R, N.

Art watched as the paper was suddenly brown again, as if it had always been that way. And then he was almost strangled by a fierce hug from Grandma. 'I knew it,' she said, a tear rolling down her cheek. 'Well done, Arthur. You know what this means?'

'Erm, no,' he said.

'It means you can attend the Faculty for the second part of your training! And, of course, it means you are free to pass to, and from, here and Amarly as you please. You won't need anybody's help anymore.'

'I won't? How?'

'A simple Transport spell. Lithogrics will do that for you, and you have it now. There's no stopping you!' She looked at him proudly.

Behind them, Evi gave a moan. Tina was cradling her in her arms as she opened her eyes. She smiled up at Tina for a moment, but then her eyes widened as she recalled what she had seen and heard. She sat bolt upright, and searched for Art.

'What was *that*?' she said. 'You need to tell me what that was, because I'm really freaking out here!'

Grandma tended to her. 'You're right, dear. We should all go home for a talk as soon as possible. Come on, up we get. Arthur – will you get Danny? I think he'll need some help.'

They all gathered their things together, and left the side room as quietly as they could. As Art helped Danny to the lift, Evi caught up with him and slipped her hand into his. He smiled. 'I'll explain everything. I promise,' he said.

She looked at him nervously as the lift doors closed with them all inside.

*

Back at Grandma's house, the front room was cosy and warm. There was a fire blazing in the grate that seemed to have appeared from nowhere, and they were all sitting round the dining table as if they were at a board meeting. It was just before one o'clock in the morning, and they were all tired, except for Evi, who was holding Art's hand and was keen to hear everything he had to tell her. The older Maga was sitting at the table too, so they had to be careful how they told the story of the night's events when they got to it, and had agreed in secret during the planning stages to refer to the *younger* Maga purely as 'the student' in his presence.

Art started by telling Evi all about his best friend Maga, who had appeared so long ago in his life, and who helped him with the Drop every year. Then he told her about finding the Fragment, which he showed her still strapped securely to his wrist, and how it had transported him to The L-Shaped Village. He told her about the extraordinary people he had met there, and the 'battles' he had had, and discovering about the 'legend' of Santa Claus, as it were, from Hité before he left. To his astonishment, Evi took it all in her stride. When Art asked her how she could just believe everything he was telling her, she just answered 'You're forgetting what I saw tonight. We could hear everything through your earpiece, including the scream just as you were coming out of the party with the sack, and that's when we ran straight over. We arrived in time to see Danny suspended in mid-air in that sphere. Once you've seen something like that, crazy things don't seem so crazy anymore.'

'Fair enough,' Art answered. He looked at his watch. 'Oh! By the way! Merry Christmas, everyone! Oh, sorry – and Happy Hanukkah Tina!'

'Hanukkah finished over a week ago, but thanks anyway,' Tina said with a warm smile. 'Carry on though – this is getting interesting.' Tina was doing a pretty good job of pretending that she was hearing all this for the first time too, to spare Evi's feelings.

Art asked Grandma to explain to Evi how the whole Santa Claus thing worked, mainly because he wanted to hear it again as well, and partly because he wasn't sure he could explain it as well as she could. Art was overwhelmed just as much as the first time when she explained that it was all about creating traditions, and trying to keep a very delicate balance between injustice and good-will between realms, and how it was all done with hundreds of different departments working in all Times simultaneously, and how it was all overlooked by one person, who by today's understanding of the tradition, could be thought of as Santa Claus. Evi was smiling as she listened, and she squeezed Art's hand every now and then.

Art took over, and explained how he had discovered about his own training as an Agent, and about 'the student' that Maga was to instruct. Maga's face darkened every time they mentioned 'the student', as he was still very grumpy that Art managed to pull the wool over his eyes. Art talked about the planning sessions with The Golden Three, which led to the Drop, which they had all just returned from.

At that moment, Grandma returned from a trip to the kitchen with a tray of Stroth-Brews and some fresh Dough-Drops. 'I'm sorry I had to do what I did,' she said, 'but I had to think quickly, and that was the only way I could think of to stop him, and *you* for that matter, from running into that trap.'

'I know, Grandma,' Art said. 'How did you know it was there?'

'I don't know, exactly, I just felt there was something wrong – I could feel it in the air. So I rushed over to the hospital, and I was right - the stink of rogue Magic was unmistakable. But by the time I had found it, the student was running right into it, and I had to stop him. I know it confused you Art, and I'm sorry.'

Danny raised his eyebrows from across the table, but everyone chose to ignore it. By now they had all realized that Danny's distrust of Grandma wasn't going to go away overnight, and they all chose to skate over the subject of Danny running into Avarice's trap because of it.

'I'm glad you were there, Maga,' said Grandma changing the subject quickly. 'I'm not sure we'd all be here now if you hadn't shown up.'

'I was protecting my student Mage is all,' he answered with his arms folded. Then he sat up. 'Hang on – if it wasn't *you*,' (he pointed to Art) 'then who *was* …' Maga gasped. 'He was there! My student Mage was there - he must've been! Who was it? I saw you Art, Grandma, Danny lying on the floor, and … who else … oh yes - some *idiot* dressed as a cheap Santa ...' He stopped mid-sentence. Then he gasped and stood up. He looked angry, *very* angry, and he opened his mouth to bellow something, but then he stopped himself. He sat down, smoothed off his trousers, and folded his arms. 'Very clever. Well done.'

Art was a little relieved he had escaped an ear bashing from Maga, but could see that he was rather embarrassed at the simplicity of the trick, so he decided to change the subject and move on. 'Have you ever seen Magic like Avarice's before, Grandma?' he asked.

'To be honest, no. But I *do* know that when you're dealing with rogue Magic, you have to expect the unexpected. That's why it's so hard to fight.' She looked at Maga proudly. 'Most Mages would have crumbled under the weight of the explosion, so they would.' Maga's chest swelled a bit at this, and he didn't look quite so sullen any more.

'Where do you think he got it from?' said Art.

Tina looked puzzled. 'Well, he was a Mage too, wasn't he?' she said.

'Avarice was no Mage,' Grandma answered. 'He was nothing more than a coward.'

'So how did he do it?' Tina asked.

'Maga?' Art said, and gestured towards him. Maga sat up straight, his chest swelling a bit more.

'A lot of Magic isn't just created on the spot. In fact most Magic is created, usually in liquid form, by a Mage, which can then be stored and used by anyone, more's the pity. Magic should only be used by a Mage, or under the supervision of a Mage. What happened tonight is the result of giving Magic to someone who had no idea how to contain it. It was the death of him, and nearly us too, not to mention every human within a square mile of the blast.'

Art thought for a second. 'But when Avarice saw Danny, I heard him say that he was pleased because he had an excuse for being there, like Dabellar didn't know he was away. Do you think he *stole* it from Dabellar?' He said.

'That's very likely,' Maga said. 'But even so, Magic shouldn't be left unguarded for anyone to take – Dabellar is still responsible.'

Evi squeezed Art's hand. 'Well, thank you,' she said to Maga. 'Thank you for ... being there. And saving us all.'

'You are more than welcome,' Maga said, raising and replacing a make-believe hat.

'There's one thing I don't get yet,' said Art.

'What's that?' Tina said.

Art looked at Grandma. 'You didn't kill Avarice after all. You're innocent.'

She smiled. 'I guess so.'

'So - why have you grown tall and ... aged like a human? You didn't do anything,' he said.

Grandma sighed. 'Time is a funny thing. To be honest I have no idea, but I suspect it's something to do with my intent.'

Tina put down her drink. 'But you said yourself you didn't know what happened that night. You didn't mean to kill him, you were just protecting Jonathan.'

Grandma looked sullen. 'Whatever the reason, and however I remember it, I struck a man and sent him to die in another realm. The Timeline obviously isn't very forgiving.' She sighed, then suddenly looked resolute. 'But I'd do the same thing again in a heartbeat, so I would. Avarice was a tyrant.'

'In the end his demise was down to his own ignorance,' Maga said. 'Don't be so hard on yourself, Dorothy. You were the very best in your time, you know that.'

Art narrowed his eyes, and looked between Maga and Grandma. 'Is there something I'm missing?' he asked.

'Now, now,' said Maga. 'Pointers.'

Evi finished her Stroth-Brew, which she had clearly enjoyed, and took a Dough-Drop from the tray. 'So what happens now?' she said.

Grandma smiled an enormous, warm smile. 'Well now that's up to Arthur. You have a choice to make so you do.'

'What kind of choice?' Art asked.

'Well, you can either carry on with your life here, or ... begin the second part of your training at the Faculty – which would mean *living* in Amarly.'

Evi squeezed Art's hand so tightly he would have cried out if he hadn't been so shocked himself, and for a while, no one said anything at all. Art looked at Evi, and could see the pain in her eyes. He looked back at Grandma. 'But, I mean ... when?' he managed.

She shook her head in mock disgust. 'Have you forgotten already how Portals work,

Arthur? No one here will even know you've been gone. You can complete your training, come back here and live your life until you're legally an adult. Then, if you choose, we can make the move a bit more ... *permanent.*'

'Art – what are you doing?' Evi said, looking worried. 'Are you going away?'

Art looked her in the eyes. 'Not from you, no. Not if you don't want me to.'

'I *don't* want you to,' she said.

'Evi dear,' Grandma interrupted. 'The invitation includes a plus-one. You can *go with him*. And as far as everyone here is concerned, you'll be gone a fraction of a second. Haven't you ever wondered how a Sprite gets its name?'

'How it *what*?' Art said. 'A Sprite is a ... sort of non-human, isn't it?'

'Well, mostly, but that's not why Sprites are called Sprites. Anyone can be one.'

Art looked totally confused. 'I'm lost. What are you talking about?' he said.

'When you visit another realm, Time can't affect you. You know that already, right?'

'Right,' said Art. 'But a Sprite is someone *from* the other realm, isn't it?'

'Actually, no.' Grandma said with a knowing look on her face. 'Long ago, those who were welcomed back from different realms were referred to as '*Spritely Ones*,' because of their youthful appearance despite their actual age. And somehow the name stuck – people called them *Sprites* for short. Usually only Agents and the odd Mage earned the title, but theoretically *anyone* who's been between worlds, even for a short while, could be called a Sprite.'

Art's mouth was hanging open, Maga was chuckling to himself, Evi was still looking a little confused, and Tina was beginning to laugh. She pointed at Art.

'You're – haha - you're a Sprite! Hahaha, hahahaha!'

'Tina – please!' Evi scolded.

'Sorry,' said Tina, and fell silent, with a suppressed grin.

Art turned to Maga. 'But ... you always told me you were a Sprite!'

Maga gestured widely with his arms. 'And I am,' he said, smiling smugly.

'Yes, but that's not ... the actual type of *being* you are though, is it?'

Maga looked at Grandma. 'He catches on quick, doesn't he?' he said.

'Well, what are you then?' said Art.

Maga chuckled. 'Oh, I don't know. We're not as vain as humans - we've never had a name for our ... what do you call it ... *species*. We just *are*.'

Grandma tapped her mug lightly on the table a few times. 'Excuse me! You're all missing the point. The fact of the matter is, Evi, that you can go *with* Art, and return at the same point in this Timeline as you left. And you won't have aged a day.'

'Hang on,' Art cut in. 'Wasn't ...' He was about to say that the younger Maga had been promised the very same thing, only to find out that his Time in the human world would also pass back in Amarly because of some regulations about Temporal energy or something like that. But he stopped himself at the last second, as the older Maga was right there, and might remember that particular piece of his past, and then the game would be up.

Thankfully, Grandma seemed to know what he was going to say. 'I can assure you that won't happen this time, Art. Your part to play in all this is too important – they wouldn't dare. So the only thing that matters now is *making* the decision. You and Evi should talk it over. Seriously.'

Danny cleared his throat. 'So what should we all do until then?' he said.

Grandma smiled. 'Well, this has been the most interesting sleep-over of my life, having you all here like this, and I say we enjoy it, and celebrate a successful mission. Tomorrow, well - *today* actually, we should all go back and enjoy Christmas with our families, and meet back here when the decision has been made. Until then – who's for more Stroth-Brew?'

They all cheered, Evi and Art a little less than the rest under the weight of their decision, and soon the table was laden with Dough-Drops and honey, Stroth-Brews, fresh warm bread, crisps and chocolates that seemed to appear from nowhere, and happy chatter. Art and Evi's hands stayed clasped together, and every now and again they looked at each other and exchanged worried glances, until one by one everyone at the table got out their sleeping bags and settled down on the huge soft rug in front of the fire for the night. Grandma finally rose from her seat, wished them all goodnight, and switched off the living room light.

Chapter Nineteen
The Freshman

Maga was the first to leave Grandma's house in the morning, shaking Art's hand fiercely before he went. 'If anyone were to have got the better of me, I'm glad it was you, Art. Farewell,' he said, and disappeared down the garden path. Art didn't know if the 'farewell' meant that he wouldn't see Maga again any time soon, but he didn't broach the subject for fear of getting upset. Then Art, Evi, Danny and Tina all gathered their things together and set off themselves. They all thanked Grandma one by one as they went, wished her a Merry Christmas, and stepped out into the frosty garden of a sunny Christmas morning.

They all walked as slowly as they could, chatting excitedly about how they were going to spend Christmas Day, but all too soon they were outside the first stop – Tina's house. Danny was the perfect gentleman, and offered to walk her to her front door so that Art and Evi could walk the rest of the way together. Tina hugged Evi and Art in turn, then curtseyed to Danny, who bowed politely in return, and off they went, chuckling. Art walked Evi to her house, they parted with a long kiss, and he watched as she disappeared into the Wise household, wondering what sort of day she was going to have.

Art's Christmas was the very best of his life so far. He spent his with his family, opening stocking presents with Walt in their parents' bedroom, then tree presents, before a glorious festive lunch which made them all sleepy in the afternoon, even Walt. But Evi woke them all up by ringing on the doorbell so she could spend part of the day with Art.

Tina spent hers with Peter, as the two families always went out for a slap-up lunch on Christmas Day if part of Hanukkah didn't fall over the festive period.

And Danny spent his feeling very nostalgic over forty lost Christmases, and decided to shower his family with gifts to try and make up for it. By now they were all used to his shocking change in character, and the whole family seemed to have grown together as a result, and more than once Danny shed tears of pride at the fun they were all having.

The day after Boxing Day, all their mobile phones went off within seconds of each other. It was a text saying that Art and Evi's decision had been made, and that they were all to go over to Grandma's house for tea that evening.

Art and Evi were the first to arrive. They filed in, hand-in-hand, and Grandma's front room was filled with the flickering light of an open fire, and a vast candle-lit table laden with food and hot drinks. Art looked around; there was still one person he hadn't seen since the Drop, and he couldn't see him now.

'Where's Maga, Grandma? I mean the young Maga. What happened to him after the Drop?'

'Oh, he kept a low profile that night. He was upstairs all along, just as we planned,' she said.

'Is he still here?' Art asked hopefully.

'Sorry, no. I sent him back early so he could spend Christmas with his family - slightly against the rules, but I don't think the Faculty will argue with me. But maybe you'll see him soon?'

Art and Evi exchanged a knowing look, but before Grandma could quiz them anymore, there was a knock at the door, and Tina and Danny arrived. To Art's surprise, the older Maga was with them too.

'Maga!' Art said with a huge smile.

'You think I wouldn't be here for this?' he said. 'This decision affects my future as well as yours you know.'

'What? You mean you don't *know* what we decide? How is that possible?'

Maga looked smug, the way he always did when he was about to tell someone something they didn't know. 'As you know, I am from further up the Timeline than any of you, especially Dorothy, so you would think that history is just laid out for me to read. But Time doesn't work like that. As soon as you come *back*, history as far as the *traveller* can remember becomes hazy, unclear. I can still remember the basic facts, but if I'm directly involved in a decision that could go either way, it's like I'm looking through a tunnel – the history around me disappears. As far as I am concerned, everything can still change. It's for that reason that decisions *aren't* set in stone, however firmly history is rooted from where you are in the Timeline. If something changes, then when I'm far enough away from the epicentre of the change to remember and the memories come back, it'll feel like they had always been that way.'

Art rolled his eyes. 'In English, please, Maga.' He said.

'I genuinely have no idea what the outcome of today is,' Maga said.

'Fair enough. I won't keep you waiting then,' Art said. He squeezed Evi's hand, who smiled warmly back at him. 'I'm going to go for it. And Evi's coming with me – I couldn't do it without her.'

'And I couldn't let him go without me,' Evi said.

Tina took her free hand. 'Are you sure about this Evi? I mean this is a big decision.'

Evi smiled. 'From what I've heard, I'd be a fool to miss it.'

Grandma applauded. 'Wise girl.'

'But what about your family?' Aren't you going to miss them?' Tina said.

'Of course I will. But I can't miss out on this chance, Tina. And talking of which – neither should you. Why don't you come too?'

'Oh, no. I couldn't leave Peter.' She smiled slyly. 'Someone's got to look after him.'

'But you'll be gone no time at all – you know that.'

'I know,' Tina replied, 'but I'd still be without *him* for a year. Besides ...' She nodded towards Art. 'Two's company and all that.'

Evi hugged Tina as hard as she could. 'I'll miss you,' she said.

'You'd better,' she chided.

Grandma clapped her hands together. 'So – the decision's been made.'

Maga smiled. 'Time is a very funny thing,' he mused. 'I sort of knew that you were going to go, but I couldn't have told you that before you said it. How odd.'

'Will you stay for some tea before you leave, dears?' said Grandma.

'Yeah of course. Besides – we need to talk about that transport spell.' Art said.

'What about it?' Grandma replied.

'Well, I won't need it, will I? Not all the time I have *this*.' Art held up his wrist, and the twine that held the Fragment in place was still there. But Art's heart jumped when he realised that the Fragment *itself*, was not. 'W ...where's it gone? I've lost it!'

'Now, now, dear,' Grandma said. 'The Fragment is not lost. If it's gone it's because it *went*. You clearly don't need it anymore. Or it's magic.'

Art looked sullen. 'So ... how will we ...'

'Look's like you'll be needing that spell after all,' Grandma said, and handed Art a folded piece of paper. He opened it, and written on it were two words he had never seen before, written in spidery writing:

An-art As-ed.

'Is this it?' he asked.

'Just translate that in the usual way, and you can go back and forth as you please.'

'Whoa. And you're sure it'll work? I mean, with me doing it?'

'Of course it will, dear. Now sit down and have something to eat.'

They all sat down at the table together, where the Stroth-Brew was free flowing, and Dough-Drops and fresh warm bread disappeared as fast as ever. They all chatted animatedly about what they had been up to over Christmas, and before long the fire had died down to a warm glow, and they were all full of food and high spirits.

EPILOGUE

Grandma watched and listened with satisfaction as everyone laughed and joked with each other around the table, but eventually she sighed and said 'I think it's time, dears.'

Art looked at Evi, and she smiled at him and nodded. Art stood up and took Evi's hand, and she rose too. 'Erm, where should we stand?' he said.

'It makes no difference dear, really.' Grandma replied.

'Erm, it sort of feels like we should be over here,' Art said, and led Evi by the hand over to the fireplace. Grandma smiled.

He smoothed out the paper with the transport spell on it, and read the words out again under his breath; *An-art As-ed*.

'Remember Art - Lithogrics is a very powerful form of magic in the right hands, but it is *paper* magic in every sense of the word. It won't do a thing said aloud.'

Art looked at her warmly. 'Can I write to you while I'm there?' he asked.

'Of course. The Calsow's have a fireplace, don't they?'

'Well yes, but ... if we're only gone for a moment as far as you're concerned, then how will you answer them? Or *get* them, for that matter.'

'Well, there's a simple answer to that,' Grandma said. 'Just agree here and now that when you return, whenever that may be for you, that you set the coordinates for ... shall we say fifteen minutes from now in this world? That'll give us a chance to communicate.'

Evi brightened up. 'You'd better write to me then, Tina,' she said.

'How many letters do you suppose I can write in fifteen minutes, Evi – honestly!' Tina laughed.

'Okay then,' Art said. 'That's what we'll do. I suppose we should get going. Are you sure we won't need *anything*? I feel weird not taking a suitcase or something.'

'Just go!' Grandma laughed. 'And enjoy it – Agent training is something to behold. Oh, if only I could be you. Now get off with you!'

Maga chuckled. 'I think it's changed a bit since your time, Dorothy. And I'm betting you had a hand in some of it.'

Art looked between Maga and Grandma again. 'Are you *sure* there's nothing I'm missing?' he said.

'Off you go, Art,' Maga said.

Art opened his arm out like a wing, and Evi took hold of it. He thought for a second, then translated the transport spell underneath the English version in perfect EllShapyan, with a silver fountain pen that Evi had bought him for Christmas. As soon as he had finished writing the last letter, the writing turned green and a familiar low rumble began beneath their feet.

'Quick!' Grandma said. 'Fold up the paper and squeeze it in your hand. And Evi – hold on as tight as you can.

'Bye, Tina!' Evi called, as their outlines began to shimmer.

'Have fun!' Tina called back.

Maga exhaled deeply. 'Ah! – brings back memories, doesn't it Dorothy?' he said.

Art narrowed his eyes. 'There's definitely something you're not telling me, you two,' he said.

Maga tapped Grandma's arm. 'Come on Dorothy – it won't do any harm, will it? He has a right to know, really.'

'A right to know what?' Art called as the rumbling grew louder. Grandma smiled slyly, but said nothing.

'Bye, bye, Art,' Maga said, waving mockingly.

'Oh, come on! That's not fair!' Art called.

Maga laughed, but then he paused momentarily, then he rolled his eyes. 'Oh, *okay* then,' he shouted above the noise. 'You know how I told you the Boss before this one was a woman ...' he said, and then glanced fleetingly over at Grandma.

Art looked confused for a second, but then his eyes widened and he gasped.

'You've got to be ... NO WAY!'

UNDERSTANDING ELLSHAPYAN

Lithogrics is the study of the creation of physical magic by the use of written language. It was also known as *paper magic* before the subject was widely studied and relatively well understood.

EllShapyan, the language of magic, is a system of some seven hundred and twenty two magical symbols, a number of which relate separately to each of the languages of the seven magical realms. Each realm has its own system of symbols, similar to our own alphabetic system, which usually relate to between thirty or forty EllShapyan symbols.

The human alphabet, however, is the exception; it relates to only *twenty six* EllShapyan symbols. The ancient manuscript recovered by the Founders shows them as:

Many believe the human realm to be magically weak in comparison to all others due to its small number of related symbols. However, while some realms share a number of symbols with each other, the human realm encompasses some of the EllShapyan symbols used by *every other* realm, and although there is one other realm which also does this, the human realm shares the greatest number of these, which some believe actually makes it the *strongest* of all realms. This has yet to be proven, but there is already much evidence to support this. For example, several notable scholars believe that belonging to a realm that shares some of its symbols with all other magical realms will give the dedicated student a complete command of Lithogrics, while others believe that only an understanding of all 722 symbols *and* their realms will do this. The human realm remains, however, the least magically explored.

Sorted into their relative realm origins, the human-EllShapyan symbols line up as follows:

Most forms of magic can be created by using the symbols from each separate realm, and their use, or misuse, can have disastrous results to the untrained user. For example, it is useful to know that each letter of EllShapyan can only be used ONCE in each word made up using the corresponding letters of the alphabet. Using a symbol more than once makes the resulting magic unstable and unreliable. To indicate a double letter in EllShapyan, it is customary to use two small dots above the letter to be doubled. Thus Art Elfee's name, as written on the envelope, appears as:

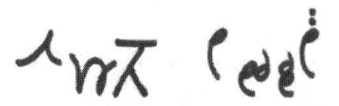

Daily practice of the symbols is necessary in order to achieve the correct skill level required to make Lithogrics work. However, not just anyone can create magic effectively in this way; the user needs a "Spark" (best translation) to have any chance of success, which resides in very few individuals, especially in the human realm. The actual translation of the word "Spark" requires an understanding on three different levels; humans have so far been unable to reach the second level. An understanding, however, is *not* necessary in Lithogrics, a mistake humans, especially the older ones, make all too regularly. All that is required is a specific type of confidence in one's ability.

About the Author

Lee Fomes was born and raised in Hampshire, in a small village called Medstead. He began writing stories of total fiction for pleasure at an early age, often airing them on his unfortunate brothers and sister when they would have really rather been out in the huge expanse of garden at the back of the house, as Lee often was. His inspiration for this novel was plenty of happy Christmases at Redcote, the family home, and many more at his own home with his wife Hannah, and his twins William and Molly, all to whom this book is dedicated. He is a professional musician in the Armed Forces, and lives in Cuxton, a small closely-knit community in Kent.

Since writing book one in the series, Lee J H Fomes has had a ball signing copies of his book around the country. Thanks to some very special people, book two is now in your hands, and Lee grows fonder of its characters by the day. He wishes to thank everyone once again for their support.